Crashing Into America

The Repentant Radical Series
Crashing Into America: A Radical Passage From India

On the Road Through Maggie's Farm: The Birthing of a Revolutionary

Breaking Blonde on Blonde: An Inside Out Revolution

Crashing Into America:
A Radical Passage from India

**A Novel
By
Robbie Orr**

**RedVolt Press
Tulsa**

What people are saying about Crashing into America?

Robbie Orr's entirely original novels capture a hauntingly beautiful time and place—the lost world of a South Indian hill station, Kodaikanal, home to several generations of American missionaries who sent their children to this wholly unique boarding school in the Palani Hills. I knew Kodai and Orr's stories evoke a flood of memories. But he then takes the story forward to what happens to young American expatriates when they come home to a sharply divided America in the 1960s. "*Crashing*" and "*Maggie's Farm*" then become an insightful parable about sex, rock 'n roll, and radical politics—all seen through the eyes of a missionary kid. The writing is clear and fluid and the story carries one along.
Kai Bird is a Pulitzer Prize-winning biographer and historian who spent two years in Kodaikanal.

What is it like to come of age inside and outside America?
How does one navigate religion, politics and even death?
Here is a novel in which Jamie, a young boy, goes from throwing snowballs to watching pinballs determine if he will be drafted
into military service and perhaps sent to Vietnam.

Crashing Into America is also a journey inside two countries.
In these political days of people moving from one land to another,
one is forced to constantly ask - Where is home and how do we avoid crashing into it?
E. Ethelbert Miller, Writer, and literary activist

Robbie Orr brings an innocent little boy, Jamie, to life in post-Independence India. The son of missionaries in India, his life is a constant search for identity. From the fear of being left alone as a young child in a boarding school in India to a young adult going back to "his America" in the throws of the Vietnam War, he starts to question his place in India, in America and in the World. "*Crashing Into America*" is a compelling story of innocence, curiosity, and rebellion. The story has an endearing familiarity to those of us who grew up in a country where our hearts belong, but our belonging is constantly questioned.
Louise Riber is a filmmaker who has spent over 60 years in India, Zimbabwe, and Tanzania.

Smart, political, intimate, authentic: *Crashing Into America* shows us how the body intersects with history, where it finds meaning and solace, and how beneath our political and religious trials, work at the soul level goes on. We grow up, mostly, despite being caught in our own projections, and to tell us we have Robbie Orr's humble yet wise narrator—part confidante, part tour guide, part warning at the crossroads.

John Colburn, originally from Mantorville, MN, is an editor and co-publisher at Spout Press, the author of Psychedelic Norway (Coffee House Press) and many other volumes of poetry.

• Do preacher's kids have more fun? Depends on whom you ask. Jamie Moore, hero of Robbie Orr's *Repentant Radical* series of novels, would say yes. Moore dances through the Sixties and Seventies, from boarding school in India, where his parents are missionaries, to Grinnell College in Iowa, where he joins the Movement, and on to the explosive scene in the Twin Cities, with side trips to Latin America. Along the way, he encounters rock and roll, friendly drugs, even more friendly women, and potential revolutionaries of varying degrees of commitment to the ideals of Karl Marx, Che Guevara, Frantz Fanon, and Mao Zedong.

• The book is engrossing and a very rapid read. It also gives a pretty thorough account of the many strands of revolutionary political thought that were current in the 1960s-70s. Jamie Moore navigates the stormy seas of feminism with aplomb – such aplomb, in fact, that I sometimes questioned his poise. But he is a fit hero for this backward look, and he has a lot of fun.

Martha Roth, author, editor, and activist who lived in Minneapolis and Vancouver, BC

Robbie Orr's tale of a US and Scottish white boy who grew up a missionary's son in India and came of age in Iowa during the Vietnam War, civil rights, and women's rights movements is rich in story and historical anecdotes. The Beatles, the Mai Lai massacre, a Black preacher, a Marxist librarian, Consciousness Raising; Orr illuminates moments when cherished beliefs crumbled and new worlds opened up. We feel the loss and the liberation.

Anne Winkler-Morey, Author, *Allegiance to Winds & Waters: Bicycling the Political Divides of the United States*

To dear Deborah, we found each other at a union convention and have never let go.
To the Rogers and Duncan cabins and The Hermitage at Clearwater Forest, where the spirit of the Northwoods brought this book alive.
To my teachers, Bob Granner and Miss Jay (Jeannette Jerehian), who gave me a love of literature and writing.
And for all activists and seekers who carry on the struggle for liberty, equality, and community.

Table of Contents

Going Home

"This is my own, my native land."
Sir Walter Scott

I

A boy of eight stands next to a steamship.
The heat of the Bombay sun in May wraps him
in its familiar blanket. The trunks and suitcases
are loaded. Pink-skinned passengers walk
up the gang-plank. He feels out-numbered
to be surrounded by people who look like him.
He remembers his dry, dusty hometown, 200 miles Southeast,
and the jungle gym tree filled with his normal brown-skinned friends
while his parents were busy all day long at school and hospital.

II

The ship slides through the hot blue sea,
through the Canal with hulks rusting
from the recent war. Every day, his mother teaches
him and his sister to swim while his father
reads, smiles and watches the baby.
They have food every few hours and ice cream and Coke.
His parents are there all day long.
The boy decides he likes going home.

III

Sailing past the Big Rock, the boy catches a chill.
He wheezes. His mother says you will suffer from this
all of your life. He knows it was wrong to run barefoot.
The ship turns north and the ocean turns colder.
The ship pulls into Southhampton harbor.
His mother sees the Union Jack and the St. Andrew's
cross flying brightly above them. Her Scots accent broadens.
She starts to recite poetry. "Is there ever a man with soul
so dead...". The boy listens.
He watches the water and wonders
about his native land. The cold, green water froths white
and reaches up for him.

Prologue

This is a story about one boy, about one generation. It is a story about home, losing, and finding a home. About WTF is home. A story about an American born and raised in India. During the 1950s and '60s, India hosted hundreds of missionary families. The former British colony had become independent in 1947, and remnants of colonial privilege were still entrenched in India's economy and culture. We Europeans who grew up in there adopted it as our home. Still, India was decolonizing, and it didn't adopt us.

Crashing Into America is also about a generation that changed the world, but not quite as much as we hoped. The Baby Boomer generation didn't live in the United States alone. They came of age in England and France, Scotland and South India, Vietnam and Virginia. Around the globe, the post-WWII generation was born into a world of change and anti-colonial revolution. They were born into the Cold War that repeatedly turned hot: Korea, Vietnam, Malaysia, and Cuba. In the States, as expatriates called their country, my generation had everything our parents didn't. Meat was on the table every day. College was cheap and available to most (white) youth. Kids got cars, movies, and TV. But, as Prince said, we were never satisfied. Sitcoms on TV like *Leave It to Beaver* were fun to watch and thrilled our parents. But they were utterly meaningless. The jobs that paid so much more than our parents and grandparents received were mind-deadening. Undermining the American Dream State was the reality of segregation by law in the South, White prejudice in the North, and fear (of poverty) across the USA. Other realities dismantled the Dream State: the draft and dirty wars, the consignment of women to the kitchen and their removal from jobs that paid enough to raise a family, and the ever-present threat of nuclear war.

Oppression breeds resistance. And we Boomers were granted the secret weapon of our rebellion by musical revolutionaries who reached across the color line and created rock 'n' roll. Chuck Berry, Little Richard, Elvis, Bo Diddly, Buddy Holly, Richie Valens(zuela), and many others built the foundation-rocking music that gave white youth what the American Dream lacked: a passion and a purpose of shaking things up.

Our Black generational cousins loved the new music as much as we white Boomers did. But they had a more clearly defined purpose. They were determined to break the back of the nightmare behind the American Dream: Jim Crow and de facto segregation. They were part of the anti-colonial revolution that transformed China, Vietnam, India, and Africa and sparked waves of change across Latin America.

Crashing Into America is a little window into that worldwide tumult. It shows how historical events combined with first love to transform a Sunday School Christian boy into a radical young man. It resounds with events and music that formed the rebellious culture of white youth. *Crashing* explores how people are radicalized and how small steps lead to transformative leaps. This novel illustrates the key message of the Women's Liberation Movement: the political is personal, and the personal is political. People don't become radicalized by ideas but because radical ideas speak to their personal liberation.

NOTE TO READERS #1- Some of you will notice that this book is filled with allusions to the songs of Dylan, the Beatles, the Doors, and many other rock 'n' rollers. When we rejected our parents' prophets, we picked our own. You may be eligible for a special prize if you keep track of these allusions. See NOTE TO READERS #2 in the back matter of this book.

Part 1: All Are Precious in His Sight

Chapter 1: God's Plan

"Where are you from?" That was my most challenging question.

It made me feel awkward and out of place. And raised other questions in my mind. Do they really want to know? How much detail should I go into? I was born in India. My parents traveled to the United States when I was one. Before I turned three, my family lived in San Anselmo, Denver, and Edinburgh, then back in Sangli, India. Where was I really from? Even in India, we moved twice a year. Or should I say migrated because of the seasons?

Following the pattern of the British colonists, missionary mothers took their children and cooks to cool hill stations to avoid the hot season from March through May. Our family would take a two-day train and bus journey south to escape the dry, dusty heat of the Deccan Plateau, only to descend to the steamy rice lands of Tamilnadu. Further south, we boarded a creaking diesel bus to wind our way slowly up thirty miles of mountain road, bringing us to the cool crispness of Kodaikanal, which is Tamil for the mountain forest. That was our annual pilgrimage. Every five years, we would go "home," which meant Colorado for my father and Scotland for my mother. During most of the year of home furlough, we lived in Denver, visiting Presbyterian churches supporting the mission work in India and worldwide. With at least three different hometowns, I did not know where I was really from.

As a child, I never thought of myself as American. My family lived in a big bungalow on the Mission Compound in the dusty market town of Sangli, India. I was just another Marathi Christian boy, but one who lived in a big house. And one whose parents bought him such luxuries as shoes and soccer balls.

One of my earliest memories is sitting in the warm lap of the woman I only knew as *Ayah* (nanny). Surrounded by singing voices, I looked up into the dark Indian sky and the vibrant stars. A harmonium and *tabla* (Indian drums) led the crowd in hymns, praising God for the wonders of the day. Dozens of families sat cross-legged on mats around a large fire in an open field. I nestled into Ayah's lap and thought about my day. It had been magical, something out of a Hindi movie. Sugandh was our family's houseboy. He had married a beautiful woman in a gold-flecked green sari. I rode to the wedding hall with him in the Raja's Silver Cloud Rolls Royce. Granted, it was the oldest Rolls that the Raja owned. But the driver was a Christian, and the Raja always liked to keep the missionaries on his side. After the wedding, I stood between the bride and groom, waving from the Rolls. We rode around the field before arriving in our front garden for the wedding dinner.

Sugandh and his bride slipped away from the wedding dinner. Ayah convinced my mother to let her take me to the sing-along. She was sure I'd be asleep in ten minutes. Instead, the rapid-fire *tablas* (drums) reverberated in my chest, keeping me wide awake. Hari was Ayah's husband and our *maestri* (cook). That night, he played the harmonium. The melodic notes pulled my thoughts high into the dark sky speckled with diamond stars. Mom always said God had great plans for me. But what could have been greater than that day?

My answer wouldn't come until fifteen years later when I discovered my own way of being American.

Chapter 2: Baba-sahib

All Europeans, as all white people were known, were all *sahibs* in those days. Rich Indians were both called *sahib* (boss). My father, Jim Moore, was an American Presbyterian missionary and Sangli Industrial School's principal. He was known as Moore-*sahib*. Noreen Ramsey Moore, my mother, was *madam-sahib*. *Baba* is the Marathi word for boy-child, so I was *baba-sahib* (little boss) or Jamie-*baba* to those who knew me well. My given name was James, after my father.

"He must have a different middle name," my father insisted. "Only snooty people have *Juniors*,"

I became Jamie to avoid being confused with my father. I was later embarrassed that it could also be a girl's name. Fortunately, very few Americans knew that in those days.

We lived on a compound owned by the American Presbyterian Mission. It was on the edge of Sangli, a market town famous for its hot peppers and turmeric. Sangli is about 200 miles southeast of Mumbai, or Bombay as it was called in those days. Sangli sits on the banks of one of India's great rivers. The Krishna River flows out of the forested hills of the Western Ghats, the mountain chain that runs along India's west coast, and empties into the Bay of Bengal.

The regional language was Marathi, one of the older North Indian languages. Sangli was a bustling market town. Its citizens were well-fed when the monsoon rains came. Then, the richer ones grew prosperous. The big cash crops were turmeric and cotton, the white and orange of the Indian flag. Under the British Raj, Sangli was one of the small princely states of India. The Sangli Raja kept order, collected taxes, and paid the British their share.

As British rule expanded across India, the poor increased rapidly. In the late nineteenth century, Protestant missionaries came to India in a big way. And provided the poorest of the poor with some benefits of Westernization. Doctors, nurses, teachers, and engineers came along with ministers. They came from Britain, the United States, Canada, Australia, and New Zealand. They witnessed for their God and Savior by providing education and health care to India's poor. An Australian missionary engineer founded Sangli Industrial School in 1901. He convinced the Raja to give him dry, rocky ground outside the town. The school provided a trade for landless peasants. In response, many of them became Christians. Most were so-called outcasts or untouchables and had always lived in poverty. In famine years, they came to the Raja begging for food. So, he was happy to have someone else take care of them.

During the Independence Movement, the rural areas of Sangli supported Gandhi and the Indian National Congress. But the Raja and his council, who were conservative Brahmins, did not. They banned the Congress in their tiny state of Sangli and hoped the British Raj would last forever. After India won Independence, the Sangli Raja refused to enter the new Republic of India. He was still holding out when Gandhi was assassinated on January 30, 1948. It became known that Sangli was home to the financiers of the plot. Nathuram Godse, the assassin, had relatives in Sangli. He had been a student at the Industrial School but was expelled for bad behavior. When the news broke, the villagers marched on the town. They began looting and burning the stores and houses of the plotters. The rioters overwhelmed the Raja's tiny police force, and he appealed for Indian Army troops. The Indian government refused assistance unless the Raja abdicated his throne. The Raja gave in. The princely state of Sangli became the Sangli District of Bombay Province. The Raja was removed from his throne. (In Marathi, it is called a *gadhi* or mattress, usually covered with gold-embroidered silk. A raja would recline in comfort and grandeur to receive their subjects.) In compensation, the Sangli Raja received a nice pension and a lot of land.

When the founder of Sangli Industrial School fell ill, the New Zealand Presbyterians asked the American church to help. My grandfather answered the call and was the principal from 1920 until 1948, when he was replaced by his son. Our mission compound sat on a hundred acres of land outside the old city walls. It housed a primary school, a clinic for women and children, church offices, a farm, and the school where eighty young men learned tailoring, carpentry, agriculture, and motor mechanics. The early missionaries drilled a deep well that tapped into the water table that fed the Krishna River. So, even before the city built a waterworks, the mission compound was a green oasis. Three large bungalows housed the missionaries. Our house was surrounded by leafy neem, tamarind, and royal poinciana trees.

In front of our bungalow was a well-tended flower garden. It had trimmed hedges and a *nag champa* tree with white and yellow flowers. A tree of unknown species from Australia was more interesting to children. We called it the whale tree. Sturdy, inter-woven branches spread from a three-foot trunk, forming a natural jungle gym. Leaves only grew at the edges and the top of the tree, where thousands of tiny leaves shielded us from the sun and adult eyes. The whale tree was our fortress, airplane, or war elephant, depending on the day's game.

When I was a baby, my father would hold me in the early evening as he walked through the garden or along the main road. He showed me off to the Christian teachers and workers on the compound and wealthy Brahmin families who lived across the street. Babies are so adored in India that there is a phrase for it, *bala puja,* or baby worship. So, his firstborn had many fans. Being the child of an important man in town helped as well.

Since my dad was born and raised in Sangli, he was well-known and respected. He had gone to boarding school in the southern hill station of Kodaikanal. War II broke out, the Japanese threatened to invade Madras (now Chennai), and Kodaikanal School was evacuated. My dad finished high school and the first two years of college in Bombay. At the war's end, he returned to the States for his engineering and divinity degrees. Just as he graduated, his mother contracted tuberculosis, and his parents returned to their hometown of Denver. My dad returned to Sangli to teach in his father's place. He and another missionary engineer took turns as principals of SIS for the next thirty years.

He was a quiet man and a strict but loving father. He'd only raise his voice when I disrespected the servants or one of my Indian friends. Any sign of racism drove him into a rage.

"We are all children of God. From the poorest beggar on the streets to the most brilliant rocket scientist in America, God loves us equally," he told me repeatedly until I was a teenager. And I said his words back to him to shorten the lecture. When I did that, he looked at me as if I'd stabbed him with a knife. "So, n, those aren't just words. That is how I must live my life. I pray that one day you'll understand the depth and equality of God's love."

Saturday night was the time missionaries socialized. My parents often had dinner parties at our house. The guests might be other missionaries, Indian doctors, village elders, or teachers. They might be professors, businessmen, or government officials. Everyone ate at the same table, and each was served the appropriate food, vegetarian or non-veg. My father would say grace, a short welcome, and nothing more except to guide the conversation if it entered rough waters.

My mother was the life of the party. She was from Scotland and was a nurse during the war. She served with the air raid wardens in Glasgow during the Battle of Britain. Then, she worked in surgery at the Edinburgh Royal Hospital. She helped operate on those wounded in submarine attacks and the invasion of Normandy. She was a Celtic storyteller with a knack for making everyone feel at home. She quickly became a vital part of the Sangli community. She ran several community clinics and built bridges with the small Muslim and larger Hindu women's groups in town. As busy as she was, she tucked me into bed and said prayers every night.

"God is love," she would tell me. "His love shines in each one of us. It is the foundation of family and friendships. His living water brings us true life instead of mere survival."

She would tell me stories from her life. And we would wonder what my future held.

"God has a special plan for you. He has chosen a special person to be your wife. As a couple, you will find God's purpose together." She told me repeatedly.

A favorite activity was visiting the farm of Yeshwant, our *mahli* (gardener). His son Daveed and I were best friends. Their farm was a piece of dry land above the river. They had two water buffaloes as draft animals and for milk. Once a week, Yeshwant took the animals to the river to wash them. Daveed and I loved to jump off the massive black beasts into the river. We'd squeal with delight and swim through the cool, muddy water.

Another favorite was the regular *bhajans* that our cook Hari would hold in front of his tiny house behind our bungalow. He had a great voice. Friends would come with *tablas* (drums) or other instruments, and they would sing late into the night. Between songs, they would tell stories. Sugandh, the houseboy, told long, funny stories that always ended with a riddle. They were about Sivaji, the great Maratha warrior-king, and his *Peshwa,* the wily prime minister. I would watch sparks rise from the fire on cool nights and float into the dark, starry sky. I felt so happy and carefree, as if I could follow those sparks into the sky and explore God's entire universe. In those days, I knew the loving and just *Raja Yesu* (King Jesus) ruled the world and the stars. He would always work for the good of those who loved him and followed His commandments.

The first time my family returned *home* (Scotland and the US) was quite an adventure. We boarded a passenger steamer of the Anchor Lines in Bombay Harbor.

"This ship was built in Denny's Shipyards in Dumbarton. Your grandfather might have laid the decks on it. And my grandfather could have built the cabinets in the dining room," Mom said proudly.

During dinner, I would gaze at the polished teak and glass cabinets lining the walls and feel a shiver of pride. Our family had built this.

In Scotland, we visited family and friends. Mom's parents had passed. They were victims of poor nutrition and lack of health care in pre-war Britain. Then, we went on to the US, where we spent a year in Denver. I got to know my paternal grandparents while my parents toured churches in Colorado, Wyoming, and New Mexico. They explained the goals of the Presbyterian Mission: Building God's kingdom around the world by providing education and medical care. They strived to be an example of the love of Jesus at work in the world. When I went to churches with them, the whole family would dress up like the people in Sangli, and I'd feel so proud to be from India.

I went to third grade at Brown Elementary in western Denver, where

Grandpa had a house. I loved coming home to watch cartoons on TV. In those days, India did not have TV, so Rocky and Bullwinkle enthralled me. They always managed to defeat the evil Russians, Boris and Natasha. I loved Tom Terrific, Looney Toons, and all the kids' shows. Then, at 5:30 each afternoon, Grandma would turn the dial to NBC News. My Grandpa suspected the other channels were too favorable to the Democrats. He was born Republican and, as it was written by John Prine, he "voted for Eisenhower 'cuz Lincoln won the war."

Grandpa was dead set against Kennedy and liked the way Nixon stood up to the communists. I began to understand what he meant. The kids who went to Brown Elementary, a public school, told me that if Kennedy won, we'd have to go to school on Saturdays and pray to the Pope. Our group of little boys decided our duty was to harass the students at a nearby Catholic school to prevent Kennedy from winning.

"Dirty Catholics!" we'd yell at them as they walked by in their uniforms.

One afternoon in October, six inches of snow fell. Grandma had already bought winter clothes for me and showed me how to put them on. I went outside to play. A snowball fight was going on in the vacant lot just up the street. Catholics vs. Protestants. The Catholic kids were pushing my friends back. An ice ball hit me in the face as I ran to join them. I flung myself down behind an old apple tree next to two friends who hadn't run away yet. My face stung so much I cried out, "Jiminy Cricket." I knew I had sinned because that was a cover for swearing by the name of Jesus Christ, but it hurt so much.

"Here, pack these stones into your snowballs. Quick, make three or four of them," our leader told us. "When I yell charge, run at them, protecting your face like this."

He raised his arm. Clearly, he was an experienced snowball fighter. "But hold your fire until we see the whites of their eyes,"

I packed a lot of stones into my snowballs because I was so mad. I only made a couple when our fearless leader whispered to get ready.

He jumped up and yelled, "Charge!"

We ran out from behind the tree, screaming like banshees and keeping our snowballs ready.

"Fire now!" our leader yelled.

Then, we began flinging our booby-trapped snowballs. I caught one kid on the side of his chin. He fell right down. The rest of the Catholic kids went running home.

"We got a prisoner," our leader proclaimed.

The kid wailed loudly. There was blood coming from his chin. Between his cries, I heard someone calling my name. Grandma marched toward us at a fast clip. Her galoshes were unbuckled. Grandpa's coat draped around her shoulders.

"Jamie Moore, you come home right now," she yelled at me from the sidewalk.

The wounded kid stood up, and red blood dripped into the snow.

"Oh, my goodness, child. Come here and let me see you."

She grabbed some Kleenex out of a pocket and pressed it to his chin. She led him to our house, and I followed silently behind. She cleaned him up and put on a Band-Aid. She then called his mother, saying my Grandpa would bring the kid home. When they left, Grandma called me into the kitchen.

"Jesus is ashamed of you, Jamie."

"I know, Grandma, but he hit me with an ice slushy that really hurt," I said, crying.

"Crying won't get you out of this. Own up to your sin like a man," she responded.

"But Grandma, he is a Catholic, and if they win, Kennedy will make us go to school on Saturdays."

"Don't talk back to your elders. The rumor about making you go to catechism is just foolishness. And anyway, Jesus said to love our enemies."

I knew better than to say anything more. Grandma pulled my wet clothes off me and pushed me into the bathroom to shower. Then, Grandma sat me at the dinner table to wait for Grandpa to return home. Luckily, he read the newspaper during dinner and didn't give me another lecture. We had pork chops with mashed potatoes for dinner, raspberry pie, and vanilla ice cream for dessert. I decided I kind of liked visiting America.

"Grandma," I said between bites. "What is catechism?"

Grandpa looked up from *The Rocky Mountain News*.

"It is the Catholic version of Sunday School and confirmation class rolled into one. That is where the Catholics learn about their religion," she said.

Grandpa nodded approvingly.

"So, if Catholics won't force us to learn their religion, why are they our enemies?"

"They aren't really our enemies, Jamie. They just have a different religion," Grandpa declared.

"So, if they aren't our enemies, do we still have to love them?" I asked.

"Yes, Jamie. That boy is your neighbor. What did Jesus say about your neighbor?"

"Love your neighbor as yourself," I said. "So, who do we hate if we have to love our neighbors and enemies?"

"You ask too many questions, son. Let me have some peace to finish my newspaper," Grandpa answered sternly.

I did have a lot of questions and didn't understand why I couldn't ask them. Mom and Dad always explained everything to me. But things were simpler in India. Life in America was much more confusing.

As our furlough in America ended, a dark dread began to swallow me. Kids in our Mission could attend school near home for their first three years. Five miles away from the Sangli Industrial school, the town of Miraj had a mission hospital with half a dozen American families. The wife of an American pharmacist was a trained teacher. She started a school for the younger missionary kids so they wouldn't have to go to boarding school until the fourth grade.

When my family returned to India in June 1961, I was to start fourth grade. My Mom was expecting a baby, so Dad took me up to Kodaikanal or Kodai ((*pronounced "Cody"*). Then, he would put me in boarding school and return to Sangli. Dad and I stayed in a mission cottage for a week. Dad would cook, and I had him to myself the whole evening. As his departure date approached, a cold pain started in my stomach. It felt like I had swallowed a sharp stone that grew larger every day.

Then, I diagnosed the cause. I learned the terrible truth about a particular disease from listening to grown-up conversations at dinner parties. The adults' tone always changed when doctors mentioned it. Cancer. That was it. I was sure I had cancer. It meant I would die, but then my dad would have to take me back home to Sangli, where I would be with Mom and him until I went to heaven.

"Dad, I think I have cancer," I said after dinner one night.

He looked up in alarm and asked me how I felt. As I explained, he pulled me into his lap. Then, he asked me to show me where it hurt.

"It might be your stomach tied up in knots. Mine hurts something terrible when I think of leaving you, son," he said.

I thought I saw a tear in his eye, but he quickly looked away. He started singing Colorado camp songs and hymns. I fell asleep in his arms.

The next day, he had me examined by a missionary surgeon who was one of the best in India. He could feel nothing in my stomach. I was highly disappointed that I didn't have cancer. They wouldn't let me go back home to Sangli for stomach knots.

"Jesus never promised us an easy life, son," my dad told me. "But he did promise that he'd always be with us. When you're sad or homesick, reach out to Jesus and pray."

"Dad, I'm not homesick. I love our home."

He ignored me and went on. "God will comfort you. Through these trials, you will slowly understand God's Mission for your life."

Then, he walked me into the cold stone hallway that led into my new dormitory.

Chapter 3: Rapture with Jesus and John Glenn

The town of Kodaikanal sits on an escarpment of the 7,000-foot-high Palani Hills. The range consists of ancient granite covered by lemongrass and elephant grass, which absorb water like a giant sponge during the monsoons. The grass-covered hills feed streams that keep the *sholas (*forested valleys) green. They contain a riot of tropical growth that rivals any rainforest. Rhododendron trees tower over thick stands of bamboo, wild schefflera, and other plants. Leopards, tigers, elephants, deer, and mountain goats roamed the hills during the 1960s. Those hills were the childhood playground for South Indian missionary kids. This natural wonderland was the backdrop to the cold, unbearable loneliness of a young child in boarding school. It was the place that made us who we were, far from our parents and even further from their homeland. Over the years, on camping trips and nighttime escapades, in class discussions and weekend dances, we slowly emerged from the ignorant fog of childhood into the assumed omniscience of our teenage years. This was where I began that awful and awe-filled process of finding answers that led to more questions, that thing called growing up.

The town of Kodaikanal was a hill station built by missionaries and regional British officials. They cut lumber for buildings from a large *shola* and dammed the stream to make a lake. They brought landless workers from the plains to quarry the granite and built cottages and a hotel. And made gardens with plants from England and Australia, including lantana and eucalyptus trees, which soon dominated the resort town.

In 1901, Margaret Eddy, a teacher from Kansas, came to India to visit her missionary son. He ran a school for the villagers nearby. She approved of his teaching the poor but was shocked at her grandchildren's haphazard education. In the hot season, the family moved up to Kodaikanal. It was a welcome relief from the brutal summer heat of the Tamil plains. There, Mrs. Eddy discovered her new mission in life. Scores of American missionary children lacked a consistent education. She rented some rooms at the Highclerc Hotel next to Kodaikanal Lake. She founded a boarding school to educate the children of the educators and doctors who were serving her Lord. The school filled a need for hundreds of missionary families across southern India. By the 1960s, Kodai School had three hundred pupils. It sent graduates to MIT, Harvard, Stanford, and other American universities. A Kodai School alumnus became President of Princeton and later US Ambassador to India. It was a good Christian school that my father deposited me in. But it wasn't a perfect place for a nine-year-old kid.

On February 20, 1962, John Glenn blasted off from Cape Canaveral. He became the second human and first American to leave Earth's atmosphere. On a hilltop in South India, a dorm mother talked to thirty little boys during their nightly devotions.

All the boys sat on a prickly coir mat in our flannel pajamas. The fiber from coconut husks was like soft barbed wire. It must have been designed to keep little boys from squirming because the strands poked you every time we moved.

"It is written in the Bible," a stern Mrs. Rivers proclaimed, "the Heavens are God's alone. Man shall not go to the Heavens except by the will of God."

Wow, my parents had read me a lot of the Bible, but I'd never heard that. Still, Mrs. Rivers taught in Sunday school and was our housemother. So, she must know.

"Jamie, do you know what this means?" Mrs. Rivers towered over me.

A frozen icicle expanded in my throat, and I stared at her in fright.

"Frantzie? ... Mickey?... Bobby?" Her rage was mounting as she turned to the back rows in desperation. "Roger, do you know?"

Roger shook his head.

"I have failed Jesus and your parents by not teaching you the Word of God. However, tonight, I shall not fail His test. Tonight, yes, tonight, the Lord is coming!"

She told us Jesus would appear right when the Gemini space capsule passed overhead. He would descend on a shining white horse and call His people to the final battle, and then we'd all go to heaven together. After devotions, there was a lot of whispered talk. Bigger kids bravely claimed it was just a story but only out of Mrs. Rivers' earshot. Mrs. Rivers was a large woman who was handy with the paddle. I went to bed scared. It was a long time before my eyelids drooped shut.

At midnight, Mrs. Rivers roused all thirty little boys. "Get up! Get up!" I heard her shouting down the verandah. I snuggled deeper under my woolen blankets.

Then, she stood in the doorway to Room 6, shouting at my roommate Frantzie and me. We were both lying confused and sleepy in our wooden cots. When I didn't leap out of bed, she rushed towards me, "The Lord is coming," she cried out, her voice trembling.

I was terrified. Was *this* my life mission to go to heaven with Mrs. Rivers? No way. I wanted to be with my parents and baby brother when Jesus came, but I jumped out of bed. I pulled on my flannel nightgown by the time she'd crossed the room. She grabbed me by the shoulders and shook me violently as her shining blue eyes drilled into mine.

"Rejoice, the Lord has come," she shouted with a chilling fervor.

Then, she was off to the next room. "Get up! Get up," she screamed as she moved on.

Thirty boys shuffled out of their rooms. The dorm rooms opened onto a covered walkway surrounding a grass quadrangle. It was cold that night, and there was dew on the grass. Even if Jesus was coming, no one wanted to get their feet wet. So, we gathered on the paved crossing area, shivering sleepily in the night air. Mrs. Rivers was ecstatic. Her white-haired husband stood beside her, looking as dazed as the rest of us.

"Boys," she shouted. "Boys, the Rapture is upon us. Soon, very soon, Jesus will descend from heaven with a fiery sword. Quickly now, kneel and pray."

We knelt and prayed. Still, I couldn't help peeking through my fingers to see the first ray of His silver light that would illuminate the whole world. All I could see was a crowd of thirty little boys. As usual, the Baptists and Presbyterians were upfront. Next came Lutherans and Methodists, with four Catholics, three Icelandic atheists, and two Hindus in the back. We prayed harder, knowing we'd soon be in either heaven or hell. After ten minutes, the back rows began farting and giggling, as they always did by the end of nightly devotions. After twenty minutes, we were all shivering in the chilly air. The unrest began flowing forward through the ranks.

Suddenly, Mrs. Rivers stood up tall and menacingly. "What are you boys doing out here in the middle of the night? Get back to bed," she shouted. Grabbing the nearest boy, she gave his backside a loud, resounding swat. "Back to bed! Back to bed!" she ordered.

We fled back to bed.

All my dorm-mates spent Sunday Quiet Hour writing letters home. As soon as each person finished, they took them to Mrs. Rivers to check for spelling and grammar errors. Frantzie and I took ours in together. It was safer that way. We were pleased to see old Mr. Rivers napping in his rocking chair. She rarely paddled us when he was around.

I handed Mrs. Rivers my green Indian domestic letterform. I'd written about getting an A on my history test and hiking to Bear Shola. She looked over my letter and made a few changes.

"Next time, please use your best penmanship, Jamie," she said.

I was moving toward the door of her sitting room when Frantzie handed her his letter.

"This did *not* happen, Frantzie," she exploded. "I never woke you at midnight."

"Yes, Mrs. Rivers, yes you did, Tuesday night. You remember, don't you, Jamie?"

He turned to me, but she was already towering over us with her hands on her hips.

"No, Frantzie," Mrs. Rivers spoke with a growing edge. It sounded like the barber's razor scraping across the leather strap. "That never happened. You are making up stories again and are bound for the eternal fire."

She tore up his letterform. "Go back to your room and start from scratch."

I stared at her. Mrs. Rivers was lying, not Frantzie. How could that be? She was an adult and a Christian. I looked at Mr. Rivers. He had woken up, but he hid behind his newspaper. I glanced at Frantzie, and he stared back at me, his eyes wide with fright.

"Go! Write your letter, Frantzie!" She snarled and turned to me with a raised hand. "Jamie, you don't believe Frantzie's lies, do you?"

Mr. Rivers put his paper down and stood up. Frantzie grabbed my hand. We ran out the door toward safety.

That was the first crack in my Sunday school faith. My Grandpa had told me I asked too many questions, but no adult had lied to me. Frantzie and I told some other kids what had happened. One of the Icelandic atheist kids said the Bible was filled with lies. An older Presbyterian kid said Mrs. Rivers was just a crazy old lady. Since we couldn't write home about it, I figured I would wait and ask my Mom about it when I went home. Of course, by then, I'd forgotten all about that crazy night. I had a new baby brother to play with, and the night of Mrs. Rivers' Rapture was buried away.

Chapter 4: Wake up, Little Jamie

I learned how to survive boarding school life by the time I was eleven. You had to have friends who would protect you from the bullies. You had to ignore the lousy food and crazy staff members. You focused on the good stuff, like good teachers, weekend hikes, and playing games with friends. And dreaming of long vacation when you could go back home.

Our long vacation was in the cooler months of November, December, and January. One November morning, I was enjoying a long lie in bed when my stomach started growling. The hands on the black and white clock read eight forty-five as I stumbled into the dining room. My father usually taught classes by this time, and my Mom would be off to her clinic. But not today. I mumbled good morning to them, slipped into my chair, and poured some tea.

Mom and Dad didn't even notice me. They were standing next to a side table bent over the shortwave radio. Through the static, I could make out that a helicopter had gone down in Kashmir. The crash killed top Indian Army generals, and the President was dead. Was it a coup? Were the Pakistanis or the Chinese attacking India again? My parents were extremely upset. They tried to explain what was going on, but to be honest, I didn't really pay much attention. I was trying to recapture my dream. In it, Sgt. Rock and I had discovered a German Panzer column sneaking through a pass to attack American headquarters. We American GIs disabled the first four tanks with grenades and trapped the whole column so P-51 Mustangs could destroy it.

My father glanced at his Seiko wristwatch and ran off to teach his nine o'clock class. My mother rushed off to the dispensary and a long line of patients. I drank strong sweet tea, cut my toast into thin strips, and dipped them into a soft-boiled egg. The strips of toast were soldiers marching into battle. I was a giant biting off their egg-covered legs. I leisurely sipped my tea. It was Saturday, meaning new comics were at the English bookstore near the railway station. I finished breakfast, hopped on my bike, and raced through the mission compound gate. I was pedaling fast toward the Post Office when our mailman stepped into my path with a raised hand. I braked hard and skidded on the gravel.

"American-*baba*, such a sad day for America and India too," he said, touching his heart. I was surprised to see tears. But had no idea what he was talking about. So, I nodded and quickly pedaled past him.

Outside the State Bank, Mr. Pandre stood guard. He had a shotgun on his shoulder, a bandolier across his chest, and a waxed mustache that reached his ears. He stopped me and gave me a big, sweaty, tobacco-smelling hug.

"*Array*, Jamie-*baba*, why did God allow such a good man to be murdered?"

Mr. Pandre was an elder at the Christian Church. Then, the Hindu bank manager and his Muslim assistant rushed down the steps with their arms open wide. I stepped back to avoid more hugs. They shook my hand, daubed tears out of their eyes with checkered handkerchiefs, and offered their sympathy.

Similar scenes continued as I rode along the dusty main road, dodging dogs and kids in school uniforms. I passed a long line of bullock carts overloaded with sugar cane. I swerved away from a big red and yellow State Transport bus. People I never knew stopped me and told me how sad and shocked they were, saying they loved the first American President to befriend India. I began to put it together: President Kennedy had been assassinated like Gandhi before him. Mr. Pandre was right. Why did God let things like this happen?

When the Bombay papers came later that day, I read everything I could about the assassination. The following week, when the Asian edition of *Time Magazine* arrived, I read it cover to cover. I read the papers daily to discover what was happening outside the close boundaries of my life. I also noticed that things changed for me in the following days and weeks. Kids that used to shout rude names as I rode by now waved and yelled happily, "'Merican, 'Merican." And every time I went with my family to an Indian home, there was a new picture of JFK next to those of Gandhi and Prime Minister Nehru.

For the first time, I realized I was different from my Indian friends, rich or poor. I was an American, and in 1963, that was a pretty good thing in India. I started asking my parents about their lives. Why had they come to India? My world expanded rapidly as I became aware of national and international events. I was ready to stop being a little kid, although I still loved riding my bike around the town and shooting birds with my brand-new pellet gun.

Chapter 5: A Hard Year's Evening

GRRN-ING-NG-NG—the opening chord echoed as if played in a giant granite cave. Within a few bars, I felt warm waves racing through me, and a big smile broke across my face. Sure, I was in boarding school on my thirteenth birthday. And the only guest at my party was Aunt Rose Klein. But I had my first rock' n' roll album.

Aunt Rose was an elderly Presbyterian missionary who taught first grade. All adults in our Mission, anyone sent out by our church, were called Aunt or Uncle. I guess it was because the missionaries only returned to the States every five years, and we hardly ever saw our blood relatives. And they did treat us like we were all part of one big family. Aunt Rose had curly white hair and blue eyes and always wore black shoes. For my birthday, she invited me to her house for dinner. The first thing she did was give me my present from Mom and Dad. It was a brand-new Beatles album, *A Hard Day's Night*. She even put it on her hi-fi.

I sat on the edge of her wicker sofa, listening to the Fab Four working like dogs, strumming their guitars, beating their drums, harmonizing, and making me feel all right. An image of blonde-haired Helen's face floated into my mind, riding the musical waves. I smiled as I dreamed of holding her tight tonight and went tingly all over. Helen's family lived five miles from mine, so I also saw her on our long vacations. She was the prettiest girl in our class. I often caught myself staring at her, but until I heard that song, I never imagined holding anyone tight. At our monthly square dances, I always anticipated that magic moment when she'd hold out her hand so I could swing her around rather than one of my missionary aunties. But the dancing the Beatles sang about was deliciously different. I shivered and knew that feeling was sinful. I was frozen in fear.

"Aren't you going to open the card from your mother?" Aunt Rose asked.

I was afraid that might bring a tear to my eye, but I tore open the envelope. A black-and-white photo slid to the floor. Wow! A snapshot signed by John, Paul, George, and Ringo.

My Mom's note said, "I hope you still like the Beatle Boys." Did I still like them? I loved them, but "the Beatle Boys?" That's what her Scots friends called them. I burst into laughter.

"Your mother wrote to the Beatles' fan club last January. And she bought the album in Bangalore three months ago. And left it with me for your birthday dinner." Aunt Rose explained.

Crashing Into America

My Mom's ability to plan astounded me. But I was more amazed by the guitars and drums that rang as bright and clear as the sun rising over the mountains. Music had never moved me like this. I loved to listen to Radio Ceylon's weekly *Top of the Pops*. That is where I first heard the Beatles, but listening on a scratchy shortwave radio was nothing like this. A stereo that hadn't played anything wilder than *South Pacific* was rocking to Ringo's crisp beats and Paul's voice telling the world that money can't buy love. An unbearable urge to jump and shout welled up from deep inside. I hadn't felt anything like this since Christmas mornings when I was little.

Aunt Rose lifted the needle long enough to lead me to the table and say grace. She then let me listen to both sides as we ate an incredible dinner of lamb chops, mashed potatoes, and vegetables. We finished off with chocolate cake and homemade vanilla ice cream. Since I was now thirteen, dessert was followed by coffee with cheese and crackers. It was a meal that couldn't be beat, except maybe Thanksgiving dinner.

"The cake was a Betty Crocker double chocolate mix sent especially for your birthday by your grandma," Aunt Rose explained.

After dinner, she turned the album over again. "Let's get up and try twisting."

My eyes opened wide, and I didn't know what to say.

"I promise I won't tell anyone if you don't," Aunt Rose smiled.

"Me twist? No way, I don't know how."

"It's pretty easy. I chaperone high school events. I watch the moves of the good dancers," the gray-haired missionary said. "I was pretty good at cutting the rug back in my day." She got up from the table and pushed back the Kashmir rug. She stood on the hand-polished cement floor in her old brown loafers. She went up on the balls of her feet, swung her heels, and then her old hips back and forth. My eyes bulged. She was moving right in time to the music. Then, she pulled me out of my chair.

"Kick off your sneakers. It will be easier in your stocking feet."

I followed her orders tentatively.

"Lift your heels and swivel them back and forth. Keep doing that while you bend your knees and let your hips follow your heels."

My stocking feet begin moving back and forth across the polished red floor. My first-grade teacher, a missionary spinster, was teaching me to twist. My four guardian angels shot their bright, bouncing energy through the stereo. Paul and John were now promising they'd be there for me anytime at all.

"There you go," Aunt Rose said, laughing. "I've watched how the kids do this but never had a chance to twist it until now. It's more fun than it looks." She giggled like a teenager.

We faced each other, laughing, spinning around the floor, and twisting the night away.

"Wow," I said with a red face. "I never thought I could do that."

"You are as good a dancer as any high school boy. I've watched them all." She gave me her bright first-grade teacher's smile.

Aunt Rose bent her knees and twisted lower and lower until she was almost squatting. Then, she worked her way back to her full height of five feet, two inches. When the Beatles swung into the rocking, *I'll Cry Instead,* old Miss Klein broke into the peppermint twist, shifting back and forth from her heels to the balls of her feet. Aunt Rose lifted one leg, then the other, her long blue skirt waving. Two or three songs later, she fell back onto the couch laughing.

"Oh, I can't dance as much as I used to."

"Aunt Rose?" I asked.

"Yes, Jamie."

"You don't think dancing is sinful? Mrs. Rivers says it is, and she is a Presbyterian, too."

"No, I don't. God meant us to enjoy our bodies."

I must have looked shocked.

"Up to a point, I mean, and of course, you must be married to uh..." She began stammering.

Right then, a honk from the driveway rescued her. After dinner, she sent her houseboy to fetch the school car to take me back. The mantel clock said seven-thirty, and I had to be back by eight.

"Don't tell too many kids about my dancing because no one will believe you. They'll think you are making up stories." She winked as she kissed me good night on the top of my short crew cut.

I sailed down the steps clutching a box with the rest of my birthday cake and Beatles record. I ran toward the waiting car and the cold dorm. But my heart was soaring high above the lake, gliding through the moonlight, looking for that new world of love and freedom that the Beatles promised. Plus, I now knew it wasn't a sin.

Chapter 6: Sweet Anna Blue-eyes of the DMZ

That birthday dinner was the highlight of the first-semester eighth grade. Still, boarding school was not too bad that year. I liked my roommates. School was getting better all the time. I hated grammar, but social studies, history, and the weekly current events discussion were exciting. Even before the Kennedy assassination, I loved history, especially about wars.

In December of 1961, I spent each day riding my bike or shooting at crows with my pellet gun. One morning, I saw a column of military trucks and tanks on the road alongside the Mission compound. I ran home and read the newspaper; India was at war with Portugal. There had been a non-violent campaign against the Portuguese for Independence in Goa and its other Indian colonies. A dozen *satyagrahis* (Gandhian activists) had marched to Goa in protest. Portuguese soldiers had machine-gunned them as they crossed a river. Prime Minister Nehru had enough non-violence. He sent the Indian Army to liberate Goa. America and Britain protested the attack on their NATO ally, but it was too late. Goa became part of India. And it all happened a hundred miles from my dusty, little hometown of Sangli.

Then, in October 1962, the Sino-Indian War exploded, and the Chinese marched into Indian territory. The following year, Kennedy's assassination and Nehru, the King of India's Camelot, died six months later. In 1965, another war with Pakistan erupted. The world seemed to spin faster every day.

A Pakistani armored division made a lightning advance across the Indian border near Ahmedabad, Gandhi's hometown. India pushed across the northern border to the gates of Lahore, Pakistan's second city. Then, it settled into a stalemate and sputtered to an end after a few months. The early losses embarrassed the Indian government. India launched a massive military buildup. That meant the construction of a reserve airbase outside Sangli.

During that winter vacation, I spent many hours hanging out at the construction site with Matt Nelson. He was about my age, and his family had come to Sangli when I was about six. His dad also taught at the Industrial School and took turns serving as principal with my dad.

The work site was a flurry of activity by hundreds of volunteers. Men worked with picks and shovels to dig up small hills. They filled metal baskets with dirt and stone. A long line of women with sarees tied between their legs walked across the dusty landscape. Each one carried a metal basket of earth balanced on their heads. They poured the baskets into gullies to smooth out a strip. There were a couple of bulldozers, but they rarely worked due to a lack of spare parts. Both our dads were engineers and good mechanics to boot. The industrial school had machine tools, so they were asked to make replacement parts for the two WWII bulldozers.

Matt and I made friends with Major Patil, a retired Indian Army engineer in charge of the project. The Major sat in a tent on the edge of the construction site, drinking tea and making decisions when necessary. But most of the time, he'd pore over maps of the Indian border region maps unavailable to civilians. Matt and I watched him plotting out the advances and retreats that occurred during the war. He showed us how he would have captured Lahore if he had been in charge of the tank column. Pretty exciting stuff for thirteen-year-olds.

During that vacation, I became further addicted to the news. Bahadur Shastri, who succeeded Nehru as India's Prime Minister, died mysteriously in Tashkent, USSR. He died just after he had signed a peace agreement with Pakistan. The Soviets said they investigated, and there was no foul play, but an autopsy was never conducted. The Major and I knew it was a plot by the Pakistani ISI (Inter-Services Intelligence). Still, the three of us couldn't figure out how they did it.

I began following the Machiavellian twists and turns of Indian politics. The Old Guard of the ruling Congress Party appointed Nehru's daughter as Prime Minister. The old boys thought they could manipulate Indira Gandhi to their advantage. Instead, she outmaneuvered and deposed each of them one by one. It was fascinating stuff. I read the papers daily, looking for a new war or political crisis. The news was much more exciting than sports.

At the end of eighth grade, my interest in politics intensified during a trip through East Asia. Every five years, missions sent us home for a one-year furlough. The missionaries toured churches to build support for international work. My parents were due for another furlough when the Presbyterians assigned them a task on our trip back home.

By 1966, colonialism had collapsed around the world. National churches were taking over mission hospitals and schools. There was less justification for Americans running the institutions. The Presbyterian Church still had hundreds of missionaries stationed across the world. Church leaders began evaluating each of their mission stations. The Mission Board asked my parents to assess medical and educational missions on their way home. My family visited Thailand, Hong Kong, Korea, and Japan.

That was all fine with me, especially since we still got to spend a few weeks on an ocean liner crossing the Pacific. The long sea voyages home to the States were precious for missionary kids because we had our typically busy parents to ourselves. We played shuffleboard, swam in luxurious pools, watched movies, and ate like kings for weeks.

In May of 1966, we flew from Calcutta to Bangkok, where we saw terrific new sights of floating markets and giant gold-leafed statues of Buddha. Then, we took a train ride up to Chiang Mai. My parents visited hospitals and schools, and I was oblivious to what my parents were doing. But I enjoyed the new foods, sights, and sounds and playing with my little brother. After we took off from Bangkok, the pilot announced that we would fly over Vietnam, and my heart skipped a beat. I'd closely followed America's escalating war to save Vietnam from the Communists. As we flew over South Vietnam, I looked down from 35,000 feet at the curving coastline green against the bright blue South China Sea. I imagined American troops tracking down bloodthirsty Communist guerrillas in the jungles below. The hills became grasslands and valleys with jungle *sholas* like the Palani Hills of South India. I daydreamed of guiding an Indian Army patrol to a secret Communist hideout. Infamous Communist bandits had kidnapped pretty Helen, my square-dancing partner, and her friends. Because I knew a hidden jungle path, our patrol surprised the Communists and rescued the girls. Of course, I got a kiss from Helen and a letter from the prime minister for my bravery.

In Hong Kong, my parents dragged my five-year-old brother Ted and me on school visits and hospitals because there were no *ayahs* (nannies) to watch him. But he was fun to play with. The family took a tour of the New Territories, and I got to look through binoculars at the guard posts and barbed wire marking the border of Communist China. It was chilling to look into a country where hundreds of millions hated America. I just could not imagine why they hated us so much.

At night, we went shopping along streets lit with neon lights of every color. It reminded me of a Christmas tree. The stores sold the latest electronics, cameras, music, and clothes. I got a brand-new Seiko wristwatch and a Beatles record, one I didn't even know existed - *Revolver*. Even my father got himself a treat.

"At $250, that is a steal," my father said, whistling brightly. "This calculator will save us hours of bookkeeping, Noreen."

In socialist India, you could never find such things, even in Bombay. The night before we left for Korea, we had an eight-course meal with Chinese folk dancers at a nightclub. The stunning women wore colorful costumes that got scantier as the evening wore on. We were finishing our dessert when dancers in bikinis took the stage. My mother hurried us out the door.

"The shows get more risqué as the night wears on," my dad said with a wink.

"Why are the shows risky?" my little brother asked.

My dad quickly changed the subject. That night, I lay in bed for a long time, trying to imagine what happened during the rest of the show.

The next day, the family flew to Seoul, where we stayed with a missionary family. Their daughter Anna had bright blue eyes and curly blonde hair. And was the same age as me. That night, the kids watched US Armed Forces TV while the grown-ups talked in the dining room. It was the first time in five years that I had watched TV, but I kept looking at Anna. She sat in an easy chair wearing white shorts, her long, tanned legs curled under her or draped over the armrests. I sat on the couch with the younger kids. Anna was buried in *The Green Berets,* a novel by Robin Moore. The funny thing was that she would catch me almost every time I stole a glance at her. Even during nightly devotions, when I opened my eyes to peek at her, she cracked open the fingers covering her blue eyes. We both smiled and blushed. How did she know I was looking at her?

In the middle of the night, I crept quietly out of the boys' bedroom to go to the bathroom. When I turned on the light, I saw two bras hanging on a line over the porcelain bathtub. There was a big one like I'd seen hanging in my Mom's bathroom and a small cotton one. I realized with shock and embarrassment that it must be Anna's. How old were girls when they started to wear bras? Then, I immediately felt guilty for having sinful thoughts.

Anna had school the next day. Ted and I had to follow our parents on a visit to a hospital. When we returned, Anna was doing homework at their dining room table.

"Do you like the Beatles?" I asked her.

"Like them? I love them," she exclaimed. "Do you have their new album?"

"Yes! I got *Revolver* in Hong Kong, but I haven't listened to it all the way through yet."

I'd only listened to parts of a few songs at the recording store's listening post.

"Neato. They haven't released it in Korea yet. Where is it?"

"Upstairs."

"Go get it; I'll tell my dad we'll use his stereo."

Soon, we were stretched out on her dad's study floor listening to "Taxman." Anna looked dreamily at the ceiling, her arms and hands traced through the air in time to the music. She wore her tight white shorts again. She turned and saw me staring at her, and we both blushed.

"This album is so damn amazing," she smiled at me.

"You swear a lot," I said, a bit shocked, but I liked it.

"All preachers' kids do, except for the goodie-goodies," she explained.

I made a note to start swearing more.

"Let's see if the next song is good for dancing," she said as she rolled over and crouched by the record player. "Come here and help me pick."

I knelt beside her, our knees touching, but she didn't pull away. And neither did I.

"Are any of these fast songs?" she asked. Her face was inches from mine, and I could smell her hair.

"Maybe this one." I pointed to *Good Day Sunshine*.

I couldn't remember how it went, but I liked it. "It is my damn favorite."

She smiled wide. "It feels good to talk differently from our parents, doesn't it?"

I agreed. Anna's hair brushed my shoulder as she lifted the needle arm and moved it over. We knelt close to each other. A steady beat of chords filled the room. Ringo fired a staccato burst from his drums.

Anna jumped up. "It's not exactly a twist, more like a marching song."

She grabbed my hand, and we started stomping around the room, swinging our arms. Mostly, we were pushing or pulling each other and laughing.

"Anna, what is this racket?" her dad said as he walked in.

"It's not racket, Dad. It's the Beatles," Anna retorted.

"Well, whatever it is, turn it off. I need to prepare for my classes tomorrow."

"Dad, you said we could listen to your record player."

"No, Anna, you told me you would listen to it, and I said that was fine until I needed my study. Now scoot."

Anna and I spent the rest of the evening watching TV with the little kids but managed to sit next to each other on the couch. We touched occasionally and whispered about our schools while the other kids complained. The adults let us keep watching TV when they put the little kids to bed. Then, they told Anna and me to go to bed at ten. I could hardly sleep that night. Our family only had one more day in Seoul. Would I only have one more evening with Anna?

During the day, my parents had planned a visit to Panmunjom in the De-Militarized Zone (DMZ) between North and South Korea. It was where fruitless peace negotiations continued for decades after the shooting war had stopped. Anna asked if she could go along at breakfast, and our parents agreed. She and I sat together on the bus with Ted. On the way out of Seoul, Anna sat by the window so she could point out all the sights. Seoul was such a modern city filled with skyscrapers and grand bridges. Ted insisted on sitting next to her so he could see. When Ted fell asleep, she moved him to the window, sat close to me, and talked in hushed tones about the novel she'd finished reading. She said it opened her eyes to what the war against Communism was all about. Anna and I shared horror stories we'd heard about the Reds as we drove into the DMZ.

"Have you ever seen a Communist?" she asked.

"No, have you?"

"There, look right there," she jabbed me.

I clambered over my sleeping brother, and we stared at North Korean guards by a checkpoint. Our arms were touching. She had blonde hair on her arms. We drove into the so-called Peace Village. A Communist guard stared at us stone-faced.

"Why do they hate us?" I asked.

"Because we are Americans and Christians."

I liked her even more because she had all the answers.

The highlight of the tour was a visit to the negotiating room. It was empty except for the steely-eyed North Korean guards on their side of the room and the US Marines on our side. Anna asked me to spend a few more days at her house as we walked out. My chest almost exploded. My family planned to visit a mission hospital in southern Korea. But Anna said I could take a fast train and catch up with them before they left for Japan. She could convince her dad. After all, we were both fourteen, and why couldn't we spend some time together?

Before getting on the bus, I asked my dad to approve our plan and rejoin them later. At six-foot-six, he towered over me. He turned his grey eyes towards Anna, who was gazing at us.

"She invited you?"

I nodded, and my heart raced. Dad was going to say yes.

"Well, she is an adorable girl, but...," he said with a small smile as my heart sank, "you better ask your mom."

"Gosh-darn it!" I said out loud.

"It would be easier to convince my mom if he agreed," I whispered in Anna's ear.

We tripped over each other, explaining to my mother how easy and fun this would be. It would be an excellent cultural learning experience, too. Mom listened quietly and then shook her head. She took our hands and led us to a steel bench, looking across the harsh wasteland.

"You are both lovely young people and are attracted to each other."

I stared wide-eyed at Anna's shocked face.

"Both of you are young and just stepping into a lovely warm sea. It is the wonderful ocean of romantic love that God has given us." We both blushed red like the stripes on the American flag waving next to the North and South Korean flags.

"However, it is also a source of temptation. You must know that underneath the glimmering surface, romance is a riptide that can take you down. You, my son, are not yet a strong enough swimmer. Jamie, if you care for a girl, your first thought must be to protect her reputation. And Anna, remember that a young woman's most precious gift is her reputation." Mom looked at us and smiled. Anna was ready to cry.

"I am glad you like each other. But remember, God has already picked the right person for you. You will meet them at the ordained time. Who knows, you may meet each other again in college. And you will be more ready for romance by then."

Anna and I sat there in stunned silence. What the heck did staying at her house have to do with riptides and reputation? I jumped up and kicked a rock hard. The rock skidded across the gravel and stopped in front of a North Korean guard. He unshouldered his rifle and aimed at the rock. My anger turned to ice. The guard shouldered his weapon and glared.

The driver honked the horn. My mother stood up and went to join my dad and little brother in line. Anna and I shuffled toward the bus parked next to a barbed-wire fence. We were both too embarrassed to say anything. I reached over and grabbed her hand. She looked up and smiled; our mutual feelings were confirmed. I generously let Ted sit by the window so Anna and I could hold hands all the way back to Seoul. We talked about our schools and favorite movies and music. She knew all the latest hits, and I learned a lot. I hadn't even heard of the Beach Boys. She laughed and teased me. We kept punching each other in the arm. I felt Anna's firm thigh pressing against mine. I squeezed her hand. My heart raced, and I kept wishing my brother would fall asleep, but he stayed wide awake the whole ride.

Anna dropped my hand as she got off the bus. We arrived back in time for dinner. Anna steered me to a chair beside hers. As her dad said grace, I twisted the eighth-grade class ring on my finger. Should I give it to her? Anna kept kicking me under the table until I jabbed her with my elbow. Her father gave us both a stern look. After dinner, the adults excused the kids to watch TV while discussing church politics. There was a big fight in the Presbyterian Church about the ordination of women. In the living room, Anna took charge and made her brothers sit in the easy chair. She scooted Ted to the end of the couch and sat next to me. Anna's eyes looked straight into mine, and I felt her breath on my upper lip. I could barely keep from kissing her. But I knew that would be wrong. Besides, Ted and her brothers spent as much time watching us as the TV. They knew something was up.

The TV was turned off. The two families headed upstairs. Anna pulled me back into the darkened living room and pushed the paperback into my hands.

"Don't let your parents see it. If my dad finds out what that book is really like, he'll kill me. Some scenes are...well..." Her face turned beet red. "It's a true war story. Parts are kind of, well, naughty..." Her lips pressed together in a mischievous grin. "But I bet you'll like it."

Then, she stood on her tiptoes and kissed my cheek. I pulled my class ring off my finger just as her father's study door opened. She jumped back. I pressed the ring into her hands, and she rushed up the stairs. I lay awake a long time, only drifting off as the Korean sunrise turned the sky bluish gray.

Ted and I followed my parents around for the rest of the trip. It rained for our last few days in Korea, and Mom got seasick on the ferry from Busan to Fukuoka< Japan. Then, our family took the bullet train to Hiroshima. The train was spotless. Japan's green countryside sped by in a blur. The doors opened only a few minutes at each station, so we stacked our suitcases by the door to get off in time. Even then, Mom almost got caught in the door.

The Hiroshima Memorial was simple and haunting. Remnants of a concrete building with the rusted ribs of a stately dome. Shadows of bodies incinerated by the first flash of the first atomic bomb. Shadows burned into the sidewalks. A boy was jumping and cremated in mid-air. Suddenly, being an American didn't seem so heroic. I wrote Anna a postcard from Hiroshima. I wrote about how glad I was that America was protecting the world from an atomic war. I thought she would like that, but the words sounded hollow, and I never sent it.

We went on to Osaka, Kobe, and Kyoto. Things kept reminding me of Anna: a girl wearing white shorts, a billboard of a blond woman, and a schoolgirl's red lipstick. I sent another card from the beautiful gardens in Kyoto. The card showed the arches leading into the Imperial Palace. Looking closely, you could see a young couple kissing under it. Before dropping the card in the mailbox, I circled the couples and wrote "Us." Later, I worried she'd get in trouble.

After two weeks in Japan, my family took a ship from Yokohama and sailed toward Hawaii. The ship journey wasn't nearly as fun as our last trip home. One evening, Mom and I stood at the stern. The setting sun made the clouds catch fire. I felt closer to Mom than I had for a long time. I wanted to tell her how I felt about Anna.

"Do you feel the presence of God, Jamie?" Mom looked into my eyes.

"Sometimes."

"No, right now. God is in the skies, the orange, gold, and red clouds, and the salt spray. Can you feel His love spreading across the ocean and embracing the whole world?"

"Yes," I nodded.

"I'm so happy you feel it, too." My curly-haired mother wrapped me in her arms.

I felt some of what she talked about but more guilt than anything else. I had been thinking how cool it would be to be standing there with Anna instead of my mother.

She held me at arm's length and looked straight into my brain. "I know you had a big crush on Anna and wanted to spend more time with her. You must learn to save yourself for the one God has chosen for you. Hold onto that faith, son. It can lead you out of temptation."

"OK, Mom. I will pray for God to guide me." I wanted the talk to end.

And I did pray, but to tell the truth, I spent much more time on that ship reading Robin Moore's novel than the Bible. Reading and re-reading the scenes Anna didn't want our parents to see. I replayed them alone in my bunk at night, changing the soldier and *Montagnard* girl in the hammock with Anna and me. I let my imagination and fingers run wild. A voice lectured me that this was the temptation Mom warned me about, but I didn't care. I wasn't just a kid anymore. Sometimes, a wave of darkness seeped in, and I prayed for forgiveness.

Then, the next day, things would change again. Music on the stereo in the young people's lounge, girls in bikinis at the pool, or a movie reawakened the world I had glimpsed with Anna. I imagined Anna and me as missionaries in Vietnam, rebuilding the country after America won the war. She would be a nurse, and I'd teach. We'd have a family. We would be different from our parents, though. We'd swear and listen to rock music.

Chapter 7: America, Where Are You Now?

Denver was the town my dad called home, even though he'd lived most of his life in India. His parents still had a tiny house on Yates Street. The whole sat at the breakfast table on our first morning back. My grandfather finished reading from *The Upper Room*, a daily devotional. When he finished, he repeated the text. "Love the Lord your God with all your heart and with all your soul and with all your mind and with all your strength and love your neighbor as yourself. There is no commandment greater than these." He prayed for us to follow these commandments and that my family would find a place to live that we could afford.

Grandma served bacon, eggs, and hash browns when he finished. She leaned over to give me extra bacon. She said, "You could just stay here. Grampy and I spend most of our time in Leadville, where he fills in until they find a younger minister. We come down here once a week to take care of this place. If you lived here, we wouldn't have to return so often."

"This house is too small for them, Eunice. There are only two small bedrooms. Where would Jamie stay? He's become a young man and needs his own room."

"We could make do," my Mom said. "And Jamie could go to that school behind us."

"I won't have my grandson going to a school with them Mexicans," Grandma said.

"It's a Catholic school," Grandpa explained. "It wouldn't be right."

"Who are the Mexicans? Redskins?" I asked.

"Jamie," my Grandpa said sternly. "You mean American Indians, but no, they are not."

"Anyway, 'red, yellow, Black, and white, all are precious in his sight,'" I said, and no one responded. "Grandma, you told me we are supposed to love our neighbors," I said, remembering her lecture after my snowball fight five years earlier.

My kind, sweet grandma's face turned a dark red. She stood up and walked into the kitchen, banging the frying pan around. Both of my parents drew in a breath. Grandpa Moore stood up and put his hand on my shoulder. I was sure I'd get a spanking for speaking up.

"Jamie is becoming wise for his years. We do need to love our neighbors regardless of their religion or background. I will pray about this as I take my morning walk."

I was shocked. Grandpa admitted I was right. Grandma, my sweet grandma, was a hypocrite. Five years ago, she was a lovely Christian woman who gave me cookies and read Bible stories as I sat on her lap. What had happened to her in the last five years?

As it turned out, they didn't have to worry about me going to a Catholic school. A church member in Westminster, a Denver suburb, rented us a house at a bargain price. Other Presbyterians pitched in with used furniture. We even got a color TV and a small monophonic record player. I got to keep the record player in my basement bedroom and almost wore out my *Revolver* album on it. I bought three more Beatles albums and a bunch of 45s. I would spend hours in that cement-walled room listening to The Beatles and the hits of summer 1966. Music and daydreams were all I needed.

During the rest of the summer, my parents went on deputation trips around the Synod of the Rockies. They would show slides of Mom's clinic in the slums of Sangli: women bathing children because there was running water, malnourished kids with protruding stomachs receiving porridge, and screaming kids getting inoculated. There are also shots of classrooms with young men studying, an instructor showing them how to use a metal lather, and church services under a neem tree. It was 12,000 miles and a universe away from churches in suburban Denver or rural Wyoming. They dragged us along when they could. I liked going along when I was little, but now I couldn't stand it. My brother and I would have to dress up in clothes from India and stand in front of Sunday school classes, answering stupid questions about India. Junior high kids would roll their eyes and whisper jokes about us. For the first time, I rebelled against my parents and insisted on staying with my grandparents. They were happy to have me and didn't make me do much work. Still, I had to watch Lawrence Welk with them every Saturday night. I spent the summer before the tube drinking pop and eating potato chips between three meat-laden meals daily. I gained thirty pounds.

My first day of ninth grade at Westminster Junior High was a disaster. Nine hundred kids rushed through long hallways that all looked the same. I kept getting lost. People pushed me out of the way. I tried to make friends, but the guys all thought I was a hick because I was clueless about the latest TV shows. And the girls thought I was just another fat seventh grader.

One thing that confused me was that so many kids looked like they were from India. There were dozens of them. They seemed northern Indians, but why were so many in Colorado? In my gym class, I finally got the courage to ask a quiet kid who seemed nice.

"Are you Indian?"

"You stupid scrub," he sneered. "I'm Spanish-American."

He shoved me, and I stumbled out of line.

"Fifty push-ups, Moore," the gym teacher yelled.

That night at dinner, I asked who the Spanish-Americans were.

"They're the descendants of the Spanish conquistadors. They settled in New Mexico and southern Colorado," my Grandpa responded.

"The Mexicans think they are better than regular Americans," Grandma Eunice said vehemently. "They used to call me 'white trash.'"

Grandma was a miner's daughter from Pueblo, and she was still in high school when she met Grandpa at a church camp. I couldn't understand what she had against Mexicans, Spanish-Americans, or whatever they were called. At least they usually left me alone and didn't treat me as bad as the white kids did.

"They are a proud people, Eunice, but I don't think they look down on us," Grandpa said.

"They always looked down on my family," Grandma retorted. Teddy and I both stopped eating. Grandma pushed away from the table and went into the kitchen. Grandpa walked into the living room and turned on NBC news.

On the screen, helicopters fired dozens of rockets into a jungle valley. "The 196th Brigade is in a major battle in Tay Ninh Province east of Saigon," a reporter announced.

Damn! I had studied the map of Vietnam, and we flew right over Tay Ninh on our way to Hong Kong. I forgot the Spanish-Americans and my problems at school. I wondered if Anna was watching the news. Soldiers jumped out of helicopters that hadn't even touched the ground. Giant balls of flame shot into the air as the US Air Force dropped napalm on forests filled with Viet Cong soldiers. A kid who looked like he was in high school spoke into the camera.

"Just a scratch," he said, talking super-fast. "Charlie ambushed us about half a klick up the road. They had us pinned down with machine gunfire. They got my buddy just before air support came in and dusted those *bleep-bleep* gooks."

What was that bleep about?

"Then, we went in and fought our way up that burnt-out hill. They dug tunnels and bunkers deep into the *bleeping* hill, but our 500-pounders blew them apart. The napalm fried the gooks. We shot the few still hiding in their rabbit holes."

The camera panned across a blackened hillside and then zoomed back in on the young soldier's face. I followed every word. Here was an American guy like me. He was fighting against the Communists; if only I could be like him.

"What was super weird, man, was that it smelled like," he paused, and his eyes rolled around in his head. "Kentucky Fried Chicken, extra crispy!" He burst into a high-pitched, staccato laugh. And his eyes burned like blue kryptonite. The last time I'd seen eyes like that was when Mrs. Rivers yelled at Frantzie and me.

"This was another major victory for the United States Army," Mr. Huntley announced. We were back in the New York studio. He read a press release from the Pentagon saying the Communists were losing the war and it would be over in the next year or two.

Then, Mr. Brinkley reported on another story. "There are bonfires all over the South, and this time it is not books being burned, but Beatles' albums."

The southern US, not Vietnam? My mind had a hard time catching up. Why would they burn the Beatles' records? Who were these people? Communists?

NBC News showed a rally in Birmingham where people were throwing albums and 45s into a bonfire. The reporter quoted John Lennon saying, "The Beatles are more popular than Jesus Christ," He pointed out it was one comment from an extended interview.

"That is un-Christian," Grandma Moore exclaimed.

"An arrogant statement," Grandpa proclaimed. "But it does describe the world today."

I hoped Grandma hadn't seen the Beatles albums in my room. I'd have to hide them under my bed. The truth was I actually did love the Beatles much more than I loved Jesus. They were so much more real to me than Jesus was. I still prayed every night, but the words seemed hollow. Especially my prayers for forgiveness. Besides, the old ways of my parents and grandparents were changing. Rock 'n' roll wasn't just a new kind of music. It was so much more. I didn't know quite what it represented. But whatever it was, that would be me.

The weather turned colder, and the leaves fell off the trees. One Saturday, my dad stayed home, and we raked the yard together. We made a massive pile of leaves and buried my dad in it. Teddy and I jumped in the leaves until it got dark. Then, Dad made a big fire in the backyard incinerator. Mom came home from a Presbyterian women's meeting and made wieners and beans for dinner, which we ate outside. It was the first time in weeks the family relaxed together.

That Monday, I rode the bus as usual. I sat next to a burly kid with a blonde crewcut. He pushed me off the bench and into the aisle. I stood up and walked toward the back of the bus.

"Don't come back here, scrub," the Spanish-American kid from gym class yelled. "This is Mexican territory."

I stood in the aisle for the rest of the way. It was clear I had no place in that school. The white kids thought I was weird, and the Mexican kids didn't want me with them. My parents tried to get me more involved with the church youth group. I participated in a few youth outings, but I sat at the back of the bus with a kid with glasses as thick as your hand. He lived in the old farmhouse at the top of the hill and was an outcast, too. We started walking to and from school but never really talked much. Most youth group kids wore the latest clothes, and I wore ones from the thrift shops. Many had their own cars. They often went bowling, which I hated. Most of the guys were cool and knew how to talk to girls. I felt more and more of an outsider.

I refused to take part in school activities. I spent the rest of the year watching TV, eating junk food, and drinking pop. I couldn't wait to go back to Kodai. Life in the States was even more confusing than on our last furlough. This country was not my home, even if most people looked like me. In India, being an American was still cool.

Part 2: Rebelling with Help from My Friends

Chapter 1: What Do You See When You Turn

Revealing my ignorance in Oxford made me a hero when I returned to Kodai.

On the way back to India, we visited my mother's brother, a Church of England parson, in a village just outside Oxford. One afternoon, he took us to tea at some famous bakery in Oxford. On our way to tea, Uncle James pointed out all the famous sights in the historic town. But I was almost fifteen, and the only sites I was interested in were all the short skirts. He parked, and we walked to his favorite teashop and bakery. And right next door, there was a record store. The store was covered with posters about the latest and greatest band, one I'd never even heard of. I turned to my older cousin Nigel, who was walking beside me.

"Who in the world is Sergeant Peppers and his Lonely-Hearts Club Band?" I asked.

He laughed kindly. He explained it was the latest Beatles record, which had come out only a few days earlier. It was a smash hit all over Britain. We stood in a queue, waiting to be seated for tea.

Wow, a new Beatles album. I turned to my parents for permission to go buy it.

"Mom, Dad!"

I made the mistake of interrupting a theological discussion. A stern look from my father told me I had to wait to speak. I hopped around impatiently.

"Jamie," my mom whispered. "Please go ahead and use the loo. You're old enough now to tell us where you are going."

A light broke through. "Sure, Mom. I'm going into the record store next door for a minute."

I turned and ran before she could say no. My dad had given me ten pounds to buy a souvenir in England, more than enough for a record album in 1967.

That little declaration of independence paid big dividends when I got back to Kodai. I was the proud owner of the first copy of *Sgt. Pepper* in the school and one of the first in India.

A few days later, I was scheduled to get on an Air India flight for Bombay via Beirut. I had to return to school in Kodai. My parents and Teddy were taking a passenger ship back to India. Then, the Egyptian Army moved into Gaza, which was supposed to be a demilitarized area. The NATO allies tried to negotiate a settlement, but the Israelis launched a massive counterattack, and the conflict escalated.

My parents' ship was routed around South Africa, and I flew back to India via Moscow. A family friend met my flight in Madras, now called Chennai. He then put me on a southbound train for Kodai Road, where passengers left the relative comfort of the First-Class railroad carriage and boarded a creaky old bus. The trip was a thrilling break into an unknown world. For thirteen months, I had been with family every day. I was utterly dependent on my parents or relatives. Then, I was flying solo across continents. I had to traverse Indian customs and immigration on my own. I took my first train journey alone. I hardly slept. I was terrified. And fucking proud of myself.

As the old diesel bus spewed toxic fumes into the air that grew cooler with each hairpin turn, a trilling of happiness echoed through the cicadas in the surrounding jungle. I knew for once exactly where I was going. And it was exactly where I wanted to be, back in Kodai.

That was really where I was from. Not Sangli. Not Denver or Westminster or wherever. I was a Kodai kid. That is where I'd left my childish ways behind. That was where I had friends who were like me. Kids who knew the taste of hot, crisp *dosa* (rice and dal crepe). They could race their bikes down mountain roads, wade through streams, climb sheer cliffs, and hike forever across hot elephant grass hills. They were who I was. After a year in America, *I was going home*.

I had forgotten how stunningly beautiful Kodai was. The lake was its central feature. It had been a *shola*, a densely forested valley between grassy hills. Early British, Australian, and American settlers dammed the stream and created a road across the dam, or the *Bundh* (enclosure). This made a meandering lake with half a dozen bays and coves. The Europeans built a hotel and boat house by the lake. Hills rose on all sides, and various missionary organizations, Presbyterians and Methodists, Baptists and Mennonites, and Lutherans of various stripes bought these hills. They built stone cottages surrounded by gardens. They cut down the jungle trees, and the Australians planted eucalyptus, wattle trees, and parks, creating an idyllic summer retreat for the missionaries who worked on the plains.

The school started in a hotel behind the boathouse. By the mid-sixties, Kodaikanal School was the largest employer in town. The school occupied the most prominent hill overlooking the lake. Boys' dormitories were built on the lakeside, and girls' dorms on the other. They were separated by the classroom buildings centered around a two-story quadrangle with high school classes on top and grade-schoolers on the bottom. Next to "the Quad" were the cafeteria and office buildings. The flag-green occupied the highest spot on the hill overlooking the girls' dorm, basketball courts, and the gymnasium.

Everything was built out of solid granite, often quarried from the hill the school was built on.

Behind the school was Seven Roads, an intersection from which five roads led down and two roads up. Roads went to the lake or down the Ghat Road to the plains. The Bazaar Road climbed to the top of the Bazaar, or "the Budge." The bazaar was the commercial center of Kodai. At the top of the Budge were a bus station, bookstore, a coffee house, and Hamidia's General Store, which sold bubble gum, belts, sandals, pocketknives, and pretty much anything a kid would need. The bazaar road descended steeply, lined by tiny shops where tailors, silversmiths, and barbers worked. A circle with meat and vegetable markets was at the bottom of the first slope.

Further down were the local vegetarian and non-vegetarian restaurants. All the big and small shops clung to a steep hillside overlooking the plains 5,000 feet below. Mount Perumal, an ancient volcanic mountain covered by elephant grass, broke the view. The plains were where our parents worked, but the Kodai hills were ours.

When I returned for 10th grade, my roommate was a kid named Bobby, whom I'd known since the first grade. He now had what passed for long hair in Kodai, a new stereo with an automatic record changer, and he loved the Beatles. He had no idea who or what *Sgt. Pepper* was and wouldn't believe it was the Beatles until he heard John and Paul singing. Then, he went wild. He raced out of our room to tell everyone we had the latest Beatles album, and soon the small room filled up. A dozen boys sat on the windowsill, beds, dressers, and the desk. The floor was standing room only. I basked in the glory. Sometimes, revealing your ignorance is a good thing.

Bobby and I had the biggest Beatles collection in the school. Since a good friend was the student Audio Visual Committee chairman, Bobby got to DJ at school dances. Canteen was an informal dance that took place once or twice a week. At the very first canteen of the semester, Bobby announced that we had a Beatles album just released in England. It was not even available in the US. A hush fell over the chattering teenager, and we began to play the whole *Sgt. Peppers* album straight through. A few people complained that they couldn't dance to some of the songs, but someone else would shush them so they could hear the music. It was like being in church, but it was our music.

Even as shy and overweight as I was, everyone treated me like I'd just won the big door prize.

A few nights later, right before Lights Out, I pulled out my Bible as I had done every night I could remember. Bobby stared at me and walked over to play Beatles '65, the first time something other than *Sgt. Peppers* hit our turntable.

"Do you pray to Jesus every night, little Jamie?" Bobby asked sarcastically.

"Well, yeah, I guess I do."

He turned up the music. In perfect harmony, Paul and John told me I was a loser.

I kept my head down and pretended to keep reading the Bible. Just then, our door swung open.

"It's Lights OUT, goddammit. And turn off the music, you fucking sophomores," Roger, the lights-out monitor, growled.

He flipped the switch and left us in darkness. Bobby turned the volume down, and we lay quiet for a few minutes.

"What does praying get you? Does Jesus ever answer?"

"Well, I've ...."

"I know what answers come to prayers," Bobby said.

He was crouching over the record player as we spoke. He moved the arm carefully in the dim light. Then, with perfect timing, turned the volume up full blast, "No reply-y-y-y," John screamed into the darkness.

Bobby turned the record player off and jumped back in bed. We could hear Roger slapping the verandah tiles with his rubber *chappals* (sandals). We had both rolled over with our faces to the wall when he burst in.

"I know it was you assholes who were blasting the music," he said as he gave us each a hard soccer kick in the butt. "Next time, I'll report you to the dorm father."

We held our breath and said nothing. A few minutes later, Bobby was back on me about my prayers.

"You know, Jamie, I used to pray every night until last year. I started thinking about why I prayed. I realized it was just empty words. I talked to the school minister, who told me to keep praying and that God would eventually answer. But like the Beatles sing. 'I saw the light. No reply-y-y.' "

He was quoting the Beatles against the Bible! And it completely echoed my experience.

I stared into the darkness for a long time.

"You're probably right. It is just a stupid habit from being a kid."

What was the point of prayer? Prayers changed nothing. Every night, I would ask forgiveness for my naughty thoughts. The only result was a hard weight of guilt pressing on my chest as I slept. The next day, I would catch myself looking at a girl's breast. There wasn't much point in making myself feel bad every night. Of course, this wasn't something I could tell my parents. At home, I still enjoyed our family devotions every night. Devotions and breakfast prayers were the only time the whole family was alone. At lunches and dinners, we almost always had guests. But I couldn't admit that to Bobby, and I certainly couldn't say that I still liked being tucked in by my mom.

My days soon became filled with friends, quick conversations with girls, tests and grades, dances, soccer, and hikes into the grassy hills. That world was now so much more important than family and Jesus. After years of increasing doubts, I turned away from my Sunday school faith one night.

Boarding school life continued in a tumult of tumbles and triumphs. Dorm life was hell one minute and hilarious the next. Some classes were fascinating. Indian Civilization opened my eyes to the ancient culture that surrounded us. I studied hard and debated politics and foreign policy in history and civics classes. I was an avowed Republican because my grandparents and father had consistently voted that way. My identity as a bright but rebellious student grew. I no longer attached the word Christian to my self-proclaimed identity as an American unless I was in front of my parents.

But I was fifteen, and girls were the main thing on my mind. Still shy as hell, I danced wildly and let my hair grow over my ears. Bobby and I snuck off campus and started smoking cigarettes to prove our rebelliousness. Once in a while, we'd meet up with girls doing the same.

Even in 1967, Kodaikanal School was a cultural outpost of small-town, white America of the Fifties. Kodai was stuck in the era of *Leave It to Beaver*. Boys and girls gave each other rings to show they were going steady. Girls still wore bobby socks, and guys sported letter jackets and flattops. Still, Kodai School students began to feel stirrings in the wind.

The Beatles and Rolling Stones were shaking things up at our dances. Families went to the States for furlough, and kids returned with incredible new records like the Beach Boys and the Supremes. A few non-missionary kids started attending the school; their parents worked for the State Department or oil companies in the Persian Gulf. Two of those kids were outright hippies, or so we thought. And I named them Cat and Chick. Cat had long red hair, and Chick wore paisley miniskirts. Within a month, the staff had made Cat cut his hair. Chick had to let the hem out on her skirts. They both started wearing Indian clothes and spent their free hours roaming the wooded hills.

When my friends and I snuck into the woods to smoke cigarettes, we often ran into Cat and Chick at the various hiding places we had made for ourselves. They smoked funny-smelling tobacco but were pretty fun to hang out with. They were both from California and brought music we'd never heard of—Jimi Hendrix, the Doors, and Jefferson Airplane. Bobby and I went crazy over it. At school dances, we'd put the new music on every chance.

At that stage, staying up after Lights Out, listening to wild new music, and smoking cigarettes in the woods was about as far as our rebellion went. It was risky because the last student who'd been caught smoking had been dragged in front of an All-School Assembly, paddled, and then expelled.

Part 2: Rebelling with Help from My Friends

There weren't any other American schools in South India, which meant you had to go and live with your parents, so it was almost like a death sentence. That kid's family returned to the States, where he dropped out of school and got drafted as soon as he turned nineteen.

By 1968, the Vietnam War began intruding on our little world. The draft, graduation, and going back to the States for college loomed on the horizon like monsoon storms. The war and the reality of America were still in the distance.

I told people that I wasn't worried about the draft. Good Americans should fight for their country, and I would volunteer as soon as I finished college. My faith in America as the champion of freedom and democracy was unshaken. In the insular culture of Kodai, there was no contradiction between listening to Jefferson Airplane and being a fan of Richard Nixon. We heard about people's cousins getting killed or wounded and anti-war protesters. But no one in Kodai openly questioned why our country was in Vietnam.

Then, we heard that Dan Carpenter had deserted from the Navy. Dan held our high school pole vault and 100-yard dash records. He was a hero to us and a classmate's older brother. They had grown up in the Kerala backwaters, steering their pontoon boat up and down muddy jungle rivers. Their Dad held revival meetings on the riverbanks. Dan joined the Navy and volunteered as a non-combatant. They assigned him to pilot duty on a landing craft. He was to drive troops up the tributaries of the Mekong River to attack Communists. Part of his duty was to fire the 50-caliber machine gun, which wasn't being a non-combatant as far as Dan was concerned. A former missionary helped him cross the border to Canada before his unit shipped out.

I was utterly shocked. Why would Dan desert and betray America? Things were getting confusing, and the storms caused by the war began shaking our little world.

As a young teenager, I followed the war in the newspapers as a fan might follow their baseball team spring training. I checked the paper daily, but it was far away. The dark clouds storming across America had reached us and begun tearing up our tropical hilltop paradise.

Chapter 2: A Dark Side of the Moon

Kodai School underwent a precipitous change during the 1968-69 school year. While the staff stayed in the Fifties, the student body jumped half a decade forward to catch up with their generation back in the States. As usual, Kodai School was well behind the rest of the West.

The composition of the student body changed; the trickle of non-missionary kids became a steady stream. In addition to business kids, the number of US Government kids increased. Hundreds of extra diplomatic and intelligence personnel were posted to Southeast Asia to support the American war and wanted their families close by but safe. Other international families also started sending their kids to Kodai. Then, we students discovered local ganja was almost as potent as hashish.

During our junior year, Bobby and I moved into a four-bunk room with Charlie Halverson and Subramanian Radhakrishnan Raghavendra (Raghu for short). Charlie was a big guy with curly blond hair and a square jaw. He was the best photographer and golfer in the school and had been with us since fourth grade. Raghu was short and dark, with a hooked nose and an irrepressible laugh. Raghu had arrived in eighth grade, not speaking a word of English. At first, we made Raghu's life hell, teasing him mercilessly, teaching him swear words to yell at girls, and making him give us his seconds in the dining room. He went along, and we defended him against teasing or bullying by anyone else. He understood the deal perfectly and soon began to give back as much shit as we gave him. We've all been best friends ever since.

Raghu was a Tamil and so could speak with the Kodaikanal locals. He soon became a favorite of the street sellers and coffee shop owners. This being South India, coffee rather than tea was the drink of choice. We soon had new safe houses to smoke cigarettes in. Our favorite was the row of brick huts just outside the school compound occupied by the halvah sellers. They came from Kerala, just across the state line from Raghu's hometown of Nagercoil. In the evenings, they would pound peanuts and cook nut brittle and halvah to sell to the students and tourists. We would smoke and tell them stories about the girls in our school that they were fascinated by. But they were much too shy to do anything beyond teasing the girls while selling snacks. The police were known to beat anyone who insulted Europeans, an unofficial law carried over from the British Raj.

One evening in March of 1969, a halvah man named Hamsa came into the hut giggling.

"Smoke this." He handed a lit cigarette to Raghu, who inhaled and burst into a coughing fit.

We passed the strange cigarette around. Soon, we were all giggling and telling outrageous stories. The cigarette had been emptied and re-filled with a mixture of tobacco and ganja. Hamsa claimed that the horse tenders by the lake had given it to him. Our cigarette-smoking hideouts, which ranged from spots overlooking the Tamil plains to small temples in the woods, soon became hangout zones for potheads. Weed was a social flood that washed away the walls of clicks and in-groups that had been part of our over-ripe Fifties culture. Raghu, being the dealmaker he was, learned that most people spent ten rupees for a few grams. He realized that we could get a kilo for 100 rupees.

So, Charlie, Raghu, and I spoke to a few friends. Within days, we raised 100 rupees, and one night after supper, Raghu and Charlie went to make the deal. They had thirty minutes to get to Hamsa's place and back to study hall without getting busted. The library was split into two sections: a large study room with three rows of eight-by-three-foot tables and the actual library with stacks of books and reading tables. I was at the back table nearest the door, watching the clock. Roger, our lights-out monitor, was in charge of the study hall that night. He sat at a small desk on a dais six inches off the floor to look over the room and detect any rule infractions: no comics, talking, or note passing unless the note is strictly related to our studies.

The study hall monitor was in a powerful position as he was allowed to see any notes being passed. He often knew the latest gossip, who had a new crush on who, and he could issue blackmarks to rule breakers. Three black marks equaled one demerit, which meant an hour of detention in the study hall on Saturday morning. If you had more than three demerits, you served your detention working on the woodpile. It was rows and rows of wire containers of eucalyptus and pine branches to be split for firewood. Fireplaces were the only heat for staff homes and dormitories, although dormitories only had fires in the living room. Wood fires were essential since temperatures could dip below 40 degrees Fahrenheit in January and were regularly in the low 50s, even in summer or during the monsoons. So, there was always plenty of work on the woodpile. Charlie, Bobby, Raghu, and I spent many Saturday mornings there.

The clock struck seven, and Roger rang the bell and glared around the room. The whispers tapered off. Raghu and Charlie were still not back. The main door burst open suddenly, and Charlie burst in, carrying his Indian Civilization book. It was 7:02 P.M.

"Halverson, one black mark for you," Roger yelled at Charlie, who lowered his head and rushed back to sit beside me.

He was breathing heavily. "Fucking Hamsa was late, but we got it," he whispered from behind his thick textbook.

Raghu barged into the library, wheezing and gasping as he staggered under a load of heavy books. He always carried all his books to and from every class and back and forth to our dorm, which was at the bottom of a walkway with multiple stone stairs and 200 feet lower than the study hall.

"Two black marks for you, Raghu," Roger thundered.

Charlie stood up in protest, "You are prejudiced, McHenry. You only gave me 1 black mark for being late."

"Another black mark for you, Halverson. And that is for talking in study hall. Raghu got two because he was more than five minutes late."

Raghu slid into his seat, and Charlie put his big book on the desk. We all huddled behind it, our heads down with pens in our hands.

"We got it," Raghu said in the barely audible whisper we'd perfected.

"Where is it?" I asked.

"In your backpack under your bed," Raghu said almost silently.

"What is under your bed?" Roger was behind us. He had the hearing of a hunting dog.

"His notebook," Raghu replied. "We are studying for the Indian Civilization test tomorrow."

"Keep it down," Roger said, walking off to check on two freshman girls whispering in the opposite corner.

"Thank God for A.L. Basham's *The Wonder that Was India*," Charlie whispered. "It always saves me."

Indian Civilization was also one of the few subjects that he took seriously. He had a brilliant mind but hated school.

The next day, we were to meet after tea for distribution. It was at one of the more remote smoking spots, the Temple in Raja's Woods. It was below the Bundh at the end of the lake and part of a compound that belonged to the Raja of Coimbatore. He was rarely at the large house, and his servants never ventured into the acres of pine trees that grew at the back of his property. A shrine dedicated to a guardian deity was in a clearing above a stream. It was the intersection of several forest paths, and tall pines rose in a circle around it.

Bobby and I stopped by Kennedy, the high school girl's dorm, to pick up Rachel. She was a government kid who'd arrived the previous semester. Her mother lived in Ceylon (Sri Lanka), and her father worked for the US government doing something in Vietnam. The three of us slipped out of the school compound from a side gate. We walked down the Ghat Road and then cut off to the Lutheran Compound as if visiting the cottage where Bobby's family lived every Hot Season. A few Lutheran staff members lived there year-round, so we had to be highly alert. We crossed the stream, and I bent down, pretending to tie my shoe. Bobby and Rachel looked around. I listened for the sound of a car or even a bike. Then, we dashed off the road and through some bushes. We found our way to the path that led through the woods to the Temple.

Mickey Carpenter, one of our classmates, was there with his girlfriend. He was the goalie on our soccer team and a nice guy, but we didn't hang out too much with him. There were also a few other guys from Wissy, the high-school boys' dorm, and more girls from Kennedy that surprised me. How did Charlie and Raghu know they were potheads? We had never smoked with any of them. Someone pulled out a Wills cigarette with the end twisted into a wick. Not having rolling papers, we often emptied the tobacco out of a cigarette and refilled it with the ganja.

I took a hit and passed it to Rachel. She was gorgeous. Bobby was lucky to have her as a girlfriend. I was still too shy, even when asking girls to dance, let alone asking them out on a date.

She inhaled deeply and tried to hold the fiery smoke in to get the full effects. She handed it to Bobby, and he passed it on to Mickey Carpenter, who took a deep hit and held it in like a pro.

"Damn! This is go-o-uud shit!" Mickey said with his slight Southern drawl.

"G-uuud shit or goose-shit?" Rachel replied.

We all broke into the ganja giggles.

Then, I heard someone crashing through the woods. "Ditch it, someone is coming."

It could be a staff member because Raghu and Charlie knew the path. I put my pack of cigs in my back pocket where I could throw them away without being seen.

Instead, Roger stumbled out of a stand of seedlings. I blanched.

"Damn, you guys sure got a good hide-out," he said.

"McHenry, what are you here for? Gonna bust us for smoking?" Bobby asked.

"Hell no, I'm in on the deal too."

"Yeah, guys, Roger is cool," Mickey said. "He got me stoned when I visited him last summer in Bombay."

The group talked and smoked cigarettes for almost an hour. Finally, Raghu ran up the path laughing, carrying his book bag. It looked much lighter than usual. Charlie came steaming up behind him.

"I'm gonna fucking goose the hell out of you fucking Dravid," Charlie yelled. He was carrying my backpack, sweat streaming down his face.

"Raghu put his books in your backpack and said it had the grass," he explained.

Raghu sat on the ground, chuckling as he pulled out packages wrapped in newspaper and string. I picked one up. It felt like a package of the hot snack mixture.

"One for each of you, nicely disguised," Raghu laughed.

Sure enough, inside the first package, buried in the mixture, was another with the unmistakable smell of ganja.

Rachel looked at her watch. "It's 5:45. You were supposed to be here at 4:30. Where the hell were you?"

"We had to make sure it was good stuff," Charlie said. "Then, Raghu parceled it up into your shares and disguised it in a package of IJ."

"Who cares," Roger picked up his package and turned to leave. "I'm just glad you crazy fuckers didn't try to smoke it all and fall off a cliff somewhere. But we'll be late for supper if we don't leave now."

"Let's go back separately," Mickey said. "Leave in small groups. We'll go up by the Raja's house and across the Bundh."

Raghu and Charlie left last but didn't show up for supper. I was getting worried. I knew something was wrong when they didn't show up for study hall. We learned there was an emergency dorm meeting. Charlie and Raghu had been busted. They were detained at the principal's house until the administration determined their fate. The next day, we heard they would be expelled for being drug pushers.

Everyone was outraged, even straight kids. Chris, who never smoked, and Roger, the football quarterback no one suspected of smoking, took it upon themselves to intervene. They told the principal that Charlie and Raghu were not dealers. It wasn't their idea. A bunch of kids went in together to buy a kilo of weed, and they volunteered to pick it up. And they told the principal that seventy percent of the high-school students smoked pot and had done it for months.

The principal didn't believe them. But he said that if they could get the students to return the whole kilo of marijuana, he would ask the School Council to be lenient. Roger and Chris went around the dorms explaining their mission. The next day, they returned to the principal's office with two pillowcases of marijuana. When they weighed the pillowcases, instead of a kilo of ganja, they found 2.5 kilos. It was obvious that Charlie and Raghu were not the only sources. They were kicked out of school dorms but allowed to attend classes for the rest of their junior year.

Bobby was to return to the States at the end of the school year. The Lutheran missions were cutting back on staff, and his dad took a new job at a seminary in Dubuque, Iowa. Bobby decided he would stay in India for his senior year. I invited him to stay with my family for during long vacation. Bobby's parents had other plans, especially after the big grass bust. So, Bobby was going "home" to Iowa. I had no idea where it was. But if Bobby was going to Iowa, I figured I should apply to colleges in that state. So, when it was my turn to talk to the high-school counselor about colleges, I was happy he advised me to apply to Grinnell College. It was a former Congregationalist college started by abolitionists in the 1850s. A previous school chaplain had come to Kodai from Grinnell, and it was known to be an excellent school. I didn't know the difference between Ohio, Iowa, and Idaho. Still, if Bobby was going to be there, I would too. I submitted my application.

Our junior year ended, and Bobby left for the States. After a short vacation, school started again in mid-June. I was rooming with Raghu and Charlie in Room 8 again. With Bobby gone, Rachel and I were both really bummed out. We consoled each other by sharing news and bits of letters from him. We soon became close friends.

On July 19, 1969, our rebellion took a different path. The next day, Americans were landing on the moon. It was the first time in human history that anyone had traveled to another entity in space. The Indian papers were full of the story. And the staff made us gather in the gym on July 16th for an all-school assembly. Kodai School students listened to the launch of Apollo 11 on Voice of America, crackling shortwave radio amplified over aging big box speakers we used for Canteen. During the next few days, every class discussed the latest news reports, the implications for human civilization, how it would impact our future, and a hundred other topics related to the moon landing.

The landing was expected to occur late on July 20th, but it would be early morning on the 21st, a Monday in India. The Indian government declared a national holiday, but not Kodai School. It was so unfair for the Indian kids to have the day off when the Americans didn't. We were probably even breaking the law. All the students were agitated. Most of our dorm parents and teachers sympathized with us and intended to spend the day following the moon landing. Rev. Stepanski's sermon was about the moon landing and how America was showing the glory of God to the world. If it was such a special day, why wasn't the school giving us the day off? All day, we talked of nothing else. Over Sunday lunch in the Dining Room, on our walks into the woods, waiting on the flag green for tea, and at the dinner table, the injustice of denying us a holiday grew more and more significant. It became an outright insult to each of us and our country. Someone suggested we have a school strike. I can't remember who it was. But we all responded, yes!

If the school administration wouldn't declare a holiday, the students would. We planned to boycott classes and spend the day at Bear Shola Falls listening to Voice of America on a transistor radio. At the evening vespers service, Rachel sat beside me in the chapel. I told her about the planned walkout. Later, we stood in the shadows outside the chapel and talked over the plan in hushed tones with her roommate, Kristina. They were entirely on board. By morning, they organized three other girls to join us, which was good because a bunch of guys chickened out at the last minute. Still, we had over a dozen juniors and seniors. Jocks, straight-A students, and rebels were all ready to walk out together.

The kitchen manager set up a transistor radio on a chair at breakfast. It was hard to hear, but the landing craft was on the moon. Neil Armstrong and Buzz Aldrin would go on a Moonwalk in the next hour or two. The group of rebels ate quickly. We made our way in twos and threes to the side gates of the compound. We slipped out furtively and gathered near the Bundh. When everyone arrived, we started the thirty-minute walk to Bear Shola. Would we be walking along a road in the mountains of South India while they were walking on the moon?

The group listened to the radio all the way. Jimmy, another government kid, had a Sony radio glued to his head. He would shout out a running commentary. We all lit up when we got out of sight of the main road. But only cigarettes. We knew we would get caught, so no one brought grass. Charlie strode ahead while his short, red-haired girlfriend struggled to keep up. Raghu had stopped at the last cigarette shop to get matches, and I'd waited for him. Then, we ran to catch up with the gang.

"The moon landing proves God is dead," Rachel said as we pulled into earshot.

"No, it doesn't," Greg, one of the jocks, responded. "The landing and all it took to get there show God has blessed America with the best engineering and science skills. God is showing the world we are better than the Communists."

I was surprised because Greg wasn't a missionary kid. His dad worked for the US Government in Vietnam. Kristina countered that God was a concept people needed until they had science. Greg argued that science showed the tremendous power of God. I'd given up on my Sunday School Christianity, but I still kind of believed in God. Kristina's explanation made sense to me.

As we walked into the forest path at the end of the road, she said, "It doesn't matter what you believe. There was a force for love and good in the world. You can call it God or Allah or Krishna or look at it purely scientifically. It is the same thing. It matters whether you are supporting a better future or trying to keep people locked in the past."

Raghu and I walked behind them, listening to their conversation. We could hear the falling water through the trees.

"Moore," Raghu whispered in my ear. "You should take Rachel to our hideout above the falls and get her to suck you."

Part 2: Rebelling with Help from My Friends

"Fuck you," I grabbed his arm, pulled him aside, and dug my nails into his dark skin, trying to draw blood. "It's not like that with Rachel and me. We're just friends, and she's Bobby's girl. I'd never betray a best friend!" I whispered fiercely.

"You're an idiot, Moore. Everyone can see she wants you," he whispered loudly.

Rachel turned to look at me. Raghu shook me off and ran up the path laughing. We left the road and walked through the *shola*. We heard a car pull up in the parking lot below before we reached the waterfall.

"It's the school van," someone shouted.

Everyone ditched their cigarettes and scattered into the bushes. Raghu, Rachel, Kristina, and I ran around the side of a small bamboo thicket. We could hear the principal huffing, puffing, and yelling as he ran up the path.

"I know you are here, boys," he shouted into the woods.

The rush of the waterfall answered him.

Then, I saw Rachel grab Kristina's hand. "Come on out. Let's show him we're not afraid to take a stand against his stupid rules," she whispered.

They both stepped out into the open. Following their lead, Raghu and I emerged. Soon, all of us were standing silently facing the speechless principal.

Rachel spoke first. "People all over the world are celebrating a unique day in the history of our planet, a day that celebrates the best of America. Why are you refusing to celebrate it?"

"Get back to school now," he yelled.

His scalp was bright red under his blonde crew cut. We walked down the path and piled into the big van on top of each other. Raghu, Charlie, Mickey, and I sat on the backbench with Rachel and the other girls on our laps. The rest crammed into the back seat and luggage space.

When the van started, Greg asked why the school ignored the Indian Prime Minister's declaration of a national holiday. Didn't that show disrespect for our host country? The principal glowered at him. We all began arguing with him at once. It was a historic day. Why shouldn't we have the day off? He couldn't get a word in sideways. He turned his back to us and stared out the window, letting our arguments bounce off his red and blond head. The vice-principal waved his arms as we drove up to the flag green. His face was bright reddish orange.

"No wonder you Indians call us red carrots," I whispered to Raghu, who cracked up.

"All the students are boycotting classes, from grade school to senior high. Half the staff has joined them," the vice-principal shouted as we piled out of the van.

We all started laughing and cheering. The principal started running toward the library. We took off behind them. It was filled with students and staff. Kids were sitting on top of desks or lying on the floor listening to a Voice of America broadcast. Several teachers stood around a radio at the checkout desk. The librarian had hooked it up to the PA system. As we boiled into the room, the principal shouted for everyone to return to their classrooms. Mr. Grant, a tall man with a goatee, stood up and took the principal by the arm. Several teachers followed them outside to discuss the issue.

While they were outside, Neil Armstrong said his historic words. Everyone gave an earth-shattering cheer, and the principal and teachers rushed back into the room. Everyone stood in silence, listening to the first man on the moon.

When the astronaut finished, the principal and VP walked out. Mr. Grant calmly announced that school was dismissed for the day. We let out a short victory cheer. Then, we continued listening to the broadcast with the rest of the world. It was a great day to be an American and our first success in organizing against the system. We fought the Law, and WE won.

After the moon landing protest, we had a big battle with the staff over the dress code. One day, the senior high girls wore miniskirts halfway up their thighs. The principal suspended them for a day. The girls marched down to the Post Office and sent protest telegrams to their parents. Our anger was building to the boiling point. That night, a group of boys sneaked out and threw volley after volley of rocks onto the principal's tin roof. Then, we raced back to our dorm and were back in bed before the dorm father and the lights-out monitor did a bed check. All-out war with the staff was on.

A couple days later, we unleashed another protest. Most guys had boycotted the barber for weeks, but we had kept our hair slicked down with Brylcreem to make it look shorter. One night, we all washed our hair and wore it long the next day. Mine almost covered my big ears. Rachel made me blush when she said I looked like George Harrison.

The principal suspended the boys and compounded us, which meant we were forbidden to leave the school compound. We couldn't go to the Post Office to telegraph our parents. We staged a sit-in at the library while some girls brought telegraph forms for us to write on. We circulated a petition to the School Council. By the end of the week, over ninety percent of the students had signed the petition. Dozens of parents sent letters and telegrams supporting us. Just before the end of the semester, the principal announced a new dress code. We won the right to let our hair grow, and the girls could wear short skirts but not more than three inches above their knees. We were fed up with their rules. But now we were winning. Things were getting better all the time.

Part 2: Rebelling with Help from My Friends

Total chaos broke out the last night before everyone left for the long winter vacation. Dozens of senior high guys and girls snuck out of the dorms. We broke into the school chapel, Union Church, St. Peter's, and the Anglican Church above Coaker's Walk. We rang the bells right at midnight. Then, a dozen of us stoned the principal's roof, throwing a handful of good-sized rocks each before we scattered and ran. We watched from hedges all night as staff and Gurkha guards raced around the town, responding to one outrage after another. When we were kids, we worshipped the Gurkha watchmen. But now that we were at war with the staff, they were part of the enemy.

We retreated to the woods for a while, then snuck down to the top of the town bazaar. The Bazaar Road went down a steep hill, but the post office road followed a ridge near the summit. Along that road was the town siren that sounded throughout the day, telling the time to the whole valley: six and seven A.M. to leave your house and then start work. Noon and one P.M. lunch break, five P.M. quitting time, and nine P.M. bedtime. We broke the lock on the siren and blasted it around three A.M. Another group tipped over the police traffic island at Seven Roads. Charley was with a group walking along Bazaar Road when they heard a car and ducked into a stand of trees. The Vice-Principal and a Gurkha guard raced towards the blaring siren. Charlie threw fireworks into the road to warn the siren crew. But we had already disappeared into the woods when they hopped out of the school car and shut off the siren. They looked around, wondering where we had gone. We silently stood behind trees, laughing to ourselves.

The staff was losing control. We were asserting that we were part of our generation. We were expressing our right to be heard, but in the full-throated roar of rebellion, we had no idea what we wanted to say. Luckily, we all left for vacation before things spun out of control.

Chapter 3: Hey Bungalow Bill

Despite our rebellion against the oppressive rule of our enemy, the staff, we student rebels, had no understanding of what was happening back in the States. Our only sources of news about America were *Time* Magazine and Voice of America. I supported Nixon and our mission in Vietnam. So, it was ironic that Republican-leaning *Time* Magazine was the medium for my first radical epiphany.

Back in Sangli, the mind-blowing excitement of our school revolt was replaced by unending boredom. I was without my friends, without a source of ganja, and with precious little music. Our family didn't even have a record player. I'd failed to convince them to bring the one the family had in Denver. My dad explained that customs duties would be higher than buying a record player in Bombay. But we never bought one. I had a growing collection of Beatles' 45s and several albums. But even to listen to my records, I had to go to Matt's house next door. Or bike five miles to Miraj to visit the American doctors' kids and listen to their music.

When I was little, boarding school was hell, and Sangli was heaven. Bike riding, lounging, tree climbing, bird-hunting. And three full meals a day plus tea-time came with all the cookies I could eat. But by my senior year, my universe had turned upside down. Going back to the plains meant exile from everything I cared about. The Indian kids I'd grown up with had become strangers. They said we European kids acted stuck-up, but we weren't. It was just that our worlds grew apart, separating or maybe segregating as we grew older.

As children, Daveed, the oldest son of our *mahli*, and I were inseparable. We played in the "whale tree" for hours. We had a soccer football team, and as the ball owner, I was captain. I'd always been tall and athletic, so I played goalie. Daveed was always my center forward. We had a way of communicating on the field so that I'd drop-kick the ball right to the spot he'd run for, and as often as not, he'd power it into the goal. We also played marbles, spun wooden tops, and rode out to the villages with my mom for her public health clinics.

Daveed and I help my dad print pictures in his darkroom. He had a camera on his neck wherever he went, both for the mission work and the family. Under the red lights of the darkroom, Dad would get a kick out of making us figure out who was who on the negatives. Who was the one with white hair and a dark face? And who was his reverse image? Then, Dad would make a print on photographic paper and throw it into the developer. We'd watch in wonder as the image slowly appeared, grey and blurry. I would gently rock the black developer tray as Dad had taught me. When the picture slowly swam into focus, it would show who was who. We always guessed wrong. Once, we printed photos of us washing buffaloes with Daveed's father. One shot showed a boy jumping off a water buffalo into the river.

"That is you, Jamie-baba. I remember you slipped off the buffalo and landed face-first in the water!" Daveed said when we looked at the negative,

My Dad made the print.

"Ha, ha," I shouted when the picture became clear. "That one is you. You are just as black and *chichi* as that ugly water buffalo."

"Jamie, I will have none of that language in my presence," my dad exploded. "Never, never use that word again."

He pulled the print through the stop bath, shoved it into the fixer, and opened the darkroom door.

"Go to your room and wait while Daveed and I finish this roll."

Completely stunned, I lowered my head and walked away. My face was burning in shame. What had I done that was so wrong? Kids used the word *chichi* all the time in Kodai. It was what Kodai kids called Indian English. When we spoke with an Indian accent, we were talking *chichi*. What was it that bugged my dad so much?

I waited for almost an hour while my dad and Daveed finished printing the family pictures. Then, Dad walked into the bedroom.

"Bend over, Jamie," he said.

Then, he gave me three sharp spanks from his strong hand. That was the only time I remember getting spanked by Dad. It was usually Mom.

"Never, never use that word. Do you even know what it means?" he shouted?

"It means dirty," I stammered through my tears.

"It means impure; it means feces. It means SHIT. That is what the British called the Anglo-Indians. No son of mine will ever call another human being SHIT!"

Hearing him swear was as shocking as the sharp strokes of his hand. The lesson was to show me that Daveed was a brother. Marathi had many different words for brother: true-brother, cousin-brother, mother-brother. Daveed was definitely some kind of a brother. We'd ride my bike to go bird hunting; he'd sit on the crossbar and steer while I held the gun and pedaled. Daveed and I stayed best friends until I went to boarding school, and we still hung out during my long vacations.

Our friendship sputtered as we grew older. During my vacations, Daveed was in school all day and had to study hard each afternoon and evening. If he sneaked out, his father would beat him. When I got into high school, I got bored with bike riding and shooting birds. He still liked it, but when he finished his tenth year, he had to study all day for a year before taking his matriculation exam. He passed it with one of the highest scores in Sangli and won a scholarship to nearby Walchand Engineering College. So, by my senior year, he was already a college student. He wasn't very friendly anymore, but my parents kept inviting him to the house for tea. He'd discuss things politely with them. But he would make sarcastic comments about everything American when we'd sneak out for a smoke. I didn't care. We really didn't have much in common anymore.

Our other soccer teammates had also gone their separate ways. Two were studying at the local business college. Some had gone to work with their fathers as stonemasons or carpenters. A few were in the Industrial School training as mechanics. My mother got us all together that November and held a formal tea for us.

Teatime was a big deal at our house. Our family had a proper four o'clock tea that included a spread of cookies and sandwiches. On this occasion, Sugandh, now our cook, baked a chocolate cake. It was decorated with blue and yellow icing, the colors of our childhood football team. There were ten figures playing soccer and the goalie with yellow hair.

"Wah-Wah!" My teammates all exclaimed when he brought it out.

I glanced over at Matt, who also played on the team. He wasn't as into football as I was. He was my co-captain since he was the other European kid on the team. He rolled his eyes, and I grimaced. This was all too embarrassing.

My mom always presided over the dining table. And this tea was no exception. She covered the long teak table with linen and set with her Noritake wedding china. Sugandh and Yeshwant served each boy tea and cake. When Yeshwant served his son, he beamed with pride. Daveed's face darkened, and he shrank into his seat.

My mother asked each boy what they were doing and what their plans were. She conducted the conversation by nodding or waving her teacup at the person expected to speak. Most of the team tucked into the cake, peanut butter cookies, and jam sandwiches. They were all proud of their adult jobs or further schooling. Only Daveed, Matt, and I held back.

"This will be Jamie's last year unless he attends an Indian college as his father did. Jamie, please explain about being accepted by Grinnell College and what you are interested in studying."

I dutifully obeyed. Then, asked Daveed.

"I'm going to place first in my class every year so I can get a good job and move as far away from this dusty little town as possible," Daveed said tensely. He then put his teacup down and closed his eyes as if to shut himself off from all that surrounded him.

Part 2: Rebelling with Help from My Friends

Well, Daveed and I still had something in common. I, too, couldn't wait to leave the dryness of our dusty hometown on the dry Deccan plateau. I used to think I was someone important there. I knew I was just a *lal gazar* (red carrot) to the jeering Indian kids I rode past on my bicycle. To most of the townspeople, we were *gore lokh* (white people), an irrelevant curiosity. Yet the small Christian community still treated us like nobility. It made me mad when they acted as if I was important because I was the missionary sahib's son. By then, I didn't believe in Jesus anymore. And their adoration made me feel like a complete hypocrite.

I was someone in Kodai, up in those cool, green hills. I was a senior. I was co-editor of the school yearbook. I wrote a column for *The Thar*, our weekly school newspaper (four mimeographed pages stapled together). There, I was one of the smart kids and one of the rebels. I was tall—almost six-four with a strong, wiry body. I was good at basketball and one of the best soccer goalies ever at Kodai School. I had a big nose, but almost every time I smiled at one of the girls, she smiled right back, so I couldn't have been too ugly. Unfortunately, I still could hardly talk to girls without turning beetroot red. I was Indian that way. I always thought about girls, but my tongue got tied the moment one came close. In class, I could be articulate as hell. I debated with teachers and students, guys or girls, on issues from the rich and wonderful history of India, racial injustice, the stupidity of poverty amid affluence to the rights of the Palestinians, Communism, and America's role in the world as the champion of democracy. Yet I could barely say hi to a pretty girl without stuttering.

The exception was Rachel Townsend, Bobby's old girlfriend. She had long chestnut hair and deep, dark eyes. She was super pretty but still easy to talk to. I guess I didn't feel nervous with her because she was my best friend Bobby's girl and so off-limits to me. Since Bobby left, Rachel and I became best friends. We went for long walks in the woods, talking about school, world events, and how we missed him. We would wander together from one secret hangout to another. Rachel and I would join in the socializing and debates if others were there. Or, if we were alone, we'd lie on the ground looking up at the eucalyptus and or pines. Rachel would always ask me to light her cigarette. She'd lean over and put her face so close to mine that I could smell her sweet-sour skin and lemon shampoo. I wanted to kiss her so badly I could hardly stand it, but she was still Bobby's girlfriend. On that long vacation, I spent a lot of time daydreaming about her and longing for her letters.

November was one long day after another in boring old Sangli, where nothing had ever changed. The weeks of boredom stretched on. I'd ride a bike every morning with Matt, the other missionary boy. We'd hunt for birds, then ride to the school Office to see if we'd gotten any mail from friends in Kodai.

Sometimes, Matt and I would ride to the river to smoke cigarettes without anyone snitching on. Other times, we'd bike or bus to Miraj to hang out with other missionary kids and complain about how boring things were.

Still, the following day would be different; it was Thanksgiving Day and a welcome change in my routine. It was the one American holiday when all the missionaries celebrated together. All the doctors and their families from Miraj and American missionaries and Peace Corps Volunteers from the whole region were coming to our house for a Thanksgiving dinner that couldn't be beat. First, I had to go to another dinner party with my parents.

Chapter 4: Tiger Hunting with a Bicycle and Gun

Our family and the Nelsons, who lived next door, were invited to dine with the Collector, the top government official in the district. He had an MBA in business administration from Harvard and a PhD from the London School of Economics. He was in the upper rungs of the Indian Administrative Service. India followed the British model of separation between the state and the government. A civil service professional ran the state's day-to-day affairs at each level. At the same time, the elected politician made policy decisions as the people's Government representative. The politicians had limited control because they couldn't hire and fire Civil Service employees. The worst they could do was transfer them to a backwater somewhere or appoint them to a plum post. Mr. Gokhale was sent to take good care of Sangli, the home district of Dada-sahib Patil, the Congress Party boss for our state of Maharashtra. Sangli was a bit of a backwater. However, it was a stepping-stone to important postings because it put the Collector in daily touch with the party boss.

Along with missionaries, the Collector invited the Peace Corps regional director and two local professors, one a leading Hindu scholar and the other a respected Muslim historian. The adults sat in the formal sitting room with pre-dinner snacks and tea, discussing questions the Collector would bring up. Given the company, he did not offer beer or cocktails even though he had a private liquor license.

After we boys sat listening for a respectful time, Sanjay, the Collector's son, invited Matt and me upstairs to the billiards room. A teak wood table covered with fading green felt sat in the middle of a whitewashed room. The room was bare of furniture other than a rack for pool cues. Sanjay was home on break from the University of Bombay. We'd met a few times before. He set up the billiards and offered me the first shot. Sanjay explained how to line up the angles and aim. I suggested we take practice shots rather than playing a game. I was not too fond of competition, except for sports, which I was good at. Sanjay ignored my suggestion, took the first shot, and pocketed two balls and then another one.

Matt got two balls on his turn and smiled with satisfaction.

As I was about to shoot, Sanjay asked, "So, what do you Americans think of your heroic army's massacre in My Lai?"

I jerked, and the cue almost tore the aging green cloth. Sanjay winced and rushed over to the table to rub it with a billiard ball to erase the mark.

"Sorry, I should have waited until you shot."

I was fucking upset. The Indian papers had reported American soldiers shooting and torturing innocent civilians. But these reports were obvious lies. From reading *The Green Berets,* I knew that America was protecting Vietnam from evil Communists. I'd seen what the Communist soldiers were like in Panmunjom. They hated us. The papers were biased because America had made a stupid decision to ally with Pakistan in the 1965 war. India had criticized the US in Vietnam, so President Johnson reversed JFK's friendly policy toward India. That was a bad mistake, but no way would American soldiers shoot women and children.

"What's your proof?" I asked after I saw I hadn't done lasting damage to the billiard table. "Those stories came from the North Vietnamese propaganda agency."

"No, those stories are based on reports by Seymour Hirsh, an American journalist."

"Show me. Even the *Indian Express* said there were only accusations."

Sanjay stepped into the hall and waved for us to follow him into his bedroom. It was an airy room with a large fan and a balcony overlooking the garden. He gestured towards a chair, looked out the door to see if anyone was in the hall, and shut it tight. He opened a dresser drawer and pulled a tabloid newspaper from under a pile of clean underwear. Sanjay threw a copy of *Blitz* on a carved rosewood coffee table.

"That's a commie rag," I said, but Matt picked it up.

"Shit! Look at these pictures."

Black-and-white photos of mass graves and dismembered bodies covered the front page.

"You don't want to believe your beloved America is killing innocent women and children. They are worse than the British in India," Sanjay hissed.

I turned the pages of the newspaper. A full-page picture of a scantily clad Hindi film starlet caught all of our attention. We heard his mother calling as she came up the stairs. He grabbed the newspaper and threw it under his bed. She opened the door and looked stern but regal in her yellow silk sari.

"Boys," she said in an Oxford accent. "Nothing good happens behind closed doors. Do come and join us as we adjourn to the dining room."

The dinner conversation was lively. The Collector kept steering the conversation toward economic development and away from Vietnam whenever Sanjay brought it up. The food was an exquisite five-course Indian meal with vegetarian and non-veg dishes. Matt and I stuffed ourselves.

By the next morning, I was hungry again. I woke to the aroma of baking bread coming from the kitchen. I was still mad about Sanjay's stupidity in believing something that *Blitz* would print. Those pictures had to have been from a Communist massacre. Then, I remembered it was Thanksgiving Day. I jumped out of bed, my stomach already growling. The kitchen buzzed with activity and laughter when I wandered in, looking for food.

Our *maestri* oversaw the big meal since it was his kitchen, but that didn't sit well with Dr. Blair's cook, Shidhoo. His *sahib* was the medical director of the most famous hospital in the area. And he was the most senior of all the missionary cooks. Previous Thanksgiving dinners were held at the Blairs' bungalow. Shidhoo had flawlessly executed each dinner under his stern-eyed control. He didn't allow joking and chitchat in his kitchen, but his pot roast fell off the bone, and his creamy gravy was the stuff of kids' legend.

At boarding school, Presbyterian mission kids often reminisced about his homemade peanut butter cookies. When Shidoo was baking, we would sneak through this kitchen on any excuse. We hoped to grab a cookie from the *pinjara* (screened cupboard) before he could spot us. The Blairs had five boys, so being at the front of the line was essential. The last ones often got nothing from the cookie raid but a swat on the rear end from Shidoo's wooden spoon. On Thanksgiving, Shidoo was given jurisdiction over desserts to spare him the indignity of taking orders from a younger man. With the title of pastry chef, he set up his headquarters in the Nelson's kitchen across the lane.

In contrast to the Blairs' cook, Sugandh was a well-known joke-cracker. He was skilled at roasting, frying, and baking. He could make an old piece of water buffalo meat as tender as a steak at Sizzler's in Bombay and whip up tasty gravies and sauces almost as good as Shidoo's. Sugandh could bake cakes and flawless lemon merengue pies all in an old cast iron wood oven. But he and his friend Roki saw work as a place to have fun. Roki worked for another doctor's family from a mission hospital on the coast near Goa.

Both Roki and Sugandh's kitchens were places to tell stories, hear the latest gossip, and tease us missionary kids. When I was little, I loved sitting on a stool in a kitchen corner and listening to Sugandh's stories. He would tell us about tigers or *rakshasas* (demons) that inhabited dark jungles. But the best stories were about Sivaji, the wily Maratha warrior who fought off countless invading armies.

That morning, however, I was more interested in breakfast. Unfortunately, Sugundh was too busy cooking to pay me much attention. As he and Roki worked, they hit jokes, the literal translation from Marathi. They hit one joke after another like tennis balls sailing off a cricket bat. Yeshwant, the *mahli,* finished the breakfast dishes. Then, he swept and washed the floor, maneuvering between the cooks' legs.

I brought an empty plate and a stool into the crowded kitchen and sat at the only corner of the counter with a bit of free space.

"Is there any breakfast?" I asked.

"You'll have to wait a few minutes, *dada* (elder brother)," Sugandh said, then turned to Roki. "Did you know Jamie-baba has a terrible sickness? Ever since he turned seventeen, his heart has been broken." He acted out each of his lines like the true actor he was. "All day, he mopes around the house moaning in pain because of all the pretty yellow-haired girls up in Kodai. He doesn't like us anymore."

"Naheen, naheen! I still love listening to your stories," I protested.

"But not as much as you love the yellow-haired girls," Roki said.

They both roared in laughter. Sugandh pulled a pot off the stove long enough to toast a couple of slices of bread on the wood flame. He buttered them and handed me hot, sweet, milky tea topped with whipped buffalo cream.

"That's all you'll get today. We are too-much busy."

"I don't think about yellow-haired girls," I complained.

"Then, why do you rush to paw through the mail every day?" He winked at the third cook. "This is Jamie-baba running to the office waiting for a letter from the yellow-haired girl." He pantomimed an eager puppy with its tongue hanging out.

"She doesn't have yellow hair."

"Then, what color is the hair of the girl who writes you so many love letters?"

"Rachel. She has brown hair, and they aren't love letters."

"Ah, Rachel, I know her. She was your friend Bobby's girl. She came with him to our cottage in Kodai many times during the last hot season. She drinks her tea like this." Sugandh perfectly imitated Rachel, pushing her hair out of the way and drinking her tea. Then, he turned to Roki. "She looks like that Italian movie star with long, beautiful brown hair and big..." He raised cupped hands to his chest. "Bobby was a good friend to run away to America and leave her for you." He turned back to me.

I slammed my cup of tea down on the counter.

"That's not how it is," I yelled and rushed out the kitchen door to roaring laughter.

Pissed off, I jumped on my bike and furiously pedaled past the Carpentry Shop toward the old well at the end of the compound. I picked up a few rocks and crept into the musty rock-walled darkness, hoping to find a rat or two to take my anger out on. I listened for scuttling sounds and waited for my eyes to adjust. Nothing, only silence. I threw the rocks into the water. Plop- plop-plop-plop. A giant furry dark rat ran up the wall four feet away. DAMMIT, missed again. My mind was red with anger.

Walking back outside, I blinked in the bright, hot sun. I looked around in disgust; there was absolutely nothing to do in this stupid town. I should have visited the mission families in the hospital with my brother and the Nelsons. At least I could have hung out with the other high school kids or read comics.

Still, I had to admit our cook was actually right. I was much more interested in my friends in Kodai, but why did he have to make that stupid crack about Rachel? Fuck it, I kicked the fence post and then rubbed my foot.

"OW, GODDAMIT, What the FUCKING HELL will I do all afternoon?" I shouted at my bike.

"PHOICKING, PHOY, PHOY." A boy's voice and laughter came from a nearby bush.

I dove into the brush, and three little boys boiled out the other side. I caught the arm of one of them. It was our cook's son and two of the Yeshwant's youngest boys, brothers of my once-best friend Daveed. I let go of his arm, turned my back on those kids, and biked to the school office to pick up the mail.

The sun had disappeared behind a looming wall of dark clouds. It rarely rained in November, but I was happy. A good storm would cool things off.

Chapter 5: A Real-live Thanksgiving Day Massacre

"Where's our mail?" I asked the school's business manager as I strode into the room.

"Salaam, Jamie-baba. It is here." He held out a sheaf of envelopes.

I started to rifle through the mail, hoping against hope for a letter from Rachel or even Bobby.

"Jamie."

I looked up quickly. Coming from the bright sunlight into the darkened office, I hadn't even noticed my dad sitting in the corner. Behind him was a picture of a smiling Gandhi striding towards us. My father's eyes had that glint of steel that told me I'd fucked up again. I was in for a lecture.

"Son, see that picture of the Mahatma?" he asked. "I met him once."

"Yes, Dad, you tell me that story a lot."

"It is apparent that you have not understood the moral of the story. Listen carefully and try to hear what it means to me this time."

He gently touched my shoulder and stared into me with his grey eyes. It was the last time he told me about meeting Gandhi. And it may have been the first time I listened to him tell the story.

"When I graduated from Kodai, I couldn't travel back to the States. Singapore had fallen to the Japanese, and they were marching through Burma. All the sea lanes to the States were closed to civilian travel, so I went to Wilson College, Bombay. One day, I was walking and saw a massive crowd on Chowpatty Beach. Gandhi-ji was speaking to the crowd in Hindi. As I was six-foot-six and the only white man on the beach, I stood out in the crowd. Gandhi-ji waved me forward and asked in English if I was in the British police services.

"No, Guru-ji, I'm an American student, the son of missionaries," I said in Hindi.

"You are a Christian missionary," Gandhi replied in English. "Are you here to help me convert these thousands?"

He waved his arm across the crowd.

"No, sir. I am here to listen to you only," I replied, still speaking Hindi. The crowd held their breath to hear his answer.

"Well, young man, you are acting more like your Jesus than most Christian pastors I've met. As I always say, I love your Christ. It's the churchy-smurchy Christians that I can't stand." Gandhi spoke into the microphone in Hindi and threw his head back in laughter. And the crowd laughed with him.

"So, what does that story have to do with your behavior today?" my dad asked me.

"I should listen more?" It was interesting that Gandhi had told the crowd he loved Jesus, but what did that have to do with me?

"Yes, of course, but what impressed me was how Gandhi-ji treated me. I was a European student who could have been there to spy on him, and the leader of the Indian people treated me with respect. And here is Mr. Kelkar, your senior and a staff member in the school. You didn't even say hello to Mr. Kelkar before you demanded our mail."

"I didn't demand it, I…"

"Jamie, don't argue with me. Please apologize, and always address everyone with proper respect in the future."

I did the needful and retreated from the office to shuffle through the family mail. No letters for me, but at least there was *Time Magazine*. The Asian edition of *Time* arrived a few days after the cover date. Still, I waited for it with almost as much eagerness as a letter. It would remove the boredom for hours. I especially wanted to read *Time* that day to clear up the lies and prove Sanjay was wrong about My Lai. I ran out of the school office, tucked the bundle of mail under one arm, jumped on my bike, and pedaled across the soccer field.

A storm had blown up, and the sky was an odd shade of green. The air was dead still. A chill crept down my back as I crossed the bumpy field. I reached our front garden when a fierce gust shook the big tamarind tree, nearly knocking me off my bike. A small branch broke clean off the young *gulmohur* (royal poinciana) tree in the side yard. Wind stripped off fronds of leaves and sent them swirling toward the Nelson's house. A wall of rain engulfed the school hall and raced across the soccer field. I dragged my bike up the steps of our verandah. Large drops of rain and hail the size of grapes pelted the roof and trees. I stepped into the house and dumped the mail in the office. After helping the *mahli* shut all the windows, I watched the storm whip the tops of the neem and cork trees along the road to the mechanic's shop. The thick trunks held firm, but the branches danced like crazy teenagers. One broke off and sailed clear across the soccer field, almost hitting the front gate.

I grabbed *Time* magazine off my dad's desk and went to my room. I tore off the brown mailer, unfolded it, and froze in horror. On the cover was that same picture Sanjay had shown me in *Blitz*. Women and children in black pajamas and water buffaloes, all dead. Except this was in full color—black, green, muddy brown, and blood-red images of death in a landscape that could have been right outside our hometown of Sangli.

The hail battered our Mangalore tile roof like machine-gun fire. I drew a sharp breath, collapsed onto my bed, and read and re-read the stories. It made no sense. The story was almost the same as in fucking *Blitz*. No fucking way would good Americans shoot defenseless women, let alone rape them, and mutilate kids and old men. Americans fucking didn't do that. Only the bloodthirsty Communists did. But this was in *Time,* so it must be true.

Maybe this was a fraudulent edition of *Time.* I looked through the magazine, but it was the same type throughout. On the same page as the My Lai story was a report of President Nixon awarding medals to some writers and artists. I flipped through the whole magazine. President Nixon fought with the Democrats who controlled Congress, college protests over the massacre, a giant demonstration against the war on the Washington Mall, Chevy's latest attempts to compete with the Ford Mustang, a dreadful review of Jane Fonda's latest movie *Barbarella*. I flipped back to the bodies at My Lai. It wasn't a fraud. Even *Time* reported the killing was done by American soldiers. But why? How could Americans do anything like that? It made me sick to think of it. It must be some horrible, dreadful mistake.

Sheets of rain obscured the back garden path a few yards away. The hail had passed, but fierce winds shook the roof. The tile roof held tight, but the storm inside me shattered my foundations. They had lied to me, the US Government, the US Army, and even *Time* had goddam fucking lied!

A small hand was shaking my arm.

"Jamie, Mom says you gotta come for tea." I stood up, letting my eight-year-old brother lead me through the extended bungalow to the dining room. Ted was chattering about the Nelson girls coming over for tea. The neighboring missionary family had four kids, Matt and then three younger girls—Joanie, Leona, and Fiona, who had always adored Teddy since he was a baby.

My mom sat at the mahogany table with the three girls, the Sangli Church pastor, and Mr. Pandre, the bank guard. Instead of a wool uniform, he wore a white *dhoti/sarong* and a black wool coat. His enormous curlicue mustache and three-inch shafts of ear hairs were perfectly waxed and curled.

I respectfully greeted Pastor Bhandare and Elder Pandre with folded hands and said, "Salaam." Back then, Christians and Muslims rarely said "Namaste." It was clear that the two men had just finished discussing official church business with Moore madam-*sahib*. They teased and joked with the kids. Mom was still in her white nursing uniform. Her dark curls bobbed up and down, and she waved her thin hands in intricate circles as she spoke. She seemed to be conducting a symphony of tea, treats, and polite conversation. A heaping plate of fresh peanut butter cookies sat next to the Kashmir tea cozies, which kept the tea hot. A silver milk pitcher was protected from flies by a lace doily.

My mom handed me a cup and saucer as I sat down and stared into space. She motioned toward the plate of cookies, and Teddy passed them towards me.

"Jamie, drink up your tea. We must clear the table in a few minutes to prepare for the dinner party." Her voice changed to alarm as she looked at me and then put the back of her soft, cool hand against my hot forehead. "Are you feeling sick?"

"No, Mom, but have you read *Time*?" I asked.

"How could I, dear? You've had it in your room all afternoon." She replied and turned to the church leaders to offer another cup of tea.

They thanked her and excused themselves as they had to get to the session meeting. My mom stood to walk them to the door.

"Only two biscuits today," she gently scolded from the living room as Ted and I reached for another cookie. "Thanksgiving dinner is two hours away."

Teddy and I exchanged glances, agreeing silently not to confess we were way past that limit.

"What are you girls going to wear tonight?" she asked the Nelson sisters when she returned.

"Our new red dresses."

"Jamie and Teddy, I want you to wear your new shirts."

A gust of wind rattled the screen doors. The girls laughed at Ted, who was fooling around again.

"No, Ted," our mom scolded. "Don't stick bread in your ears." She pulled part of a sandwich out of his tiny hands. "That was funny when you were two, but you're a big boy now."

"Mom, *Time* says the stories are true," I said, desperately trying to have a serious conversation.

"What stories, Jamie? Ted, sit up in your chair. You must ask to be excused if you are done with your tea."

"Ask to be excused," I ordered him, hoping all the younger kids would disappear so my mom and I could talk. "Go play in the tree. The rain has stopped."

"Yeah, let's play train in the tree. I'll be the engine driver," Ted shouted to the Nelson girls, who all stood up in a rush.

"Did I hear anyone ask to be excused?" my mother said in her formal Edinburgh accent. The kids all sat back down.

"Sorry, Aunt Noreen. May we be excused?" Fiona, the oldest Nelson girl, asked.

"Yes, you may, but the tree will be wet from the rain, so you must stay inside."

"Aww." Teddy was almost ready to cry.

"Let's go to our house to read our comics," Fiona said.

They all rushed out the door. Finally, I could have an adult conversation with my forever-busy mother. She'd been a nurse during the Battle of Britain and had seen her share of wounded and dying. Maybe she could help me understand My Lai.

"The stories in the Indian papers are true, that Americans massacred villagers in Vietnam. *Time* said it was US Army soldiers who shot hundreds of old men, women, and kids. But it can't be. Americans don't do things like that." I was shocked at my own voice. I sounded like I was seven years old.

My mom paused, and her dark-brown eyes widened as she looked at me for a long time before speaking.

"You'll turn nineteen your first year back in the States," she said. Her voice had a strange tone, and something I had never seen before flickered in her eyes. "War makes good people do dreadful things."

She took my hand in hers and bowed her head. "Dear Loving God, we cannot understand this evil war and why you let it continue. Please place your loving hands on Jamie and protect him from such horror. And please, PLEASE let this war end soon."

Heavy rain started again, a steady drum roll against the roof, and the wind whistled under the tiles, shaking the pressed tin ceilings. Cooking and laughter continued in the kitchen. Despite the rain, the *mahlis* shuttled back and forth between the two houses carrying trays laden with freshly baked rolls, pies, and meringues. They protected the goodies with black umbrellas crooked under their necks,

My mom went to the office to work on her accounts. I helped expand the teakwood table and covered it with a fresh linen tablecloth. The night watchmen burst into the kitchen with terrible news. A construction site in Miraj had collapsed, with hundreds killed and injured. As it was an emergency, I took him running through the house instead of around the verandah. He told the story to Madam-*sahib*. A few minutes later, my dad rushed in, dripping wet.

"Noreen!" He shouted as he raced through the office. "There's been a terrible accident in Miraj. A building site collapsed, dozens are injured, and…." he looked at me, "and worse. Archie Blair called from the hospital. He wants all our vehicles to help transport the injured. Bob Nelson already left with the truck. I'll go in the jeep. Can you bring the Ambassador?"

"Oh, Dear God, please reach out your healing hands," my mom prayed as she jumped up to get her first aid kit. "What about the children? What about the dinner?"

"The doctors' wives are coming to have dinner with all the kids. We'll join them when we can," my dad said.

I stood up. "I want to come with you and help."

"No," he said. "There are many dead bodies, Jamie,"

"I'm not a kid anymore. Soon, I could get drafted, and then I'll see plenty of dead bodies."

My dad drew his breath in sharply but said nothing.

"No, Jamie," my mom said softly but firmly. "Tonight, you are the man of the house. Please care for the younger children and welcome our guests. Go ahead and start dinner without us."

I was only "man of the house" when the adults had more important shit to do. Still, I returned to the kitchen. I helped the servants set the adult table in the dining room with the Noritake china, real silverware, and crystal goblets. We rolled back the Kashmir rug and improvised a table with boards and sawhorses for the kids in the living room. I covered it with sheets and set it with our daily dinnerware. I vowed not to sit at the kids' table.

The guests still had not arrived when we finished, so I took a break with the cooks. I stood with the cooks around the *bumber*. The gardener was stoking a wood-fired copper boiler to heat bathwater for my family. The rain had stopped, and the sky was clearing. Sugandh offered his friend Roki a Scissors cigarette. I took the packet out of his hand and pulled one out.

"No, baba." His voice was shaking. "Madam-*sahib* will be so angry."

"She won't find out unless one of you tells her," I replied. "They still think I'm a boy, but I've been smoking for over a year."

I sat on my haunches behind the *bumber* and asked them to warn me if anyone was coming. I pulled on my cigarette and let the cheap tobacco buzz my head. I wondered what Rachel thought about the war now. Had she changed her mind like I had? Shit, I actually couldn't remember talking much about it with her.

By seven-thirty, the guests started arriving. By eight, the food was flowing. I sat with other high school kids and mothers at the adults' table. Most of the talk was about the accident and the death toll. The roast chicken, dressing, potatoes, and chicken curry all smelled incredible, but I picked at my food with a fork.

"Jamie, you have hardly touched your food," Mrs. Sawyer said. She was the wife of the orthopedic surgeon.

"Have you got your *Time* magazine yet?" I asked her.

"I haven't had a chance to look at the mail all day, but I heard about My Lai, a terrible tragedy. Margaret, could you pass the rolls to Aunt Betty?"

The conversation continued as the missionary families finished the main course. The little kids had already been excused to play games in the bedroom. The rest of us sat talking at the adult table until the men and the mothers who were nurses returned. After they had washed up and sat down at the table, Dr. Blair gave a brief report: twenty-four dead and thirty-five critically injured. The cooks stood along the walls in starched white jackets, ready to serve the reheated food on a signal from my mother. First, we had to have another blessing from Dad, the senior minister of the group. He prayed for the victims of the accident and gave thanks for the good fortune that all mission compounds had been spared. He thanked the Lord for his bounty towards us and our home country, leading us in the Lord's Prayer.

"Now," he said after the forever-and-ever-amen. "Let's remember America, our traditions, and the wonderful gifts God has given us. Could each adult tell a story about a Thanksgiving back home?"

"Home." The States wasn't home to me. But I was interested in a distant way by the stories of shooting wild turkeys in Minnesota, getting stuck on snow-filled country roads in Illinois, and turkey dinners in Colorado cabins, farmhouses, and New York City apartments. It all seemed like something out of an old and irrelevant *Reader's Digest*. Not one of the adults mentioned Vietnam.

The Blairs' cook had refused to serve the desserts until Dr. Blair and the other men had eaten. As the stories went on, lemon meringue, pumpkin pie, made-from-scratch chocolate cake, and homemade ice cream were served to oohs and aahs. The children rushed back to their places. Pies and cakes were incredible treats in those days of sugar rationing. White sugar was one of India's few hard currency exports and was kept in locked steel cabinets. The Nelsons had been burglarized one night when they were away. The thieves had pried open the steel cupboard for the silver and cash. They were so tantalized by finding three pounds of sugar that they started eating it immediately and lost track of the time. The watchman had seen a door ajar and surprised them, mouths stuffed full of white sugar and giggling at each other like kids.

I looked at my plate and picked up a fork. I ate because the desserts were there, and I wouldn't see them again until Christmas, but my appetite hadn't returned. I felt my teeth cut through the delicately browned meringue while my mood deepened. Everything seemed strange and removed. America, whatever that was, seemed far, far away. Would it ever be my *home?* Instead of Norman Rockwell Thanksgivings, my head filled with images of bodies at the construction site in Miraj and mass graves in My Lai. For some reason, the most haunting image was a water buffalo split in two, black on the outside and bright red on the inside. I had to get out of that place.

I looked over at Matt Nelson. I raised my eyes toward the Nelsons' upstairs, and he nodded. We excused ourselves and walked out of the brightly lit dining room and into the darkness of the garden between our mission bungalows. It was a cool, clear night; the rain had passed as quickly as it had appeared that afternoon.

As Mat and I crossed the driveway, I asked. "Did you read *Time?*"

"I try to read nothing but comics and car magazines during vacation," Matt replied.

"A fucking massacre, man, hundreds dead. And it was the US Army. Can you believe that? Nineteen-year-old Americans shooting down and raping women and killing babies?"

"Shit, no, I never heard about that." Matt grew tense.

"It was covered up by the Army; even the President knew about it and kept it quiet. They fucking lied to us, our President, and a Republican too. Man, I watched my dad go into the consulate in Bombay last November and vote for him. He said he had a plan to win the war, but he lied to my dad, to my grandpa, to fucking all of us, man. I mean, how can we beat the Communists if we're as bad as they are?"

"Seriously fucked up, man. Sergeant Rock would've never done something like that," Matt said sardonically, thinking of our favorite comic book World War II hero.

"No, exactly. Americans don't do bad shit, or we didn't, I mean. Something is going seriously wrong. It's all so strange."

Matt and I were about to turn eighteen, and the draft loomed in the darkening future. I felt America had betrayed us personally; this wasn't the America we grew up believing in. Soon, Matt and I could be in that meat grinder ourselves. He was someone I could talk to about Vietnam. We climbed out a window from his second-floor bedroom and sat on the roof. Our smoking hangout was shielded from view by the leafy branches of a giant tamarind tree. We could hear anyone coming toward the house. Above us, the dark tropical sky shimmered with stars. I stood on the window ledge, reached under the eaves, and pulled out our stash of cigarettes.

"Strange is right. Fucking strange days are upon us, man. Hey, I got something you have to listen to." Matt reached through his window and flicked the switch on his stereo. He handed me an album cover to look at. It was a circus strongman and a midget, but I couldn't figure out who the band was.

"It's by the Doors. Debbie Nicholson lent it to me," Matt said. Dr. Nicholson was a successful eye surgeon from Los Angeles and a two-year volunteer at the mission hospital. His family had arrived in October, and his teenage kids had all the latest records.

"It is a strange day, man," Matt said. "A storm smashes a hundred people in Miraj, and our American boys shoot a hundred women and kids in My Lai. This song explains it all."

The record dropped from the changer. The needle settled onto the vinyl with a loud hiss. Eerie notes floated out the window. Rhythmic bass chords. Then, snare drums joined in. The music tracked down our thoughts, grabbed our minds with stone claws, and threw our souls across the tops of the neem and tamarind trees. The leafy branches shielded us from the prying eyes of the present. Still, Morrison's throaty voice sent electronic warnings about our future. A long chain named The Draft rattled in our hungry heads. The song froze the moonlit night in a frieze of cold stone.

"Damn, somehow the Doors explain what the hell is going on better than any news article," I exclaimed.

"That's why I don't read the news, man," Matt replied.

We smoked one Wills cigarette after another and watched the smoke curl into that dark star-speckled sky. Maybe I should go to college in India. Or Scotland, where they couldn't draft me. I was born in India to a British mother and an American father. I had a three-way choice of citizenship. I wondered if I still wanted to be an American. The next day, I would write a long letter to Rachel.

Chapter 6: Buffalo River Home

Five weeks later, I stood on a rise above the Krishna River. We were on a family visit to Yeshwant's farm a few miles north of Sangli. Despite the freak November storm, the land was drier and dustier than ever. But down by the river, it was cool and green. Behind me, I heard the rhythmic woop-woop-woop of an irrigation pump.

Over the years, Yeshwant saved money from his small wages. Each month, my parents contributed to each servant's provident fund, a retirement account. They were pretty upset when he turned forty and insisted on a large loan from his provident fund. They argued that the money was for his retirement. He told them he had already put money down on two acres of land in his parents' village. His family had never owned their own land, and this land would be his retirement. He had dug into the soil and knew it would produce.

Everyone thought it was the worst land in the village, on top of a hill and dry as a bone. The village elder took a bus into town and waited all day to see Moore-*sahib*. He said Yeshwant was wasting his money. Yeshwant and the elder sat in my father's office. The elder shouted that Yeshwant was as dumb as the old boulders on that hill. The sahib must see how wasteful it was to loan him the money. But the gardener stood his ground for the first time in his life.

People thought it was too high above the river to irrigate. Still, the *mahli* had watched the mechanics at the industrial school fixing large diesel pumps. He knew they could pull water up a mountain, let alone this tiny hill. And he took the elder and my father to the flowerpots on the front verandah. The pots on the left had soil from our front garden. The ones on the right had dirt from his field. He fertilized them both with buffalo manure. The flowers on the left were sparse but colorful. The flowers in his soil overflowed the clay pots; their leaves were dark green, and the pinks, purples, and yellows dazzled the eye.

"*Sahib*," the *mahli* said to the missionary, "This is the dirt where I can build a home for my family. And with a pump, we will not break our backs lifting water from the river."

The elder and the missionary engineer knew they had misjudged the barefoot man standing before them. A few years later, he grew vegetables, millet, sugarcane, peanuts, and three kinds of legumes.

Daveed and I stood behind a tree at the edge of their green fields. We smoked cigarettes and watched our families down by the river. His dad was showing off a brand-new pump. My dad was showing him how to adjust the throttle. Daveed was now studying business and accounting while his younger brother Sunil was a motor mechanics student. His dad was a gardener and cleaner, the lowest rung of servants. But he was pulling his family out of poverty step by step. Even his daughters would go to school to become nurses. Across the river, a farmer drove a cart pulled by water buffalo down to the river.

"Remember when we used to help your dad wash your buffaloes?" I asked in Marathi.

Daveed took a drag on his cigarette. "That was the old days," he replied in slow but enunciated English. "I would never swim in that muddy river with a buffalo now."

"Really?" I switched to English, ground my butt under my heel, and stepped out from behind the tree. "Those were fun days."

I remembered long-ago trips to his little village. The road was so rutted that it took the jeep almost an hour to travel four miles from the main road.

"It was fun when your family visited because it was like a holiday for my family. We had to work in the field every afternoon after school when you weren't here. We ate the same rice and dahl every day. We only ate chicken curry on Christmas or when Moore-sahib came. And we only ate what your family left behind. I will never raise my children like this," Daveed hissed.

The intensity of Daveed's anger felt as hot as the lava bubbling in my gut. All vacation, I felt ready to explode. Things were changing deep inside. It scared me. Maybe it was like that for him as well.

Down by the river, my mom waved for us to join them. We walked down the bank.

Sugandh had made bamboo fishing poles for Teddy and me but needed bait. "Run to your house and get meat scraps," he ordered Daveed.

"I'm a college student and not one of his errand boys anymore," Daveed snapped back.

His dad jumped up and slapped Daveed hard across the face. "Run and get the scraps, boy! As long as you are my son, you will never disrespect your elders."

Tears of rage sparkled in Daveed's eyes; he turned and walked deliberately up the hill. Daveed's little brother returned with scraps from a freshly butchered chicken a few minutes later. Sugandh baited the hooks, and I cast and sat on a rock. My parents and Yeshwant walked up the hill to his house. Across the river, kids were swimming, a man washed his water buffalo, and women spread laundry to dry on rocks. One of the kids climbed onto the buffalo and dove into the river.

Part 2: Rebelling with Help from My Friends

Just then, a police launch came down the Krishna River. A man with a rifle stood at the prow. My mind flew 2,000 miles east to My Lai and a picture of a small boy trapped under a dead water buffalo. I pulled out the letter from Rachel, which I'd gotten just before Christmas. She still hadn't received my letter about My Lai, but she'd been to an anti-war demonstration in San Francisco with her sister. Her father nearly kicked them out of the house because there was a picture of them in the local paper. It showed them standing next to a guy with an NLF flag. Were his daughters supporting the enemy? Rachel didn't admit it to her father but now thought the NLF were the good guys. They convinced her dad that the photograph was just a coincidence. They were walking by the protestors on the way to a store. They completely supported America but thought the war was going on too long. Her dad agreed with that but said if he ever saw them with an enemy flag or burning the American one, they'd be kicked out of the house on their ass.

One of Daveed's sisters called us to the house. Teddy, Sugandh, and I walked up a steep path to their stone and mud house at the edge of the village. Our cook and the Moore family sat on freshly washed rugs under a neem tree behind the house. The *mahli* squatted on his haunches beside the kitchen door, and Daveed stood beside him. His mother served the visitors robust sweet tea and crispy coconut-filled *kuranjis*. After we drank tea, the adults talked about religion. Daveed's mom was still in the kitchen cooking *chappatis*. Teddy and I stood up and walked over to Daveed. We all slipped off our *chappals* and walked through the small, smoky kitchen.

"This is where I sleep," Daveed said proudly, pointing to a *charpoy* cot in the next room.

"Where is your parents' room?" I asked.

"This one. This is where we all sleep," one of the little sisters said.

Daveed's face blushed darker. "But you all sleep on the floor. I have a bed."

"No, you don't. Mother and Grandmother sleep on the bed," his brother shot back. Daveed's face darkened. He slapped his brother, turned on his heel, and stalked out of the house. It took us a long time to find him; he was throwing rocks into the muddy Krishna River on a high bluff. When we returned, my dad was reading the Marathi Bible and motioned for me to sit down between him and our cook. My mom and Teddy sat across from us. He said a long prayer, thanking God for everything in the world.

We ate fresh *chapatis*, ground buffalo *keema* cooked in a red-hot special masala, and a *methi chi bhaji* (fresh fenugreek leaves stir-fried with spices). I wolfed down the food. Daveed and the rest of his family watched us eat, the adults reminiscing about the old days when we were little.

During a break in the conversation, my mom said in English, "When I was praying this morning, I felt God's presence. And a thought came to me that Jamie should stay in India for a year after he graduates. He could postpone his entry into Grinnell by a year, go to college in Madras or Bombay, and then return to the States with us in the summer of '71."

I was shocked because it was the same thought I had on Thanksgiving night. Staying in India another year could be all right. I'd have another year to decide what to do about Vietnam and the draft.

"Let's talk about this later," my dad said.

I chewed on a spicy bite and thought about Kodai. I couldn't wait.

"Two more days," I said, "and we'll be on the train to Kodai."

Ted started to tear up. Mom shot me an evil eye and changed the subject.

"Will we have time to stop for the boys to have a swim on the way home?" she asked my dad.

"Can we, Dad? Can we?" Ted said excitedly.

"We will see," my dad said. "First, I want to present something to our hosts." He reached into his shoulder bag, pulled out a package wrapped in brown paper, and presented it to Yeshwant. It was a framed 8 x 10 photograph of that old shot of Daveed and I taking a flying leap off a water buffalo standing chest-deep in muddy water. Everyone laughed in delight except Daveed and me.

I stepped outside and looked down at the river. A boy was driving a pair of water buffaloes down to the river. What the fuck was it about those ugly beasts? The people depend on them to pull their plows and wagons here and in Vietnam, but they look so wicked. Is that why the soldiers blew them apart along with the people of that village?

Darkness flooded through me. All the anger I'd ever felt toward the staff, toward kids who'd bullied me, toward Mrs. Rivers, the anger of being lied to all my life, came rushing through a gorge in my skull like a cold spring flood, a flood of pure hatred of the American war in Vietnam. It was the war that was completely fucking up my world. I wished I had a big knife to cut the war out of history and throw it into a deep, dark hole. Then my friends and I would be free.

Chapter 7: Not So, Hard Traveling

A thick, grey column of coal smoke split the blue Deccan sky. The missionaries and their kids and servants gathered around the first-class carriages. We stood on the concrete platform at Miraj station, ready to board the steam train for the 700-mile journey to the hill station of Kodaikanal. The train whistle blew. I hugged my mom and dad, took Ted by the hand, and climbed into the carriage. I turned around smiling, happy to leave my dusty hometown behind. Tears streaming down his face, Ted reached through the steel bars on the window. Both Mom and Dad were ready to cry. It was Teddy's first time going to boarding school. I felt like a total turd.

Kneeling next to Teddy, I put my arm around him as the steam whistle blew. The train started moving as Mom and Dad walked alongside, faster and faster, now almost running, until they stood at the end of the platform with all the other missionary families waving goodbye. Ted and the Nelson girls pressed their heads to the bars, trying to catch one last glimpse of their families. I even teared up a bit. Then, I remembered the package Mom had given me for just this moment. I handed out the cookies and comics. The little kids smiled through their tears, and one of the girls started reading a comic to Ted.

The chaperones were in the next compartment, so Matt and I snuck into the bathroom for a beedi (cheap Indian cigarette hand-rolled in a leaf). My mind raced as the harsh tobacco tore through my head, and I watched railroad ties zip by under the open toilet. We were on our way back to Kodai! It was the one place on earth where I felt fully alive. It was the final semester of my senior year, and in a few days, I'd see Rachel.

A two-day train journey brought us to Kodaikanal Road, the station at the bottom of the hills. Kodaikanal, Tamil for "gift of the forest," sits on the southern escarpment of the Palani Hills, part of the Western Ghats that line the coast of India. Built as a hill station for British officials and Western missionaries to escape the broiling heat of a south Indian hot season, the town is now a popular tourist destination served by the paved Ghat Road. Back in the old days, the missionaries and British Civil Servants rode up the Coolie Ghat in shoulder-borne chairs carried by *coolies* (laborers) along with luggage and provisions for the summer months. The Coolie Ghat rose 5,000 feet in six miles. It was a three-hour journey from Kodai Road station on a long and winding road. The bus unloaded our group at the school gate about nine-thirty that night. Coolies carried our luggage to the dorms. I walked with Ted to the boys' side of the hill. At the gate to his dorm, Phelps Hall, I bent down to give him a goodbye hug, but he held on tight.

"Jamie, please take me to my room."

"Sure." I lifted my kid brother onto my hip. Ted squeezed me tight, then slipped down to walk by himself. He still held my hand. A sight I hadn't seen in years stopped me cold. The mountain moon shone into the quadrangle where we experienced old Mrs. Rivers' anticipated rapture. I felt myself shrink in size and age until I was nine, walking to Room 6, holding my dad's hand to get past the ghost of my old housemother. The cold stone walls and the chilling air sucked the warmth from inside me.

"Where is my room way, Jamie?" Ted tugged on my hand and brought me back to reality.

I held his hand tighter and tried to shake the thoughts out of my head, but as I helped Ted unpack, a cold fear settled on my shoulders.

"Ted," I said, kneeling down to look into his blue eyes. "Have you met your housemother, Mrs. Johnson?"

"Yes, she is sweet. Mom and I had tea with her last May. She showed me the rooms and where the boys play with their Matchbox cars. She is really nice," he replied with a small smile.

I turned to Teddy's roommate. "How often does Mrs. Johnsone spank you guys?"

"Almost never. Billie Bennett got spanked once for yelling out the f-word, but that was after he'd had three warnings."

I helped him get his PJs on. I let him get by without brushing his teeth. Then, I hugged him goodnight and tucked him into bed. I felt incredibly sad for the little guy as I walked out the door. Even with a good housemother, there would be times when lonely little boys would turn their fears outward and rip into each other with sharp claws, just like we used to do. I looked up at the moon shining down and shook my head. Teddy still believed in Jesus. Maybe nicer and saner adults would help him keep those beliefs, comforting him for a few more years. I felt there was some kind of God, but now I knew all those Sunday School stories were fairy tales.

As I left that cold dorm, I ran down the steps toward Wissahickon, the senior high boys' dorm. A surge of excitement split open my chest. Tomorrow I would see Rachel!

Chapter 8: Lighting a Fire

The next day, I was reminded that our war with the school staff was still on. It was a Wednesday, the night for Canteen, an informal dance for high-school students.

Raghu and I were spinning the records as usual. We had picked out a fantastic playlist that included Hendrix, Cream, and the Stones, records I hadn't heard for months. We were hooking up the turntable and adjusting the amp when Reverend Stepanski leaned over the counter that separated the dance floor from the serving area. Stepanski was a short, wiry man with swarthy skin. He was the school chaplain and American football coach. He liked showing off his muscular arms.

"How are you boys doing tonight?"

"Pretty good, sir," we both replied.

"I thought you both excelled in the scrimmage against the juniors today."

We nodded and kept working. We didn't like Stepanski much because he gave us push-ups every time we laughed or goofed off in practice. Raghu came up with his nickname, "Chimpanzee," and everyone called him that behind his back.

"Raghu, you have a great throwing arm. And the way you run reminds me of Jim Thorpe."

"Who is that, sir?"

"He is from my home state of Oklahoma and one of the greatest American athletes ever. Be like him, Raghu, and you could win a football scholarship. He's a different kind of Indian, though," Stepanski smiled. "He's Cherokee like my mother. Remember that name, boys, Jim Thorpe."

"Yessir," we grunted. Mr. Stepanski gave up trying to talk to us and turned away.

"Chimp Thorpe Chimp," Raghu whispered, but a little too loudly.

Stepanski spun around on his heel.

"What did you call Jim Thorpe?"

"Nothing, saar," Raghu said, his South Indian accent thickening. "Just repeating name, saar, so I can remember the name. Jhim Thorp, Jhimp Thorp."

Stepanski's eyes drilled into Raghu's momentarily, and then he walked away. We leaned down behind the counter to let out our laughter.

A few minutes later, Rachel walked in with her roommate Kristina, a tall blonde all the guys were crazy about. But Rachel was the one I couldn't take my eyes off. She wore a white miniskirt, hiked up well above her knees, and flashed me a big smile as they sat at a corner table. We kept looking at each other and smiling. There was something different about her; she wasn't wearing glasses.

I put on the first song, "Fire," by The Jimi Hendrix Experience. I asked Raghu to put on the next few records since he never danced and walked across the floor to take Rachel's hand. She kissed me on the cheek as she stood up.

"What happened to your glasses?" I asked.

"I got contacts in the States."

Jimi's driving guitar vibrated through our bodies. Rachel and I started slow, holding hands and moving to the beat. Then, we rocked and jumped all over the floor, but when Cream began to play, she pulled me close and said, "I can't move to this beat. Let's slow dance."

She wrapped her arms around my waist, and I put an arm around her shoulder. She leaned her hips into mine. Pulling her head back, she looked me in the eye.

"When I was in the States, I broke up with Bobby," she said, laying her head against my chest.

I raised my head instinctively. Thank God, my shroud of loyalty was ripped in two, but this was no betrayal. Rachel had chosen me. I shivered as Jack Bruce's words surged through my head, and our bodies moved to Clapton's guitar. Rachel squeezed a thigh between my legs. I laid my cheek next to hers and squeezed back. Our hips swayed side-to-side to the beat of Jack Bruce's bass. Breathing faster and faster, we retreated from the hard crowd. We moved into a dark corner of the room. I pulled her even closer. As Eric and Jack's final guitar chords rang through our ears and Ginger Baker's drums shook our intertwined bodies, I felt my own needs leave the station.

She held me close, waiting for the next dance. Keith's fingers swung down like an ax on the twanging strings, and Mick yelled, "Watch this." The driving beat of "Jumping Jack Flash" told our bodies to move, but neither wanted to let go. We moved our hips back and forth, trying to slow dance to the rapid rhythm. Then, I felt a tap on my shoulder.

I turned and looked into the hard eyes of Rev. Stepanski.

"Keep three inches' distance between your bodies. Those are the rules," he said.

He put one vice-like hand on my shoulder and the other on Rachel's and pried us apart. I thought I saw his long fingers reach towards her breast. I whipped around, knocking his hands away. He spun my skinny body around, twisting my arm behind me.

"You watch yourself, son," he growled as his fingers dug into my arm and forced it up my back.

A blast of bass static shook the room. Stepanski startled and lost his grip. I slipped away to fix the short on the bass speaker. Raghu was holding a wire in his hand and smiling at me. After that, Rachel and I danced with one eye on the chaperones, moving in to grind our hips and separating before someone saw us. We took breaks at the table with Kristina, Charlie, and his girl, Carmen. For the last dance, Rachel and I wedged into a corner on the last dance and clung to each other. Her hair gave off an intoxicating scent I couldn't identify.

"You smell incredible. What is that?"

"Patchouli," she whispered into my ear.

We swayed to "Are You Experienced?" by Hendrix. I finally somewhat was, and my chest was on its own moonshot. The music stopped, and the lights came on. We walked out the door, arms around each other's waist, her head on my shoulder, a patchouli-lemon scent infusing my brain. The Reverend stepped out of a shadow and shone his flashlight in our eyes.

"You are pushing it, kids. Remember, I am personally watching you two. When you say goodnight, I must see light between your bodies."

He shone his flashlight up and down our bodies. Rachel glared at him. I pulled her away, and we walked to the senior high girls' dorm. We found a place in the shadow of a fir tree as we embraced.

We kissed carefully but passionately for the full ten minutes before they blinked the lights, and chaperones began to pry couples apart. I pulled back because I didn't know what I would do if Stepanski touched Rachel again.

"Tomorrow, let's go where we can be alone," she whispered as she left. At the door, she turned, blew me a kiss, and slipped inside.

I ran down the steps to the basketball court, jumped high in the air a few times, and then swung on a hoop before running back to my dorm at full speed. When I got back to the room, Raghu was playing Richie Havens' "Freedom! Freedom!" I couldn't believe how things had turned around in the few days since I left Sangli. It would have been the best semester of my life if stupid Stepanski hadn't gotten in our way.

Chapter 9: Crouching Tiger

After lunch, Rachel and I slipped off-campus the next day through a side gate below Kennedy Dorm. She had a new Cannon 35mm that her dad had given her for Christmas. She now carried her camera everywhere she went. We walked toward the Carleton Hotel, where her mom was staying. She used the telephoto lens to scan the principal's house and yard. Then, we doubled back down the steps and across the football field. We took the back way to Coakers Walk, a popular tourist attraction that wound around the top of the escarpment, a drop of 5,000 feet to the plains below. On a cloudless sunrise, you could see the sun glinting off the Bay of Bengal 100 miles to the east. Rachel and I wound our way up the mile-long walkway, holding hands, leaning against pine trees or daisy-covered stone walls, and kissing hard whenever no one was in sight. As it wasn't tourist season, we were alone most of the walkway. At the top of the walk was St. Peter's Anglican Church. Since it was Saturday and we were off school property, it was usually a safe refuge. We lay under a tree, talking and making out, until we heard a car. We jumped up and walked down the driveway. Reverend Stepanski drove by, glaring at us. He was probably visiting the Anglican pastor about some stupid church business.

We ran up the road as soon as we were out of sight. Looking over our shoulders and seeing no sign of Stepanski, we slipped into a stand of eucalyptus trees. We scrambled down a steep incline and along a narrow footpath. I pulled Rachel through a dense stand of wattle saplings and into a grassy clearing. I spread out a cotton blanket that I had around my shoulders. We kneeled and kissed, crouching in the jungle, my face reflected in her dark eyes.

Rachel pulled her head back. "What was that?" She said in alarm.

The wind rustled through the trees, and a eucalyptus branch fell.

"Falling branches," I said.

Rolling backward, I pulled her on top of me. I couldn't stop kissing her lips, massaging her buttocks and legs. She slipped my shirt up and unbuttoned her blouse.

CATACK— a sound like someone stepping on a twig. She rolled off me and pulled her denim shirt down. I got up to investigate. I saw nothing.

"You're just jumpy because of fucking Stepanski. We come here to smoke every day. It's safe," I said.

Rachel buttoned her shirt. She sat silently while I got up and checked around again to prove we were alone. When I returned, she had her camera out to take a close-up of a eucalyptus leaf.

"It's all clear," I reported. "No sign of Stepanski. How would he know where we cut off the road?"

"Maybe you're right. That asshole has got me nervous. I need a smoke." She shivered as she offered me her pack of Marlboros, a treat in India in those days of strict import controls.

"He is such a creep. Whenever he looks at me, I feel icky."

"Forget him." I lit two cigarettes and put one between her lips. She took a drag, leaned over to touch foreheads, and looked deep into one another's eyes. We both started laughing.

"You know that Airplane song?" She giggled as smoke streamed from her full red lips.

"Which one?"

She took another drag and leaned over. She kissed me, exhaling her smoke into my lungs.

"Make love laughing, baby." Then, she stood up and picked up her camera. She took a close-up of some eucalyptus leaves lying on her embroidered shawl. She turned and pulled me to my feet.

"Let's go into the woods, to a place only Kristina and I know."

We walked hand in hand along a faint trail leading to a ridge's top. Looking behind us, she pulled me through a thicket of young eucalyptus trees. We scrambled down into a hollow and then ducked behind a rock outcropping. The sunlit hills stretched out above and below us. We could see all the way to the plains. Rachel took out her camera.

"I forgot how beautiful this place is. I want to make sure I remember it after we leave." She carefully took a series of pictures to capture the 180-degree vista.

Then, Rachel led me along a pencil-thin ledge of a cliff that fell away 1,000, 2,000 feet. I felt dizzy and forced myself to look only at the path. I followed her around a corner. A stream cut through a *shola* of mahogany, wild fig, and giant rhododendron trees. It flowed along a grassy meadow filled with daisies and over a thousand-foot waterfall. We spread our blankets on top of the grass under a tree. The sun slanted toward the Arabian Sea behind the Western Ghats.

"Here we are safe." Rachel sat cross-legged. My eyes followed her skirt as it slid to the top of her thighs. She dug around in her shoulder bag.

"Here, my sweet baby James, we don't have to worry about prying eyes." She pulled out a pack of Sheikh Condoms. "My sister in Berkeley showed me how to use these."

The pressure in my eyes rose to the popping point.

"Making love is a natural and beautiful thing, but a girl has to protect herself."

"How could she … show you?" I blurted out and then didn't want to hear the answer.

Rachel broke into laughter and started kissing me. "Frozen bananas, silly."

Greatly relieved, I fumbled with her buttons. She slipped off my t-shirt. We were grinning so much it was hard to kiss. We raced for the unknown with eyes wide open.

"I've never…. Have you…?"

"No. Bobby and I were close, but I wasn't ready with him." She unzipped the side of her skirt and…

"Stop right there," a harsh voice ordered.

We both jumped up, looking for the source. Stepanski swung down from an overhanging branch and dropped into a fighting stance.

"Get dressed. Get DRESSED NOW!" He literally jumped up and down as we pulled on our clothes.

He marched us back along the cliff trail and through the eucalyptus forest. The sun was setting into a bank of clouds. A golden pink glow settled over the green land, but all I could see was the cloud of darkness filling the entire world from a bottomless pit in my stomach.

"You forgot I was a Green Beret. You think I can't track stupid kids in the jungle?" Stepanski smiled.

I clenched my teeth as he clamped his long fingers over her soft shoulder, touching a spot that, minutes ago, I had been kissing. He shoved Rachel into the front seat of his car and me in the back, then sped right to Kennedy Dorm. He ordered me to stay in my seat. I hated Stepanski and Kodai School.

Chapter 10: House of Detention

Stepanski took me to my dorm and told me to stay there until further word. Mr. Weyden, our house father, entered the social room where I played ping-pong. He said Rachel and I were room-pounded until the Executive Committee could meet and decide if we would be kicked out. We were confined to our rooms except for meals and classes. He took my ping-pong paddle and walked me to my room.

They were making my own fucking room into a jail cell. As soon as Weyden left, I took my cricket bat and attacked a chest of drawers. Hit after hit, the solid drawers rattled but wouldn't break. My roommates walked in.

"Moore, what the hell are you doing?" Charlie asked.

"I'm fucking room-pounded, and so is Rachel," I shouted as loud as I could. "Fucking Stepanski busted us making out by St. Mary's."

"Fucking asshole staff," Raghu yelled.

"The goddam school thinks we are Christian robots," Charlie said. "We'll show them who we are."

We pulled our windows open and started cursing into the afternoon sunshine.

"FUCK! DAMN! SHIT! HELL!"

We got no response, so we put on a Stones record and turned the music up loud. I lay on my bunk, tears welled in my eyes as I tried to blink them away. Maybe they'd kick us out of school. What would I do? Getting kicked out would be a death sentence.

"Paint it, paint it, PAINT it black," Mick Jagger sang, and the three of us shouted along.

After a while, Charlie turned down the music.

"Listen," he said. "The fucking staff is declaring war on us, and they have the power to kick us out. But only if they fucking catch us. We are going to fight back. Fucking Stepanski is getting sugar in his gas tank tomorrow night."

They locked me up, but I couldn't have asked for better cellmates than Raghu and Charlie. Raghu had come back to school with a brand-new RCA Victor, an Indian-made record player. It didn't have the best fidelity, but it was music. Raghu went around the dorm and borrowed the latest albums kids had brought back from the States. We repeatedly played *Disraeli Gears, Are You Experienced, Strange Days,* and Dylan's *Greatest Hits.* Raghu skipped the Saturday night dance and stayed with me. He snuck into Jimmy's room and borrowed the brand-new records that he wouldn't loan us—*Soft Parade* by The Doors and *Volunteers* by Jefferson Airplane. We played them until we figured Jimmy might return. Raghu slipped them back into Jimmy's room in exactly the same order. We turned our lights out early and covered for Charlie until he finally dragged his butt in way past lights out. He'd been making out with his girlfriend, Carmen. She lived in an off-campus dorm where the good-night routine was not controlled like in Kennedy.

The moon shone through the window when I flipped the stack of albums over one more time. Drumbeats shook my stomach; a quavering guitar kidnapped my mind and fanned a fire deep inside. A strange brew crawled right inside me. A pause. A drum-rap. And then a soft tap on the door.

"Almost midnight, time for you boys to shut the music off." Mr. Weyden stuck his head in. He was a mellow Mennonite doing his Conscientious Objector service by teaching in India. Unlike Stepanski, you could tell he hated disciplining us.

"Sorry, sir." I shut off the music, crawled into my lower bunk, and stared at the blackness.

"Moore," Raghu whispered after a few minutes passed.

"Yeah?"

"I been thinking."

"Yeah?"

"Before the Ape-man busted you, did you fuck her brains out?"

"You stupid asshole," I jumped out of bed and pummeled the laughing Raghu with my pillow until he grabbed it away.

He started humping my pillow and moaning, "Oh Rachel, Oh Rachel."

Charlie roared in laughter. I started punching Raghu hard in the back, but he just laughed louder. Eventually, I gave up and went back to bed. I ignored their giggles and had almost drifted off to sleep.

"Hey, you guys know why Jim Morrison's voice sounds so raspy?" Raghu called out.

"No."

"He's a cocksucker, and he got pubics caught in his throat. Ha, ha, ha."

Charlie and I both laughed at that one.

"That's what Moore is gonna sound like if he keeps sucking Rachel's pussy. Ha, ha, ha," Raghu rolled back and forth on his bunk, filling the room with his deep laugh. I jumped up, punched him hard in the gut, and grabbed my pillow back.

"You're a fucking *dravid* asshole," I yelled and jumped back into bed. I wrapped the pillow around my head to block out Raghu's stupid jokes, turned my head to the wall, and listened to the Beatles in my mind. John was singing to me that I had to hide my love away.

Chapter 11: Our Only Friend

On Monday morning, the principal's assistant pulled me out of physics class and took me to the office for my sentence. Rachel was leaving and pulled me aside.

"Hang tough and don't say a thing. Keep silent. They aren't allowed to hit you."

She leaned over and kissed my cheek.

"Rachel, you are dismissed. Jamie, come in here right now." Our steely-eyed principal in a crew cut stood at the door. I followed instructions and said nothing, not even name, rank, or serial number.

Both of us were on probation for the rest of our senior year. Rachel was kicked out of the school dorm, and her mom had to rent rooms at the Carleton Hotel. They could afford it since her dad was a big-shot advisor in Vietnam. The Executive Committee was softer on me because the Presbyterian Church supported the school. I was dorm-pounded until my mom could come up for the hot season. We were spared the death sentence of expulsion.

I walked back into physics class and gave everyone the peace sign. "Dorm-pounded the rest of the semester, but we're both still here," I smiled.

The class broke into a cheer.

"Take your seat, Mr. Moore," the stern-faced, ex-Canadian Forces physics teacher shouted.

That afternoon, I returned to my dorm while most kids headed off campus for a smoke. At least I could sit outside in the sun instead of in my cold dorm room. I checked the mail, and there was a letter from Bobby. Usually, I would have loved to hear from him, but today? His letter was all about Rachel. He wrote about how Rachel had broken up with him, but she had it all wrong. He would convince her to get back together when she returned to the States that summer. He went on and on about how sweet she was to kiss and feel up. How was I supposed to respond to that? Rachel had made her choice, and now she was with me. Still, he was my best friend.

I pulled out an Indian Overseas Letter form to write him back and put on The Doors' first album. Morrison uttered a guttural yell and sang about eating more chicken than a man had ever seen. I picked up the pen and could still smell Rachel on my fingers.

"Goddamit!" I ripped up the letterform and rushed to the bathroom to wash my hands. The red Lifebuoy soap frothed pink as I rubbed my fingers fiercely in the icy water. Returning to my room, I ran into Mr. Weyden, our dorm father.

"Jamie, I got a note from Mr. Grant. You are to go to a special yearbook meeting at his house after dinner instead of study hall," he said.

Then, he went on to give me a lecture about how sex was a beautiful but addictive drug. I nodded agreement every sentence or two, but my mind was racing. Rachel was on the yearbook committee. Maybe I would get to walk her home.

When Mr. Weyden left, I turned up the sound. Jim Morrison told me to take it as it came. The driving bass and drums made me feel alive for the first time since Stepanski swooped out of the trees. Morrison made so much more sense than Weyden and the rest of the staff. The record hissed across the gap. Hollow guitar chords echoed around an empty palace, drums hissed like snakes, and dark crystal lyrics pulled me into a slow dance of melancholy madness that mirrored exactly how I felt inside.

It was the end of everything we'd planned. Waves crashed over and through me, clearing away the wreckage. The guitar rhythm picked up. As the music sped faster and faster up a mountain road, my mood began to lift. I was fucked up, but I wasn't as crazy as Jim Morrison or the hundreds of thousands of people who were buying his records. Too excited to eat, I skipped dinner and headed for the Grant's place early.

The Grants were among the few teachers who were genuinely friendly with students, unlike most of the staff, who treated us like inmates. Mr. Grant was a music and literature teacher and an advisor to the yearbook. He played guitar and organ, sang, wrote poetry, and couldn't have been over thirty. Mrs. G was even younger, with dark hair, a pretty face, and an infectious laugh. She taught first or second grade. They both seemed more like students than staff. I would have gotten kicked out if it wasn't for them.

They always had music playing at their house. They had a lot of Beethoven and Bach and that kind of stuff. But they also played folk music, some of which was pretty cool, especially the early Dylan. They might like to hear something new, so I took along The Doors' first album.

The Grants live in staff housing along Lake Road but on the other side of the hill, below the classroom buildings and the girls' dorms. I decided to walk along the lake as the waters always cheered me. Besides, it would lead right by the Carleton Hotel, where Rachel stayed with her mom. The twilight drained from the sky in the few minutes it took to walk the Lake Road from our dorm to the Kodaikanal Boat Club. The boat club was where the road turned back towards the staff housing. Behind a stone wall, a manicured garden rose up the hill to the Carleton Hotel, the only first-class one in town. The hotel lights reflected in the dark lake, a smooth sheet of obsidian. I kept my eyes on the balconies. Which room was Rachel's? Every time a door opened, I stopped breathing. But no sign of Rachel, so I walked quickly through the chilly night. She would probably be at the yearbook meeting,

The Grants were still at the dinner table when I arrived. Mr. and Mrs. G got up, gave me an extra big hug, and insisted I eat even though I said I wasn't hungry. I took a bite of mashed potatoes and realized I was famished. I wolfed down my plate of fried water buffalo steak and potatoes.

"Who all is coming to the yearbook meeting?" I asked Mr. Grant.

"Only you," Mr. G smiled. "I thought it might help if we talked with each of you alone."

"Sounds good," I replied, smiling. I was happy they were thinking of me, but I was disappointed Rachel wouldn't be coming.

Mrs. G put the youngest ones to bed. I helped the older kids finish their homework while Mr. Grant worked on his lesson plans for the next day. He would strum a few chords on his guitar, then put his head down and write for a while. I really dug their family scene; it was so different from mine. I began daydreaming about Rachel and me being in a house with a few little ones.

After the kids were all in bed, Mrs. G brought in a pot of coffee and a tray of cookies, and Mr. G pulled up a chair at the table. No other students from the yearbook committee were there.

"Jamie, I am so sorry this happened." Mr. G said.

"Me too."

"I want to tell you I don't think any less of you or Rachel."

Less of us? Why would he think less of us? I shouted in my head.

"We know how easy it is to get carried away with romance, but you are risking your future."

"We were going to use protection," I blurted out.

"I'm glad you thought of that," Mrs. G suppressed a smile and handed me a steaming mug of sweet South Indian coffee. "But Jamie, condoms can slip. Sex is a powerful drug."

I went beet red again. What the fuck? Had they been talking with Weyden? "But we didn't do it."

Mr. G put his hand on his knee. "Jamie, heavy petting and intercourse are not that different."

"But we didn't, we haven't..." I could not believe I was talking with two staff members about sex. But at least they weren't condemning me like Stepanski.

"Do you love Rachel?" Mrs. G asked.

"Yeah, of course, she is so cool and super pretty."

They both nodded at me. I remembered they were in the same Mission and close friends with Bobby's family.

"But... but…" I stared at the bottom of a coffee cup. "I am a complete turd—stealing my best friend's girl, ruining her reputation."

Guilt flooded over me, but there was something more, much more. An earthquake of anger shook me apart.

"It's like there's a monster inside me," I set the coffee cup down hard. It cracked apart, and the café-au-lait spread across the black teakwood table.

"Oh God, I'm sorry." I jumped up.

Mrs. G pushed me back into the chair. "Relax, Jamie, these are cheap cups from the bazaar. They break all the time."

"Jamie, what you're feeling is normal. Remember Romeo and Juliette? They thought they couldn't live without each other."

"Mr. Grant, we're not gonna kill ourselves."

"I sure hope not." Mr. G let out his deep, rumbling laugh. "But I do want you to remember you aren't the first human to face an existential romantic crisis. It is what all teenagers have to go through."

I sat there feeling stupid. Mr. G picked up his guitar and began strumming.

"I know it doesn't make it any easier, but you should've seen what a fool I made of myself when I was first smitten by Caroline." He glanced at his wife, who shook her head at some distant memory. "I lived through it because I had music."

I nodded my head rapidly. "That's exactly right, Mr. Grant. You do understand us. I'd die if I didn't have music."

Mr. G's fingers started to pick out a melody I didn't recognize. Mrs. G began to hum along, and they both broke into song. Their voices moved together and apart, riding high and low over the cresting waves rolling off the guitar. "The Captain fell in love with a lady like a dove." Their eyes danced along.

"You'll get through this," Mr. G said. "It isn't a monster inside you. It's just a disease we all have to survive."

"Yeah, it's called puberty," Mrs. Grant said, and we all laughed. "Is Rachel close to her mom?"

"Her mom seems cool, but I don't think they talk much. She says her mom is kind of superficial, just into fashion and all, not what's important in the world."

"What is important, Jamie?" Mrs. G asked me.

"Well, like talking about love, what you want out of life, the war, the environment, music, and the stuff we read about in American Literature."

"Flattery will get you nowhere, Jamie," Mr. Grant smiled.

"No, but it's true. Until I took your classes, I was not into good literature."

"My point," Mrs. G said, "is that Rachel might need a good woman-to-woman talk."

I wasn't sure what that meant but wished I could have a good talk with Rachel. As I stared into the fire, I realized all my anger was gone. I felt safe and warm in their living room with two adults, staff members even, who cared about me and Rachel instead of fucked-up rules. For a few minutes, I was floating in a clear mountain lake. Then, that deep quaking again shook the stillness; sadness welled up from a crack deep inside, like that oil spill on a California beach, and slimy darkness covered everything. The only thing that could drive it away was music.

"Have you heard the Doors?"

"I've read about them," Mr. Grant said.

"I thought you might like to hear them. They're one of the few things that keep me from going fu… fu...fully crazy."

I put on side two of The Doors' first album. A thumping guitar and drumbeat music rolled across the small living room. I closed my eyes as Jim let out his throaty yell, "I'm a backdoor man."

"That's a Willie Dixon tune," Mr. G said. "Lots of bands are electrifying the blues these days."

"Electrocuting them, you mean," Mrs. G said.

"Yeah," Mr. G said, laughing. "Remember the Newport Folk Festival? Pete Seeger grabbed an ax. We thought he was ready to chop Dylan's head off for playing that electronic abomination."

"He just wanted to cut the power cords," Mrs. G laughed.

"Why would anyone do that?" I was shocked. Who the hell was Pete Seeger, and why would he try to stop DYLAN?

Mr. and Mrs. Grant looked at each other.

"I think it's called the Generation Gap," she laughed.

I ignored that comment and sat back in the wicker armchair. Shaking cymbals announced the beginning of "The End." "This is the song I wanted you to hear."

The three of us listened in silence. Mr. G's fingers moved noiselessly over his guitar, feeling the notes. Mrs. G closed her eyes, but when Morrison shouted and screamed, she jumped up and shut it off.

"Jamie, how could you make us listen to this violent filth?" She stalked out of the room.

A cold fear stabbed deep inside me.

Mr. G strummed on his guitar for ages and then said. "Don't get too upset, Jamie. I know that album means a lot to you, or you wouldn't have brought it along, but you must admit it is pretty shocking."

"It's just that old story from the Iliad or Odyssey or something like that."

"Well, it is a Greek story, but most songs don't glorify rape and murder."

"Morrison isn't glorifying it. He's singing about the anger we all have. We are all really pissed off. When Morrison screams. I feel YES! That is exactly how I feel. He throws it out there for all the world to see."

"All of us? Who is that? You and Rachel?"

"Well, yeah, Raghu, Charlie, and all the students."

Mr. Grant strummed his guitar, an old song I vaguely remembered. Was it "Goodnight Irene"? An old, sweet song, but even there, the guy wants to drown himself. So, what's the difference?

"Jamie, it's disturbing how much you let this music influence you."

"Mr. G, the music isn't influencing me. It just explains what is locked inside me. You've said that music expresses our soul."

"But Jamie, you aren't making your own music. You're just absorbing somebody else's thoughts, letting them change you."

What the fuck? He was the best teacher there, but he didn't get it. "Mr. Grant, that's not what's happening here. Something is changing us, our whole generation, but it isn't the music. If it wasn't for rock and roll, I'd go crazy. And it isn't just me. Look at what's happening in Vietnam, in the streets of America, England. It isn't the kids. The whole world has gone crazy."

"These are challenging times for sure, Jamie. And as old fashioned as it sounds, you would do much better to look to the Bible for guidance than rock 'n' roll."

"I learn more from Jim Morrison than Jesus!" I retorted. A hot, red fog filled my brain. I grabbed the record off the turntable.

"I'm sorry that we offended you, Jamie," Mr. Grant said. "And remember that there are others who are offended by your actions. I am not condemning your music or your reaction to the war and segregation. I want you to see the larger picture. And in a few months, you will be in the States and make all your choices."

Even the Grants couldn't understand. The things Morrison, Clapton, and Lennon were screaming about were surging deep inside each of us way before any of us students had ever heard their songs. Their music didn't cause our feelings; it only opened the door to set our wild things free. Rock was our lifeline; it could keep us from drowning in a dark, raging river. A good line in a song could bring you back to the surface to suck in a lungful of fresh air before you got pulled back into the murky waters rushing toward the edge of a 2,000-foot cliff. Maybe music wasn't our only friend, but it was one of our best. And it would always understand.

Chapter 12: Manic Depression

My war with the staff settled into a grim siege in the first week of February. Outside of the two classes together, modern literature and physics. and lunch and tea and studying in the library. Rachel and I rarely saw each other. It was killing us. The staff closely watched us, even some of our friends. I always thought about Rachel, swerving from anger to guilt to deep, dark lows. To bring some sanity to my life, I threw myself into schoolwork; I spent hours on the school yearbook and our mimeographed school newspaper. I studied hard for my classes. I read every newspaper and magazine I could find about the war, the civil rights movement, the student protests, the riots, and the strange happenings of the hippies. I also wrote a lot of poetry echoing Jim Morrison's apocalyptic visions. Despite the quality of those poems, the Grants and Weydens kept encouraging me to write. They liked my bad poetry better than "The End."

Rachel and Charlie were photographers for the yearbook, working in the darkroom instead of the evening study hall. Rachel loved the mystical way pictures emerged from the void of the dark chemical baths. First, conceptual fuzziness appeared on the white photographic paper. It sharpened into a black-and-white image in the developer. At the right minute, you had to move it into the stop bath to keep it from going too dark. Then, it goes into the fixer to preserve the image. Rachel saw photography as a perfect metaphor for her life. You go out and capture images of the world and then work to sharpen them up and make sense of them.

One night, a substitute oversaw the study hall. She had not gotten the news about Rachel and me, so she gave me a pass for the typing room, which wasn't supervised. Instead, I ducked into the darkroom. Charlie stepped outside to watch for staff members, and Rachel and I started making out madly for the first time in weeks.

Suddenly, Charlie rapped on the door and barged in. "Cool it, you idiots. Stepanski is coming."

Rachel crawled under the large sink that held the chemical baths. Charlie pulled the curtains tight just before Stepanski marched in.

"What are you doing here, Moore?"

"Working on captions for the yearbook pictures, sir. I'm the editor, and we have to…"

"Don't give me that crap. Where's Rachel?"

"Rachel? She's not here, sir. Left before Jamie came," Charlie replied. "She…felt pretty sick, said something about her time of the month, sir."

"Humph," Stepanski grunted. He liked it when students called him "sir" but was never sure it wasn't sarcastic. He opened the door to the storage closet, looked around the small room, and walked out. It was too close a call. Rachel and I both knew we couldn't risk that again. My depression took a turn for the worse. In Jimi's words, I was a full, screaming mess.

Chapter 13: What's Going On?

One day in February changed my whole world again. There was an all-school assembly in the chapel. Raghu, Charlie, and I sat in the first row of the chapel balcony, which was the hallowed territory of juniors and seniors. Rachel was sitting with Kristina. Jimmy, the new kid from the States, came up the stairs and sat right next to her, which kind of pissed me off. Rachel and I weren't sitting together because the staff watched us like hawks. It sucked that Jimmy was taking advantage of that.

Charlie unslung his Canon and took a few shots for the yearbook. Stepanski was standing with two Americans. Black men. You rarely saw Black people in India back in those days. One was short but powerfully built. The other towered over Stepanski and looked like an NFL linebacker.

"Civil rights activists," I whispered. "Preachers and I heard they're Black Panthers."

"Damn straight. I hope they have sharp claws and tear fucking Stepanski to pieces and then eat his bloody FLESH," Raghu said and threw his head back and laughed as he clawed the air. His ebony skin and bright red tongue made him look like Kali, the goddess of destruction.

Reverend Stepanski glared at the balcony, and I elbowed Raghu in the ribs.

"Quiet, you stupid *dravid*. You're going to get us busted," I hissed.

Raghu giggled to himself as the pastor stepped into his pulpit. "Let us begin this assembly with a word of prayer to our Lord."

He prayed for forgiveness of our sins. He prayed for wisdom to ward off temptations of the flesh. He prayed for strength to fight the Evil One. Stepanski was packing a whole sermon into that prayer. Raghu slid to the far end of the bench and stood behind a pillar so only the balcony could see him. He mimicked Stepanski's shaking, folded hands, and his rolling head. The whole balcony was snickering, desperately trying to contain ourselves. Rapid footsteps sounded on the stairs. Raghu knelt, bowed his head, and folded his hands. It was the principal. He glared at each of us, trying to discern who to punish. He pointed to Charlie, Raghu, and me and tapped his eyes, letting us know he was watching us. He stayed at the back of the balcony to guard against any further irreverence.

"So, children," Stepanski continued, "I am proud to introduce to you Rev. Johnson and Rev. McFarland, ministers of the Lord from Missouri, next to my home state of Oklahoma. They will tell us about their Christian work in inner-city St. Louis."

"How are you all doing?" Rev. Johnson asked. He smiled like he was the happiest man in the world. And the whole 95% white crowd smiled back at him politely.

"Where I come from, when someone asks a question, he expects to hear an answer. How are you all doing?" The Reverend repeated.

"Good," the assembly replied.

"That's better. Now, who has heard of the Rev. Martin Luther King?" he asked.

All our hands shot up.

Rev. McFarland, who looked like a wrestler, stepped up to the podium. "How about Malcolm X?" he boomed.

I proudly raised my hand with Rachel, Charlie, Raghu, Kristina, and others. A dark cloud gathered on Stepanski's face.

"So, do you all know what Jim Crow is?"

Many people put up their hands. Rev. Johnson strolled down to the pews, looking at each person with a hand up, then shook his head before moving to the next. He strolled to the back of the chapel and turned around.

"Have any of you ever drunk from a 'Coloreds Only' drinking fountain? Has anyone ever seen a 'Coloreds Only' drinking fountain? Has anyone been refused service in a restaurant because of their skin color?"

I happened to glance at Stepanski; he was the only staff or student who nodded his head.

Rev. Johnson turned back to his partner. "These good folks have never met our Jim Crow, Reverend McFarlane. Should we introduce them?"

"You guys stand up, you three who look like an Oreo cookie in reverse." Rev. McFarland pointed up at Charlie, Raghu, and me. We stood up.

"In Mississippi, Alabama, across the South, you three can't eat together in a restaurant without going to jail. You can't drink out of the same water fountain. You can't even pee in the same toilet," Rev. McFarland said.

The little kids all began to giggle.

"Have you all seen pictures of police dogs attacking the marchers in Montgomery and Rev. King giving his speeches?" the short reverend asked in a friendly tone.

"Yes, sir," everyone answered, nodding their heads.

"So, why were we marching?" the happy reverend asked the assembly.

A dozen hands shot up.

"Oh, come on, we already know you all don't know bull tweedy about Jim Crow, so why you even gonna try to tell me why we're marching?" he shot back. His voice echoed off the stone walls of the chapel.

Our hands disappeared. We all blushed.

"Well," boomed the tall preacher. "We are marching because there are still segregated second-class schools all over the United States. There are slums in Chicago and houses in Mississippi that compare to those in Bombay and Tamilnadu. The system is still ripping us off and keeping us down. We are marching because we ain't gonna be nobody's good niggers no more."

Everyone was shocked at his language, but we shook our heads in sympathy.

"Here in Kodai missionary school, you never use the word nigger, do you?" Rev. Johnson was all smiles again.

Everyone agreed in silent relief.

"You don't discriminate against the Negro." Everyone shook their heads.

"I have even seen the only two Black students in your school eating together with Indian, Thai, and white students," Rev. Johnson continued.

Everyone nodded.

"But," Rev. McFarland slammed his fist on the pulpit. He waited for a disturbingly long time before he continued in a quiet voice that cut deep and cold, "What do you students call the Indians?"

The first and second graders squirmed. The upper grades fidgeted.

"I have walked around this Christian school and watched you kids playing marbles and tops. When you get mad at your friends, what do you call them?" McFarland's voice boomed.

Some of the staff looked at the offending children.

"I have sat outside the bakery watching you high school kids fool around and swear and call each other that same name as if it were a cuss word." Rev. Johnson looked at us in the balcony.

"Students, WHAT DO YOU CALL THE INDIAN PEOPLE?" McFarland shouted.

No one answered. My ears were burning. I glanced at Raghu. He was transfixed, gripping the rail.

"You and I know what word you use." McFarland's voice dropped so low that everyone leaned forward to hear him. "Have you heard it, Reverend Johnson?"

"Yes, I know that word." He said, and now his smile was gone. "But none of them want to say it here and now, not in the house of the Lord."

Silence filled the hall.

"If all of you are too ashamed to stand up and admit it, I will say the word. You call them *dravid*. You stupid *dravid*. You are such a *dravid*." Johnson mocked us in a high-pitched voice. "Now, please explain to me, dear students, exactly how *dravid* is different from the word 'nigger'?"

Everyone sat in stunned silence. Filled with shame, I looked at Raghu. He stared straight at the two Black preachers. Stepanski sat back in his preacher's chair, gripping the carved armrests, his knuckles white against the dark teakwood. The two Black men let the silence grow, their eyes traveling the room.

"Students, children, we are all children of the Lord. Racism is a sin," Rev. McFarland broke the silence. "To perpetuate a lie that so-called white people are better than others is a sin against humanity. What Sunday School hymn do you all sing? 'Red and yellow, black and white?' Racism is a sin against God, disrespecting his children."

"Yes," Rev. Johnson spoke out with a strong, clear voice. "But what is a sin? Is it not a wound against one of God's creatures? Racism comes from a self-inflicted wound white people have deep in your soul. It hurts so bad that you try to feel better by hurting someone else."

"So, it is," Rev. McFarland nodded.

"Children, how many times a day do you cut each other down? How many times do you yell at your *dravids*?"

"Reverend, I believe the polite word is 'servants,'" McFarland interjected.

"I am so sorry for not being polite," Johnson replied with exaggerated courtesy. Then turned back to us. "How many times do you yell at your servants, the people who get paid a pitiful wage to cook, bring you food, and clean up after you?"

"And rac-ism," McFarland said, enunciating each syllable. His voice was a steamship whistle that rattled the windows of the chapel. "Racism is not genetically implanted in babies. It must be taught. And teaching racism to children is one of the greatest sins." He stared at the pews filled with staff members.

"'But no,' you are saying in your mind. 'I have never taught such things.' Maybe not," the tall pastor's voice became low. The congregation leaned forward to hear him. "Maybe not in words," he whispered, then shouted: "By their deeds, ye shall know their hearts! We have seen the Indian kitchen and maintenance staff lined up each evening. Before they leave, men and women are each body-searched by your Gurkha guards. An OUTRAGE." He slammed his flat hand against the carved rosewood lectern. "It is an absolute insult to a proud and ancient people. A people that you ignorant educators arrogantly assume you are superior to. This land gave the world mathematics, meditation, and metaphysical philosophy while you Europeans lived in caves.

"You all live a life very familiar to me," he continued. "You come here in the name of Jesus Christ to spread God's love among the people of India. But you live at the top of a system created by British colonialism. You live above the Indian people and benefit from their labor, their cheap labor, I must add. My mother cleaned house for a white Baptist minister so I could go to college. How many of your servants' children are going to college?"

I thought of Daveed. He could attend college through Yeshwant's discipline and hard work on the farm.

"Our struggle against racism in the American South is only one part of a worldwide struggle. Across the world, people of all colors are standing up. We won't stop until we free all God's children from the Pharaoh's chains of power. So, you don't need to worry about racism in the American South. That is our job. You deal with the racism right here in your school, in your church, and in your hearts."

A sub-zero silence gripped the chapel. The two Black men looked around the hall. After a few painful minutes, Mickey Carpenter, a senior whose family was from Georgia, stood up. He took his glasses off, and his voice cracked. "Sir, how can we start to understand our own racism?"

"Thank you, thank you, young man, for asking that question," Rev. McFarland said. "It is hard, challenging to understand your racism. Jesus said it was harder for a rich man to enter heaven than for a camel to pass through the eye of a needle. He might have been talking about a white man trying to understand racism. But with God, nothing is impossible.

"To understand racism, your position in the power structure must be analyzed. Racism is not the same as prejudice. It is a system of prejudice enforced by political and economic power. You start by putting yourself in the other's shoes. Talk with the beggar at your school gate, with the sweeper who cleans your bathrooms. Try to understand their view of the world, young man."

"And you read, you educate yourself politically," Johnson said. "You read Gandhi and Nehru on British colonialism. Read Frantz Fanon and Ralph Ellison about the psychology of racism, and W.E.B. Dubois and the Reverend King."

Mickey pulled out a notebook and wrote down all the names. Mickey's brother Dan had gone AWOL from the Navy, making us question the Vietnam War. As soon as he was finished, Rev. McFarland watched him and added, "And Malcolm X and Eldridge Cleaver."

I turned around and whispered to Mickey, "Let me see those names."

Stepanski stood up, shaking. He strode into his pulpit.

"Reverend McFarland, I completely agree with your stance against racism. However, are you suggesting that these children read books by a convicted criminal?" he asked, shaking with anger.

McFarland turned to him. "Yes, I am, Rev. Stepanski. Was Jesus not a convicted criminal?"

The blood drained from Stepanski's face. His jaw moved, but no words came out. He sprang out of the pulpit with his fists balled. McFarland looked at him. Johnson turned toward him and spread his arms wide, whether in love, as a challenge, or both. Stepanski spun on his heel and walked toward the rear of the chancel. A silent cheer went up from the balcony.

"Reverend Stepanski," the Reverend Johnson called in a loud, clear voice. "Reverend, let me apologize if you feel I have insulted you."

Stepanski stopped at the head of the stairs that led out of the Chapel.

"We meant no disrespect at all, especially to you. We know people of Native American heritage are also victims of racism. And we also know that the Word of God comes from imperfect humans. Otherwise, no one would have ever heard it. So, we must listen to the truth whether it comes from Eldridge Cleaver, Malcolm X, or Rev. King."

McFarland walked over and put his arm around Stepanski's shoulders. He spoke into his ear. They both turned and joined Rev. Johnson in the middle of the chancel.

"Reverend Stepanski, could you explain the kind of racism you had to live with as a Cherokee child growing up in Oklahoma City?"

Stepanski stood silently. He looked at the crowd and then back to the two Black pastors.

"It is hard to discuss, but I have been excluded from theaters and restaurants. I was often told to sit in the back of the class. And kids called me monkey or chimpanzee. And the fact is that derogatory name has followed me here, to this school." He glanced up at the balcony. "But my mother was related to Jim Thorpe - the All-American football player and Olympic champion. He showed the world that our people were as good as anyone else."

I listened in silence. God, how racist we students were, calling him "Mr. Chimpanzki."

Later that day, a bunch of us sat on the flag-green, waiting for the dining room to open for tea. The Indian tricolor and the Stars and Stripes whipped against the blue sky. Jimmy's Panasonic cassette recorder played a tune, asking, "What's going on?"

It was the first time I'd heard Marvin Gaye.

Raghu jumped up. "Here is Reverend Stupid-pantski,"

He acted out the Green Beret pastor's ordeal in exquisite detail. As Raghu retold the story, his mobile face reflected the expressions of each of the three reverends. Everyone rolled on the grass in laughter. Then, Stepanski himself walked out of the principal's office.

"Moore, what are you doing here? You are to be in class or in your dorm,"

"Just finished class, sir," I jumped up. "Now I'm waiting for tea, sir. Doors open in five minutes, SIR."

Stepanski walked up to me and put his face two inches from mine.

"You are pushing it, Moore," he barked. "Take one more step over the line, and you won't know what hit you."

His eyes seared something deep inside me. He spun around and walked down the road. This fucking school, the staff was always just a couple inches off your back, pushing you, forcing ideas down your throat. Racist ideas, but we were fucking racist too. Shit, I didn't know Stepanski was Cherokee.

"Bastard," Raghu said a bit too loudly, and Stepanski spun around.

Raghu stood up and continued with an exaggerated South Indian accent. "Can I hawe extenshun on my Religion Shtudies paper, saar. Pashtorrrd Shtepansski, please? I am sick from a cold and need more time, Bashtord saar."

Stepanski's stern eyes bored right into Raghu, who smiled pleasantly and held his gaze for a full minute.

"No!" Stepanski exploded, broke eye contact, and strode away.

We barely contained our laughter till he was out of earshot.

"You got balls, Raghu," Charlie thumped him on the back. "That guy is a real bastard, but you're the first one I know who's ever said it to his face."

"He is a bastard," I blurted out. "But I didn't know he was American Indian and got discriminated against."

"That doesn't give him the right to be an asshole," Charlie replied.

"But remember what those Black pastors said? We are racists when we call Raghu a *dravid*!"

"Forget that, Moore," Raghu said. "I know you don't mean anything bad."

"No, it is wrong for us to use that word to put people down. It is a racist word, and when we use it, the poison seeps into each of us," Rachel said, looking right at me. "This school is part of a racist system."

"You are right on, Rachel. And so are those Black pastors. Our whole society is full of racism, from this school to the US Army to the prisons. The whole fucking system is racist." I was shouting and was a bit shocked at the anger in my voice.

Rachel moved across the grass toward me.

"Racism is part of our country," she said, grabbing my sleeve, "because the United States was built on slavery and oppression. Read Malcolm X."

"You already read Malcolm X?" I asked in awe. She was close enough so I could see myself in her pupils and smell her lemony hair. "Where did you get his book?"

A bright smile spread from her lips and into my eyes. She pulled out a copy. "Jacob, the librarian, turned me on to it. He's been stocking the library with all kinds of radical books. Most of the staff has no idea what's in that library." She laughed and leaned even closer and whispered. "Jacob is a Marxist, you know."

"Fucking commie from Kerala," Charlie chimed in. "All those Malayalees have communism in their blood. It's passed by the fucking mosquitos, just like in Vietnam. Nixon's gonna have to invade Kerala next."

Everyone laughed, but Rachel and I kept staring at each other. That energy between us had grown even more potent. This electricity made holding back from jumping her right on the flag-green even harder. Jimmy started telling a story he'd heard from a Vietnam vet.

"The helicopter gunners would shoot up the fucking water buffalo for the hell of it. A fifty-millimeter gun makes those black beasts explode like a big fat sausage on a hot grill. POOF."

My thoughts flew from the flag green to kids diving off a buffalo into the muddy waters of the Krishna River. I saw Daveed's buffalo explode. A dark, red tide flowed across the river, drowning the green valley. A tidal wave of red-hot anger spilled out of my head and flooded the fucking flag-green.

"That is fucked up, man," I shouted at Jimmy.

Rachel nodded, "Really fucked up."

"It's barbaric like My Lai," Kristina joined in.

"Hey, I'm not saying that was cool or anything," Jimmy replied. "I'm just telling a fucking story my cousin told me. Besides, you guys are being racist to Stepanski because he's an Indian."

"He's not an Indian," Raghu said. "He's a chimp."

"That's exactly what I mean. You're saying that because Stepanski is Cherokee."

"No, we're saying it because he's an asshole," I lied to defend Raghu. But my face was burning because I knew Jimmy had hit our racism straight on.

"No more calling Stepanski racist names," Rachel said.

Jimmy shrugged his shoulders and turned away from us. Then, he cranked up the volume on his Panasonic portable. Rachel and I lay back on the grass, shoulders touching. An unnamable fury surged through me. My mind was exploding as guitar chords blasted a call to arms. Drums joined in with a strident rhythm; hundreds of feet stamping in the street, hundreds of hands ripping up paving stones. Mick Jagger screamed and railed about a palace revolution. The music drowned out everything, sweeping me away in a dark red tide.

The dining room bell rang for tea, and everyone jumped up and rushed to the door. I couldn't move. I wasn't hungry anymore. The tidal wave inside had busted down the remaining walls of the house I was born in. My missionary world was falling apart. The heavy teak beams of our old bungalow in Sangli, the hand-hewn granite blocks held together by mud and sand plaster, came crashing down. Everything that had kept me from exploding into madness was washing away, shattered in exploding bombs and machine-gun fire in my head. It wasn't just the school but the War and not just the War but the whole fucking worldwide SYSTEM. I wanted to blow it all up. A touch on my shoulder pulled me back from the edge of darkness.

"Hey, let's go to the library, and I'll show you the books Jacob turned me on to."

Chapter 14: Circus Sands

After that day, Rachel and I spent a lot of time in the library. It was one of the few places we could be alone together. The staff trusted Jacob, the librarian, and he trusted Rachel and me. We would study at a table in the back, occasionally sneaking into the stacks to make out. If a staff member came into the library, Jacob would cough loudly and greet them by name. Rachel and I listened for the signal while we were making out or reading some radical text, and we'd move apart or grab a different book.

Rachel and I enjoyed each other's bodies but also loved the flooding seeds of world revolution penetrated deep into our minds. We read the histories of Vietnam and India. We read and argued about Frantz Fanon, Che Guevara, Betty Friedan, Norman Mailer, Erica Jong, Regis Debray, Marshall McLuhan, and many others. We learned a new perspective on current events from *Frontline*, a leftist magazine that Jacob subscribed to. Poverty, racism, and war ruled the world. Still, the civil rights movement and the anti-war protests in the US and Europe, the war in Vietnam, the Chinese Cultural Revolution, the guerilla wars and protest movements in Latin America, and the independence wars in Africa were all connected in a sweeping wave of change that would create a brand-new world.

At night in the dorm, I listened incessantly to *Bob Dylan's Greatest Hits* and his early protest songs. My old beliefs were gone, like "Positively 4th Street." I'd lost my faith in God, the Sunday School Jesus, and the goodness of America, the home of the brave and free. And I was dissatisfied with my position of white European privilege. I loved being in India, but my social position was nothing I'd earned.

Rachel and I were busy being born, not dying! We replaced those old myths with new truths about a shockingly brutal and unfair world. We were on our own, like rolling stones, but exploring together and trying to find a new way home. Every night, we were in the library until it closed. We read and talked about the latest war news, the demonstrations in Berkeley her sister went to, our relationship, and how superficial and confused our parents were. Her dad was furious about his daughters' anti-war views. He said the protestors were all ignorant about what the Communists did. They'd killed a lot more innocent people than the Americans, but I'd heard those lies before.

The times were changing, and Rachel and I chased a new truth as we listened to Dylan on earphones with her new cassette tape recorder hidden under the library table. His harmonica solos and poetics led us through new jingle-jangle mornings when the chains would all be broken. We both planned to work with the anti-war movement when we got to the States. She saw herself as a radical photojournalist, traveling the world and exposing the horrors of the System. I imagined myself in demonstrations at the Pentagon and going to jail together. Our dreams ignored the fact that she'd been accepted into UC Berkeley and I was going to Grinnell College in Iowa.

As we studied and talked and made impenetrable love, we understood it wasn't only our anger or Kristina's, Charlie's, Raghu's, or Mickey's. People around the world were furious about the system. Our little group of teen rebels in the post-colonial outpost of Kodaikanal School was not alone. We were part of a wave engulfing the world from Portland to Paris, Montgomery and Mexico City to Madras, and Santiago to Sydney, a revolutionary movement, a fire sweeping the globe. We could not wait to get off our isolated little mountaintop and join it, but first, we had to graduate.

Rachel and I followed the rules except for our anatomical explorations in the library. Our immediate motivation was Senior Sneak, the annual getaway trip before graduation. The location was always a secret until the bus loaded and drove down Ghat Road. The Weydens, Miss K, and the Grants were chaperoned for this year's trip, so we knew it would be a blast. Kids who were dorm-pounded couldn't go. Mr. Grant did say that they might make an exception for kids on the honor roll, and we both had A-averages. Still, they kept us guessing until the day before we were to leave. Stepanski called us both into the principal's office.

"We are proud that both of you have concentrated on your studies," the principal smiled paternalistically. "You have followed the rules and qualified for the National Honor Society again. Given your past behavior, we can't admit you to the Society. However, because we have seen a change in your attitudes, we decided to let you both go on the Senior Sneak."

Rachel and I broke into broad smiles.

"Furthermore," the stern-faced principal continued. "Because of the serious mistakes you each made earlier this semester, you came very close to ruining your lives. To help you resist further temptation, I have asked Rev. Stepanski to travel with you and guide you on the right spiritual path."

"Yes," Stepanski chimed in. "Every afternoon, Jamie and I will meet for prayer and discussion, and Mrs. Grant has agreed to do the same with Rachel. Also, you must pledge not to wander alone."

We agreed. It was a small price to pay. I was ecstatic. Finally, we could be alone together again. I wondered if Rachel still had her condoms. To be safe, I got Raghu and Charlie to slip into the bazaar that night and buy some.

The next day, I got a letter from my mom saying Grinnell College had agreed to delay my admission by a year and that she and my dad had figured out they could pay my way at Madras Christian College, where a friend of mine studied. I would be near Kodai and could come to Sangli for my longer breaks. The idea still appealed to me, but now I wanted to join the anti-war movement in the States and become part of the worldwide revolution. I wrote back that I felt I should return to the States and be part of the peace movement. I knew they would be upset because they supported Nixon, but that was now my calling. Besides, Rachel would be in the States, and I wanted to be at least somewhat near her, though I didn't put that part in the letter.

A few days later, the Class of 1970 was sitting around the pool of the Government Rest House at Mandapam, a fishing village on the Bay of Bengal. Just before sundown, a bunch of us decided to walk down the beach. A wind was blowing in from the sea. Rachel and I waded along the edge of the surf, holding hands, occasionally trying to push each other into the water. Most guys and girls alike wore white cotton pajama pants and *kurtas* (loose-flowing Indian shirts). The group climbed to the top of a small rocky hill. In the distance, we could see the guest house. The sun was setting behind us, painting the clouds above us a deep pink. We sat down and pulled out *beedis*.

"Keep your smokes cupped and your back towards the guest house. You never know if fucking Stepanski is watching us through his Special Forces binoculars," Kristina warned.

Rachel and I lay on the rocky ground, watching the clouds. Raghu sat next to us. He pulled out a pack of Scissors cigarettes. "Who wants to get bombed?"

In the pack were ten cigarettes, emptied of tobacco and lovingly repacked with the best ganja in South India. With the ends twisted, they looked like sleek missiles ready to blow our brains apart.

"Let's go down in that gully by the beach," Charlie suggested.

Most of us followed his lead while a few of the straighter ones stayed on the hill, keeping their eyes peeled. A year earlier, they would have been narcs, but now they were our lookouts. Until the end of our junior year, our class of forty kids was split into exclusive cliques: The In-Crowd, the Out-Crowd, jocks, Bible-thumpers, clothes horses, and the straight-A students. But our senior year changed everything. It wasn't just grass or new music from the States that broke down walls. The changes sweeping our so-called *home* country reached across the oceans to the little missionary school in the Palani Hills and claimed Kodai school students. We became part of our generation.

A giant banyan tree stood in a gully in the sand, which must have rooted itself to an underground stream. Next to it stood a small shrine dedicated to Ganesh, the Remover of Obstacles. About twenty of us sat in a circle passing the joints. Rachel grabbed a cowgirl hat from Charlie's girlfriend, Carmen, and sat in the sand. She and I leaned against the wall supporting Ganesh, heads touching and looking at the purple sky. She put her lips on mine and blew in a lungful of smoke. The stoner smile hit us both at the same time.

After we smoked, the super-Christian kids who were our lookouts walked down to the beach to join us. The sun had set behind us overhead, and the sky was cloudless and a deep blue. Over the sea, a dark wall of clouds was coming straight at us.

"That wall of clouds is our future," Tom said. He was one of the Bible-thumpers. "It is a wall we all have to jump over even though we have no idea what is on the other side."

"Yeah, it's called graduation, but it's more like a fucking tidal wave ready to wash us apart," Charlie said. He put his arm around Carmen and pulled her closer. She was returning to Germany, and he was heading to Minnesota for college.

A line of dark waves and a wall of clouds rushed towards us; we talked about our plans and who was going to which college. We would be scattered from Australia to Germany, Sweden to New York, Montreal, Minneapolis, Ohio, Iowa, Wyoming, California, and points in between. Raghu was the only one staying in India until he got accepted to a school he wanted. Greg, one of the straight-A students, said his older brother quit UCLA to travel but got drafted immediately. Carmen said she read that student deferments were going to be canceled.

"Don't worry, the war will be over by next year," Tom reassured us.

"Shit, you don't believe Nixon has a plan to end the war," Rachel challenged him.

"He's already pulled out thousands of troops, and the Vietnamese are taking over combat operations," Tom replied.

"Yeah, but the war is far from over," I said.

"I had a dream that I died in Vietnam," said Greg.

"You guys are all bumming me out," Jimmy said. "I'm returning to the beach house and bringing some music."

Jimmy had a ton of the latest cassette tapes his older brother sent him from LA. Raghu volunteered to help him but left me another joint to tide us over.

"The US is being forced out of Vietnam. Nixon and Kissinger are just trying to save face. It is part of the Third World revolution," Rachel said.

"It is a worldwide revolution," Kristina responded. "Look at what's happening across Europe: in Germany and Sweden, France, and Britain, a revolution is breaking out. All across the States, Blacks and other minorities are tearing down racism. Women are breaking down the prison of sexism. It was a new version of the French Revolution of 1789—Liberté, Égalité, Fraternité."

"Yeah, but now it is Liberty, Equality, and Community," Rachel agreed. "Back then, it was all about brotherhood between men. Women were there to be fucked, and now the times are changing."

"But some of the first modern feminist writings came out of the French Revolution," Kristina corrected.

"Right on, sisters," Carmen replied, raising her fist. "Let us women keep on coming." She pushed Charlie down and jumped on top of him.

The wall of clouds drove the last light from the sky, but stars were coming out behind that dark wall over the ocean. Rachel took the blanket from around my shoulders and spread it on the ground. We lay down and started kissing.

"Let's smoke some more," she whispered. "I only got a couple of hits."

"Anyone else wanna get high?" I asked, sitting up.

Charlie, Carmen, and Kristina followed us down the beach in deference to the non-smokers. We lay on our backs in a five-pointed star, our heads touching. We passed the joint around a few times; it was pure flower tops and scrambled your head immediately. Charlie started to giggle as he raised and lowered his legs. One foot was bare, and the other was clad in a Kolhapuri *chappal* (sandal).

"Chappal-foot," he said, giggling, and then raised his barefoot, toes spread wide in a pinching motion.

"Alligator," Carmen giggled.

Soon, we were all raising and lowering our feet in time and chanting in unison. "Alligator, Chappal-foot. Alligator-chappal-foot," until we all burst into laughter.

"This is silly. Let's go off on our own," Rachel whispered to me.

We picked up our blankets, shook the sand off them, and walked over a dune behind the Ganesh shrine. This was going to be our chance. We found some boulders that sheltered us from the wind a hundred feet over the dune. Rachel and I spread our blankets on the soft sand and looked at the beach. Most of the class was still sitting there. We saw three points of light in the darkness behind the shrine where Kristina, Charlie, and Carmen were smoking.

I pulled my kurta up over my head and gently pulled Rachel down. She pulled her t-shirt off, her chest naked against mine. I pulled her tight against me with one hand and fumbled in the back pocket of my jeans with the other.

"What are you doing?" she asked.

"I'm ready," I said and waved the packet of condoms.

"Don't worry. I'm on the pill," Rachel said. "My sister sent me some in a packet of M&Ms."

And we made love, fully and completely, for the first time. Then, we lay silently, listening to each other's breathing.

"Rachel, I love you. I am so happy we have each other."

"Me too."

"It will make going back to the States so much easier."

"Iowa and California are a long way apart." After a long pause, she said, "We won't be able to see each other that often."

"Yeah, but during the summer, I'll be in Colorado. That's only two states over. So I can come to visit you before we start college. And after my first year, I'll transfer to Berkeley."

Rachel sighed and laid her head on my chest. The moon shadow of the boulders lengthened.

"Do you want kids?" I asked.

She sat up and stared at me.

"Oh, not now. I mean later, much later," I said. "When we're older… I'm just wondering."

She lay back down next to me but stared at the sea. "Well, yeah. Someday, Jamie, but not anytime soon…we are still so young. I have a lot of things I want to do before being tied down."

"Yeah, you're right. We… I mean… you… I mean, people don't have to have kids right away. They can be together for a long time before getting married or having kids."

"Jamie, you've never had a serious girlfriend before, have you?"

"Not one like you, Rachel."

"I've never had a boyfriend like you either, Jamie, but we don't know what the future will bring. You've gone to Kodai all your life. I've lived in three different countries, been to so many different schools, and had a lot of boyfriends."

That cold stone appeared in my gut.

"None of them meant as much to me as you do. I mean that. You are sweet, smart, and respectful of me. But things change so much when you go to different schools. I don't know how to plan for what will happen when we return to the States."

I held her tighter as I felt her slipping away.

"I mean, we'll stay in touch, and I want us to stay friends forever," she said.

Friends forever? I had a different idea, but I was so stupid.

A flashlight bounced over the boulders above us. We flattened ourselves against the ground.

"Moore, you gotta come back," Raghu spoke in a loud stage whisper as his flashlight found us.

"Turn that damn thing off," Rachel hissed as she reached for her jibbah.

I threw my Indian blanket over her legs and pulled on my jeans.

"Hey, Miss K and Mrs. G walked by us and said they were supposed to make sure you guys were with the group." Raghu shone the flashlight on us again and then snapped it off.

"Oh shit," Rachel and I both said.

We scrambled to our feet as we heard Raghu and Jimmy laughing.

"Don't worry. They went back to the guest house to get guitars, and Kristina went with them to get wood for a bonfire. It also gave us time to warn you guys and a few other couples."

We dressed quickly, and Rachel grabbed my hand and led me down from our hideaway. The dark tropical sky looked like a curtain in front of a spotlight pricked by a million pins. We approached our friends dancing in the sand, singing "Mr. Tambourine Man" along with Bob. A few yards away, a curl of phosphorescent green broke along the shore. Stretching to the horizon were endless rows of dark ocean swells, but hidden deep within each was a secret light,

Everyone joined the dance, our hands waving free at the sparkling sky. We sang together, burying the sorrows of today deep beneath the sands below our bare feet. The wind picked up, and the dark waves kept coming.

Part 3: Jamie Moore's 115th Nightmare

Chapter 1: Captain Arab's America

The waves that rushed across the Bay of Bengal were poised to sweep us off our green mountain refuge. They would slam us against the concrete and glass walls of airports worldwide, alone and confused. We, the children of foreigners born into the womb of Mother India, had grown together, sheltered and wild. Nurtured by that ancient culture, we Kodai kids grew up in hills covered with elephant grass and jungle *sholas* filled with rhododendron trees towering over underbrush thick with bamboo and wild schefflera. We lived vicariously off the rock & roll, rhythm & blues, the images and news coming out of the US of A. But our presence in India was a remnant of the decaying British Raj, which had welcomed and encouraged the sizeable American missionary movement. After independence, India began sloughing off American missionaries, but it took decades before they were all gone. Despite our origins, we were still part of India in 1970. Our parents played essential roles in hospitals, colleges, and schools across India. And their children were part of the package. But the radical sixties changed missionary kids.

Sustained by spicy sambhar and dosa, inspired by Gandhi, Eldridge Cleaver, and Sri Aurobindo, we were Rolling Stoned and Beatled till the crying winds of Jimi Hendrix and Jim Morrison blew the smoldering teenage embers of sex and rebellion into open flames. Nourished with mutton curry and egg parathas, rich south Indian coffee, tobacco, ganja, and occasionally hashish, we learned American history from a Canadian and Indian history from an Englishwoman. We grew up without TV, but we read Marshall McLuhan. Within and without the sixties, we were Americans who weren't from America.

We were desperate to leave the restrictive rules of Kodai School but scared of "going home." We knew it meant the end of the world as we knew it. During our last weeks, Rachel and I would lie under a spreading eucalyptus tree, smoke cigarettes, and make out and share our dreams of joining the Revolution while looking up at the starry south Indian sky. The world was spinning out of control as we watched. Yet we couldn't wait to get off our isolated little mountain and become part of the new American Revolution.

Then, two weeks before we graduated, came the shocking news. **Four Dead in Ohio**. And two more in Jackson State. College students who'd been protesting the war were shot and killed by the National Guard and State Patrol.

No fucking way. What was happening in America? The news came in brief articles in *The Indian Express.* A week later, *Time Magazine* arrived. Rachel and I were the first to read it. The cover picture was a color photo of a student kneeling beside her dying friend. We read it right before our AP American History final. It was hard to concentrate.

That night, new dreams stalked me. I was running up slippery temple steps next to a muddy jungle river. Each step grew taller, and my legs grew heavier as a crocodile grew closer and closer until I'd wake with a start, sweating and breathing hard. Or I'd dream of hiding in pitch darkness with friends as a madman hunted us. When he appeared, I would open my mouth to scream a warning, but my voice froze deep in my throat. Or I would fly over jungles that looked like India in a helicopter. I would have a gun in my hand and a helmet on my head. Then, the chopper would explode as I woke.

I did not share these dreams with Rachel, Raghu, or Charlie. We just got high and listened to music. *America* by Simon & Garfunkel was our theme song for graduation week. We were all poised to go looking for whatever it was. The week was one long, stoned night in the woods of Kodaikanal. Only graduation day stood out. Exuberant and triumphant, the Class of '70 wore new clothes as we marched into the school gym. I wore a red, raw silk jacket. Rachel wore a red silk dress that stopped six inches above her knee. Mickey and I gave a humorous class history and then broke into a speech condemning racism at the school. Mickey's band played a cover of "We Got to Get out of This Place" by The Animals. And we marched across a stage decorated with a giant peace sign as our grim-faced principal, a Naval Reserve Lieutenant, handed out our diplomas.

Then, one final night in our mountain paradise prison. Sleepless and stoned, a group of us walked across the Bundh. The dark black lake reflected a full moon so close we could have touched it. We climbed over a wall on the Coimbatore Raja's compound. The compound was deserted. So, we explored the Raja's gardens in the moonlight, forsaking the safety of the woods. The group wandered along paths through rose bushes and flowering trees lit by the full moon. The moon lit up the big house, and we smoked on the verandah. Wandering around the back, we discovered a full-sized cricket pitch. We played an imaginary cricket game until we got bored. We lay on the pitch and looked at the tropical moon to which we were saying goodbye. Couples periodically snuck into the long, dark shadows of towering eucalyptus trees, making the best of our final night together. As the eastern sky lightened, we all walked to Coakers Walk to watch the sun rise above the Bay of Bengal. We caught the rare sight of the first flash of gold-red sun on the distant water.

Then, it was time to walk away from a world we could never return to. Rachel's mom had a taxi booked for 9 A.M. We walked into the Carleton

Hotel at 8:55. Rachel's mom insisted we sit down and have breakfast. The cab could wait. The English breakfast of eggs, grilled tomatoes, baked beans, toast, and even bangers—the sausages I had so often dreamed of—all tasted like sawdust. The old, jagged stone that first appeared the night my father put me into boarding grew sharp and cold in my stomach. I felt like I was nine again, walking away from everything I loved and into a hard unknown.

Rachel's mom finished her coffee. "Time to go, or we will miss our flight from Madurai."

I didn't even know you could fly out of the ancient city of Madurai. She and I followed her mother but ducked into a hallway for a final flashing kiss. Then, she was gone. I walked home alone. We would leave the next day for Sangli, so I could say goodbye to my hometown, and the servants and school staff could say goodbye to me, the *sahib's* son. Then, Bombay and the world.

The waves we'd seen on the beach pulled apart our tight circle of first friends, washed us away, and smashed us onto the rocks of strange countries our parents called home. Charlie, Mickey, and I had planned a Grand Tour of Europe on our way to the States. Rachel was traveling with Kristina to Sweden and then flying to DC, where she'd meet her mom and dad and drive across the country visiting relatives before heading to UC Berkeley in the fall. I was to spend the summer in Colorado before going to Grinnell College in Iowa. Raghu was still applying to colleges and trying to get into America.

Before my parents saw me off at Bombay Airport, my mom made one more attempt to convince me to stay in India. "Son, I am worried about you. I keep having bad dreams about you in America. My Scots' intuition tells me to hold you and keep you in India."

"Mom, we have our European trip planned. I'm ready to go home and be part of the peace movement. Besides, we already have my ticket."

"We can change the ticket. Look what happened to the protestors in Ohio. And the draft?"

"Noreen, darling," my dad intervened. "I agree one hundred percent, but we've talked about all of this before, many times. Jamie has made his decision."

I hugged them and walked to the line, waiting for emigration clearance. I turned and saw Teddy crying into our mother's chest. He had grown a lot recently. My dad had an arm around her but was watching me. He gave me a wave and a smile. He looked proud but worried.

Mickey, Charlie, and I soon found ourselves on a plane flying over the moonscape of Iran and landing in Turkey, packets of ganja stuffed into our underwear. Three lost boys stepped off the airport bus before the Istanbul Hilton. Charlie and I bumped into each other, trying to avoid the revolving door. Neither of us remembered how to step through the whirling blades of steel and glass.

"You stupid fuckers," Mickey said. He'd lived in the States during his junior year and walked straight through the whirling door. In the dim coolness of the hotel lobby, we met friends of my parents who took us out for lunch and to a youth hostel. We spent our days sightseeing and our nights smoking ganja. Totally ignorant of Turkey's harsh treatment of drug users, we smuggled in an ounce of hallucinogenic-grade ganja wrapped in silver foil packets. We stuffed them into the crotch pockets of our tightey-whiteys and left five days later with a half-ounce. Only after the movie *Midnight Express* came out did we realize how utterly foolish we had been.

The Grand Tour of Europe continued with wasted days and nights in Geneva, Frankfurt, and Stockholm before arriving in London, where we stayed at the YMCA Hostel in Piccadilly. Since we'd run out of ganja, we spent forty-eight hours in London drinking gin mixed with Coke and going to movies. We took in *Z, Easy Rider, and Midnight Cowboy*—a trio of films designed to scare the crap out of any young immigrants heading to America.

A black-and-white snapshot shows three skinny, long-haired white boys wearing Indian jibbahs standing in Piccadilly Circus. Our eyes were filled with fear, but we smiled bravely and held up packs of 555 State Express, James Bond's cigarette brand. We escaped from London a day early, flew to New York, and landed hard.

My parents had arranged for a friend from the Presbyterian Church headquarters to meet us. The family would put us up for a few nights in Stony Point before we went our separate ways: Mickey to Atlanta, Charlie to Seattle, and me to Denver. Instead, we arrived at JFK a day early. We walked through customs and emerged into a muggy New York summer day.

Alone and confused, we set our bags down on the sidewalk. I still felt a heavy weight pushing down my shoulders. A thick smog blanketed the traffic-scape of bus lanes, highways, and the monorail, still new from the New York World's Fair six years earlier. I took a deep breath and burst into a coughing fit. I had to sit down and could not stand.

"What's that?" I gasped.

"I think they call it America," Mickey said, laughing.

Mickey said he knew how to get us from JFK to the Port Authority, where we could call my parents' Presbyterian friend. We got to the giant bus terminal. I was taking a piss in a grimy restroom when a little man who looked like Ratso Rizzo approached me and asked if I was lonely. I wet my jeans in a rush to leave. We all tumbled into a hallway where a couple of short-haired white guys asked if we wanted some grass. Charlie and I turned toward them, smiling when Mickey grabbed us.

"You stupid motherfuckers," he hissed as he shoved us into an elevator. "They are probably narcs, Or they were gonna rob and beat the crap out of you. We aren't in India anymore, Toto."

This wasn't exactly the America I'd been so anxious to find.

Chapter 2: Threw Myself in Jail for Carrying Harpoons

Denver had a massive anti-war movement and even a Black Panther chapter. I was going to Denver to live with my grandparents. The summer would be enjoyable. Or so I thought. I hadn't noticed that they lived fifty miles east of Denver, where my grandpa was the minister.

A few days after our hard landing in New York, I was listening to my Grandpa's Sunday sermon in the First (and only) Presbyterian Church of Bennett. He had left the mission field after WWII to be close to his aging parents. He was over seventy but still worked as a pastor, helping struggling churches in small towns. And you really couldn't get much smaller than Bennett.

The town had a grain elevator, a Cenex station, a laundromat, two churches, and a school. It also had a couple of boarded-up restaurants, which shut down when the Interstate was built a mile south of town. Now, the action was at the truck-stop café and a Nickerson's restaurant off the I-79 exit. Gray dust rose from Bennett's gravel streets with each passing car, bike, or tumbleweed. There was no place to go except the laundromat, which had a pop machine and a color TV. I now knew Sangli was not the most boring place in the world.

The only thing that caught my eye was the girl in the choir. She looked at me every time I glanced at her, which was most of the church service. She had flowing chestnut hair, almost like Rachel's, but redder. Thinking of Rachel depressed me even more because she was still driving across the country. There was no way I could get in touch with her.

Grandma took hold of my arm during the social hour after the service and pulled me over to the girl. She introduced us and slipped away as soon as we started talking. Her name was Lillian. She was a sophomore at CU in Boulder studying biology and planned to go to med school. She wore make-up and seemed pretty straight, but she was probably the only person my age in town.

The next day, I got up super early to start my new job with Mr. Schwarzkopf, a rancher my grandpa knew. His son was in Vietnam, and he needed help for the summer. The first morning, he drove his pickup across dusty range land, up steep hills, and down dry arroyos. We repaired breaks in his fences. The temperature hit 100 degrees. My feet were sweating and sore in the new work boots my grandparents bought me. Finally, it was lunchtime.

We sat in his pickup to eat our baloney sandwiches while listening to the news on KOA clear channel radio.

"Finally, our boys are kicking their asses in Cambodia." The rancher's ruddy face broke into a grin. "We would have already won this damn war if Johnson had let the Marines do that back in '65."

"But why are we even over there?" I blurted out.

He put his dusty Stetson back on and looked at me long and hard.

"You, of all people, should know that we are shedding our blood for freedom to worship our God. I remember your dad preaching about the Indian church and its trials. Your grandpa has talked to me about the Communists in India. You may be a longhair now, but your family are good Christians. So, I know God will bring you through this phase."

My throat went tight, and my brain went red. What the hell was he thinking?

Yet something made me pause. Mr. Schwarzkopf's son was over there fighting, risking his life. Arguing about the war with his dad was not the brightest idea. I bit my tongue. The rest of the day, he kept needling me about Vietnam and how my hair was a danger the way it kept blowing in my face. I cut myself on the barbed wire three times. And by the end of the day, my feet were a mass of blisters. The sun was touching the mountains before he finally called it quits.

On the drive home, he turned to me and grinned. "You're costing me more in Band-Aids than cash." He punched me in the shoulder. "But for a greenhorn hippie, you did all right."

I stared out the dusty windshield, mad as hell. Here I was, doing my best to get along with this redneck rancher, and he was insulting me. The sun dipped behind the mountains when he dropped me at the church manse. I was aching all over, dirty, and hungry. After I showered, put on new Band-Aids, and ate my Grandma's fried chicken and fried potatoes, I was exhausted. I fell asleep on the couch while we watched *Gunsmoke*.

Tuesday was the same, except I fell asleep watching *Perry Mason* in the evening. One hot, muscle-aching, skin-breaking hour followed the next until the sunset. Then, the rancher dropped me back at my grandparents' house. But on Wednesday, we quit at 5:30 because of church choir practice. The redneck rancher was a soloist.

When I got home, I learned Rachel had called. Her grandma had a stroke, so they had cut short their trip and flown straight to San Francisco. She left her grandma's number and told me to call after six California time. I sat on the front steps, reading and re-reading the message. I was drinking my second Coke when I saw Lillian and her mom pull up across the street.

"Hey Jamie," she called to me, "want to join us for choir?"

"I'm not much of a singer," I said.

"Join us afterwards for cake and coffee," her mom said.

I nodded and went into the house to wash up for dinner.

Grandpa had already eaten as he had a committee meeting at the church. Grandma served me fried pork chops, canned beets, and homemade mashed potatoes made with buttermilk. After having seconds, I got up to help myself to a piece of pie. Grandma left cleaning in the kitchen and poured us a cup of coffee.

"I heard Lillian McGill invite you to join the choir."

"I can't sing, Grandma."

"Lillian is a fine girl with a strong faith. Do you think she's pretty?"

"Yeah, she is pretty, Grandma, but so is my girlfriend Rachel."

"I talked to Rachel on the phone today. She seems like a good girl. Are the two of you engaged?"

"No, that's kind of old-fashioned, Grandma. Rachel and I are committed to each other and the movement."

"What's the movement?"

"You know, the freedom movement for worldwide justice and peace."

"It's sad, Jamie, but peace has become a four-letter word around here."

"But Jesus called for peace, and the Vietnamese are fighting for their freedom like America did."

"Yes, Jamie, I understand. Remember, I was in India when Gandhi led millions of people to independence. I saw truckloads of poor farmers coming to Sangli in dirty white pajamas. They lined up across the parade ground from the Raja's police and the British Army. They marched toward the government building and got beaten and jailed. They had courage. When I see the Viet Cong in their black pajamas, I see them as Gandhians with guns."

"Exactly, Grandma, and that is what the peace movement is saying."

"But America is there to protect, not take away their freedom...."

"No, Grandma...." I started to tell her about the French colonialists,

"And there was something else I always wondered about until I figured it out," she continued.

"What's that, Grandma?"

"Why do they wear black pajamas. Black clothes are so hot in the sun. Then, again, the white pajamas of the Marathi farmers got so filthy. Even when washed, the pajamas looked dirty, so black does make more sense."

"But Grandma, I'm talking about the anti-war movement..."

"Jamie, people don't take kindly to that kind of talk around here, but you and I are talking about girls, not the war. Tell me about Rachel."

A big smile crossed my face. I hadn't had anyone to talk with about Rachel since leaving India. Even on the trip, Charlie and Mickey groaned and

117

made fun of me when I mentioned her name. I talked ten minutes straight about Rachel's family, how much we'd learned together, how funny she was, and what her smile, eyes, and hair looked like. I left out her other parts, but they filled my mind as I talked with Grandma.

"Well, Jamie," Grandma said as she finished her coffee, "I want to say that Rachel seems like a fine young woman. She and you have been good for each other, but you are both young. You will both attend college in different states. And you will meet many bright, pretty girls. But what's important is understanding what God has in mind for you. I was head over heels for the pastor's son when I was even younger than you. He proposed to me, but my ma said we were too young. And we should wait while I kept my eyes open for what God had planned for my life. I was mad at the time but am sure glad that I waited. Your Grandpa gave me a life I never imagined when I lived in that old farmhouse on the edge of Pueblo."

I saw the years fall off the white-haired old woman as I listened. A brown-haired girl with laughing blue eyes told me about square dancing and ice skating at a church camp in Estes Park. She met a charming college student two years older who stole her heart away and took her to India in 1930.

I stared with my mouth open wide.

"All I'm saying is that God has a special person in mind for you, Jamie. Keep your eyes open and let things go where they may with Lillian. Is it too hard a thing to ask?"

"No, Grandma. Keeping my eyes on Lillian is not a hard thing at all."

She let out a peal of laughter. "She is an attractive girl. Now you go into Grandpa's study, call Rachel, and head to church for cake and ice cream."

I sat down in a big leather desk chair. Three different Bibles and other books were open on his desk. I picked up the phone and dialed her number.

"Hi, how are you?" A voice I'd been dying to hear for weeks came across the long copper wire from California.

"Tired and aching and fucked up from farm work but feeling really good right now. How are you?"

Rachel had already been in Berkeley for a couple of weeks. Her voice sounded tired, and she didn't seem excited to talk with me. Things were intense because of her grandma's stroke. She had met all kinds of radicals at a party at her sister's apartment. She met this incredible guitar player who often opened for bands at the Fillmore West. He was also a member of the Revolutionary Union and had been an SDS organizer for years. He'd even been on Mississippi Freedom Summer. He showed her around the movement in Berkeley. A women's underground paper needed help with photography. She'd gone to a demo and took pictures of cops on horses chasing a young kid down the street. One of the pictures had been printed.

"Well, how old is he?"

"Who, the kid who got chased down by the cops? Twelve, maybe ten."

"No, your SDS organizer friend."

"Oh, twenty-five or so. Why? Does it matter"?

"You seem pretty impressed with him," I said.

"Jamie, you're jealous. He's just a friend and someone I can learn a lot from."

I was jealous but almost more that she was in Berkeley while I was stuck in Bennett.

"You are still my best friend and lover."

A huge rock lifted off my chest. I could hear that rich timbre in her voice, meaning she felt deeply about what she was saying. I sat back and listened to the words she was using to talk about us. Then, I just heard the sound of her voice and lost track of what she was saying.

"… but we don't own each other. Ownership is a bourgeois concept."

I'd never heard her use that word. We were each other's first and were committed. I asked what that meant now. She didn't answer but switched the conversation to me.

"But how are things in Colorado? It must be cool being in the mountains."

"Bennett isn't in the mountains. The eastern half of Colorado is a flat, dusty plain like the surface of the moon. I drive around the moon all day working for a redneck rancher."

"You shouldn't condemn him just because he thinks differently. Did you know the word redneck is a putdown of poor whites by middle-class people? It's the people who have to work all day in the sun whose necks are burned red. Ray would say farmers are members of the working class. Even if they are pro-war, the Movement has to win them over."

"Who's Ray?"

"The radical guitar player I told you about."

She changed subjects and told me about her trip to Sweden and all the cool radicals she'd met there. And how sad she was about her grandma dying. She'd been a reporter for fifty years and covered politics and labor. Rachel was surprised to learn about all the radical writing her grandmother did in the twenties and thirties. A big anti-war demonstration was planned, and the Jefferson Airplane would play. India already seemed so far away, like a dream she'd had once. I could come out to visit sometime in late July or August. After twenty minutes, she said she had to hang up and go to a meeting.

I hung up and looked at the American flag on my grandpa's desk. The office was hot and stuffy, and I could barely breathe. I walked on down the hall. The Doors were playing in my head. Music—that was the problem. I had nowhere I could listen to music. Grandma and Grandpa didn't even have a stereo. I had a few tapes Rachel made for me before I left. As soon as I got my first paycheck, I would buy a cassette recorder and some more music. I walked through the kitchen. Grandma was in the basement doing laundry, so I sat on the back steps. Thunderheads were gathering over the mountains. The sun slid behind their dark shadows.

There was nothing between Bennett and Denver but dusty prairie and wheat fields filled with dried-up stalks. The record player in my head switched to a Dylan song I'd heard on the underground radio station.

Desolation Row was precisely where I was. The thunderclouds grew darker and towered over the land. Dylan's song and images from Eliot's "Wasteland" filled my head. I was a lost rat scuttling through dried grass as sharp as glass. I had to get out to Berkeley and visit Rachel, but it was apparent she wasn't crazy about seeing me.

From an open window, I could hear the church choir singing "Blest Be the Ties that Bind." I was bound by Christian love, all right! Bound to a dull summer with old grandparents who could not understand me. The choir stopped singing, and I walked outside, thinking about Lillian.

Why not go talk with her? She was pretty and seemed to like me, and Rachel said we didn't own each other. I wasn't in Kodai anymore. I couldn't believe Rachel was moving away from me so quickly. She said we were still lovers, but like Dylan said, I didn't need a weatherman to see how the wind blew.

I jumped and kicked at a tumbleweed that blew across the dried lawn. One sandal flew up, and my foot stuck in the prickly ball. Dammit! I had to stand on one foot and pull the stickers out of the other. I hobbled across the road to get my sandal. The choir practice seemed to be over. Hopefully, Lillian didn't see my stupid move. I smoothed the wrinkles on my t-shirt and headed for the church basement, looking for Lillian, cake, and ice cream.

She wore an indigo-blue dress that reached halfway down her tanned thighs. It set off the red in her hair. She was talking with Mr. Schwarzkopf, my rancher boss.

"There you are, Jamie. Come have some cake and ice cream," she said as she took me by the arm and turned to the rancher. "Keep that thought, we'll talk later."

Lillian steered me through the crowd of choir and church committee members, talking and eating cake. They were all at least twice as old as we were. She held my arm to her side as we walked and spoke into my ear.

"Augustine was telling me what a good job you are doing."

"Who's Augustine?" I asked, turning to her. My lips were inches from hers. We looked at each other and paused. Her eyes were hazel green with yellow speckles. We both saw our reflection in the other's iris. We knew what we'd do next if church people hadn't surrounded us.

She shook her head, and her auburn hair brushed my face. "I'm sorry," she said, blushing. "What did you ask me?"

"Who is Augustine?"

"Mr. Schwarzkopf, the rancher you're working for. He said you were doing well for someone without experience."

"Really? He was saying that to be nice."

"No, he meant it. He never says something just to be nice." Lillian put two pieces of chocolate cake and several scoops of vanilla ice cream on a plate and handed it to me. "Let's go sit at that corner table."

Chapter 3: Busting Out

That Saturday, I slept until almost noon. I was drinking coffee when Grandma pointed out that Lillian had been driving around the town all morning in her little red Camaro.

"She drives by our house every ten minutes and is alone, Jamie. I think she's looking for a friend to ride along." Grandma smiled. "Why don't I serve you coffee in the backyard? She'll see you next time she scoops the loop."

I was soon in Lillian's '69 Camaro convertible, heading for the next town where they had an A&W root beer stand. We spent the afternoon together and went to a drive-in that evening to see *Kelly's Heroes*. We spent more time making out than watching the film.

When we returned to Bennett, I began thinking my summer wouldn't be so bad after all. I felt guilty about Rachel, but she was the one who said we didn't belong to each other.

During the service the following day, we kept smiling at each other. As soon as it was over, we sat together in a far corner of the social hall, telling each other details of our lives until a male voice broke the spell.

"Hey, you two, I don't mean to intrude, but I heard some news you'll both be interested in."

"Hello, Mr. Schwarzkopf," I said politely.

"Hi, Augustine," Lillian beamed.

"NBC News is reporting that they have indicted the Ohio troopers for the riot at Kent State."

"That's outrageous," Lillian exclaimed.

Her eyes locked with mine. We must have had the same shocked expression.

"Good, somebody needs to pay for those murders," I burst out. Lillian's reaction was the same as mine.

Lillian now looked even more alarmed as she stared at me.

"Murders? It was self-defense. The rioters attacked the guardsmen with gasoline bombs."

"Where did you hear that?" I asked.

"My brother knows people in the Pennsylvania Guard. They had intelligence that there would be an attack by underground revolutionaries."

"I read every story I could, and there was nothing like that." How could Lillian believe those lies?

"Jamie, you can't believe what you read in the liberal media. I've listened to experts from Washington prove that the media is still controlled by communist sympathizers."

"What experts? Where?" I said a bit too loudly.

Men in suits and women in white hats with flowers were turning to stare at our escalating argument.

"Lillian is right, son. You have to be careful talking that peacenik stuff around here. Some veterans will tear you limb from limb." Schwarzkopf put a hand on my shoulder. My head went red. I gritted my teeth to keep from shouting and stood up quickly, knocking my chair over. The whole room turned to look.

Grandpa came over, took me by the arm, and led me to the door. "You've had some long days, Jamie. Why don't you take a walk and then go home and get some rest? I'll suggest to Mr. Schwarzkopf that he gives you the morning off tomorrow to catch up on your sleep."

I nodded my head and walked outside. Another storm was gathering over the mountains, but I didn't care. How could Lillian be pro-war? I followed a road that led north out of town, walked for a long time, and then turned around. My feet were sore, and I was thirsty. When I returned to town, all the cars had left the church parking lot. Grandpa had rescued me from a weird situation, but how would I survive a summer in this town just when I thought things were turning around?

The following day, I slept till ten o'clock. I was still in my PJs when Lillian called. She was on a work break. She apologized for calling me naïve and was sorry she'd gotten so angry—her temper was one of her weaknesses.

"I have a bit of a temper, too," I admitted.

"I noticed," she giggled. "We can fight sometimes and still be friends. Even if you are wrong, I can practice Christian forgiveness." She burst into a throaty laugh before I could get mad.

"Yeah, we can just agree to disagree," I said.

"I'd like to see you tonight. I have some news to talk about, Lillian replied.

The rancher came to pick me up at noon. He'd been at the John Deere dealership in the next town getting a part for one of his tractors. He sort of apologized by saying people had to draw their own conclusions and mentioned Christian forgiveness as well. Lillian and the rancher mentioned Christian forgiveness, a sign that Grandpa must have spoken with them.

"For now, son, let's agree to disagree," Mr. Schwarzkopf said, extending his hand.

I shook it. "Sounds good, sir."

Work was a bit easier that day as we spent most of the time driving along the fence line without finding a single break. The rancher told me stories about his college days with my father.

Lillian and I went to Nickerson's Restaurant by Interstate 70 for pie and ice cream that night. We both avoided talking about Vietnam. Instead, she asked me a lot about India and my parents' work. I told her what going to high school in Kodai was like. It was fun to talk to someone who cared about India. We got on well if we stayed away from politics. I was again sitting on top of the world.

"I have some good news/bad news, Jamie."

"What?" I asked, my stomach starting to tense.

"The good news is that I've been asked to join our Boulder chorale group on their tour of Europe."

"Oh, that is great news."

"Yeah, they rarely take sophomores on the trip. I was on a waiting list, and another soprano got sick. The bad news is that I am leaving this weekend."

The bottom dropped out, and my summer roller coaster continued. Lillian and I talked until the restaurant closed, and then she drove me home. She climbed across the console and pushed my seat all the way back. We were both all over each other. Breathing hard, we were ready to blast off when she climbed back to her seat, holding my head to keep her lips locked on mine. Then, she turned the key in the starter.

"I'd better go before we do something else we'd have to ask forgiveness for," she said, smiling. "See you tomorrow."

As I looked at the taillights of her pickup, I was missing her already. At the same time, I couldn't believe I was falling for a Republican. I'd betrayed Rachel and myself. Rachel was joining the Revolution, and I was ready to spend my summer making out with a pro-war choir girl. What was wrong with me?

Was I ready to give up my new beliefs for a pretty face? Was I that horny? I had better save money and visit Rachel to connect to the movement rather than the church. But was that really it? What did I believe? What is the difference between who you are and what your lovers and friends think? No, it wasn't just Rachel. I'd never go back to believing the myths about America and democracy and Jesus loving all the children of the world.

Grandpa was watching Johnny Carson but switched the TV off when I came in.

"Glad to see you home, son. I've been wanting to have a talk with you."

I sat at the dining room table while he went into the kitchen and got each of us a cup of coffee, black but weak like most church people seemed to like it.

"Son, people around here are mighty upset about the protestors."

"I can see that, Grandpa. And a lot of us are pretty upset about the war."

"Many people see protest as siding with the Communists, which gets their back up. Jamie, I can understand your point of view. Remember, Grandma and I were in India, too, and we know a lot about the evils of colonialism."

I was shocked he used the word.

"There is a lot of anger at the changes sweeping our country. And folks in Bennett…"

"But Grandpa, our movement is for peace and justice for all. That's what America is supposed to be about, right? And we have the freedom to express—"

"My heart agrees with you, Jamie, but my job in this small town is to understand my congregation and to minister to their needs. I'm trying to build up their tolerance."

"Should we tolerate evil? Napalming of children and killing old women and babies is evil."

"War is evil, and both sides have committed atrocities."

"That is why we want to stop it."

"In college, Jamie, you can act on your conscience. But I must ask you to be cautious with your words while you are in Bennett."

"Jesus didn't stay silent when he saw evil in the temple."

Grandpa's face grew red, and he stood up.

"My parishioners may be misguided, but they are not evil. And do not lecture me about Jesus, young man. I am going to bed before I lose my temper."

I had trouble sleeping that night, so I read Norman Mailer's *Armies of the Night* about the march on the Pentagon until the dawn came streaking in. The next few days were a daze. The rancher worked me hard each day. Each evening, Lillian and I spent the time getting closer and closer until she would push me away, still smiling.

Saturday morning, Lillian left for Europe, and I slept until noon. Then, I drove into Denver with my grandpa and mowed the grass at the old house on Yates Street. They took me to a mall where I bought a cassette recorder, Simon & Garfunkel's Bookends cassettes, and some Dylan albums, including one I'd never heard before. We ate dinner at their favorite restaurant, The Drumstick. It had a model railroad running all around the walls but didn't serve alcohol. I was back to my life as a kid. When we got home, I went into my basement room. I played my new Dylan album and *Bookends* over and over that night. I had to leave Bennett and look for the real America. It couldn't all be like this dusty Podunk town.

After church the next day, Grandpa and Grandma took me to Nickerson's Restaurant for dinner with Lillian's parents. Col. McGill was a retired Navy pilot originally from Kentucky and is now the church moderator. Things started out boringly enough, with them talking about church politics. The debate was about women becoming ministers. To my surprise, Grandpa was all for it and was trying to calm Col. McGill's concerns. I chowed on the roast beef and mashed potatoes. Grandma gave me half of hers. We all enjoyed the pie a la mode.

A blonde waitress re-filled our coffee cups.

"Bonnie is a pretty young woman, isn't she," Mrs. McGill said.

Col. McGill winked at me, "Jamie prefers auburn hair."

I blushed.

"And my daughter is also pretty interested in you, young man. Despite your long hair, I know you have a strong Christian upbringing. Your father and I have met several times, and he is a good man."

"You know what I saw in Aurora at the mall yesterday?" Mrs. McGill interrupted and shivered her shoulders. "There was this beautiful blonde girl, as cute and sweet as can be. And she was hanging on the arm of this big hairy, black ape! It just made me sick."

"Mmm," Grandma Moore muttered in a non-committal way.

"I don't know what this country is coming to," Col. McGill said. "The President will straighten it out if the Democrats don't tie his hands. He's finally cracking down on those crazy radicals, but I don't know what we can do about the niggers."

My eyes widened, and I stared at Grandpa Moore, who gave me a cautionary look. I stood up quickly.

"I feel sick," I announced,

I walked around in the 95-degree heat, which didn't help my nausea. I sat in the shade, fuming. Life in Bennett was becoming pure hell. Racists and warmongers, only one person my age, and even she was a Republican and now gone for most of the summer. The concrete of the freeway shimmered in the heat. America was supposed to be in the middle of a revolution. Still, this town was even further behind the times than Kodai. These people didn't even know enough to be ashamed of their racism. I could not take much more.

Fifteen minutes later, the two couples came out of the restaurant. The McGill's didn't even look at me as they got into their big Buick. Grandpa waved me over and asked me to sit in the front with him. Grandma climbed into the back seat of the '65 Chevy Impala.

"There is a lot of racism in this town, son," Grandpa Moore said as he drove into town. "I understand that, and I tried to explain your situation, growing up as a white minority, and our love for the Indian people. They said they understood your feelings but that you owe them an apology for rudeness."

I glared at my grandfather. "Rudeness versus racism—which is worse?"

"Confronting every ignorant comment creates walls that are hard to tear down. To change hearts and minds, you have to engage."

I stared out the window. Engage with racists? What did my grandpa understand about the racist system? I watched brown wheat fields roll past in the heat. They were so ugly compared to green rice paddies.

Later that afternoon, Bobby Steinmetz called. He was excited that we were both going to college in Iowa. Bobby was entirely over Rachel. He was dating a girl from his church who turned him on. He worked weekends at a bowling alley and had another summer job at a dairy farm outside Dubuque. Yesterday, the farmer had said he could use an extra hand for a month or two. It didn't pay much, only $1.50 an hour, and it was challenging work. But we'd work together, and I could stay with his parents free all summer.

The rancher was paying me that, and I had no reason to stay in Bennett. I asked Bobby about the anti-war movement in Dubuque. He said his high school walked out as part of the national strike after the killings at Kent State. They had a draft resistance center at one of the churches. I could be part of the movement in Dubuque.

"What is Dubuque like? Is it flat and dusty and dry as shit like eastern Colorado?"

"No way. I know what you mean about Eastern Colorado. Our church took a trip to Vail last winter, and it looked like the moon."

"Exactly!"

"Dubuque isn't like Kodai. It is a small city with a beautiful view of the Mississippi. Every Saturday night, they have an outdoor rock concert in a park overlooking the river. Dubuque has hills and valleys, lots of woods, and green all summer."

A river, green hills, woods, and rock music settled it for me. I couldn't step out for a walk without people whispering about the hippie grandson of the Presbyterian minister. Besides, Bennett was filled with red-necked, racist war-lovers. I now knew why the underground paper I'd picked up in Denver always spelled it "Amerika" with a swastika in place of the *r*. Like Simon and Garfunkel, I'd get on a Greyhound and go looking for my America.

"Shit, Bennett is like Sangli, dry and dusty, but worse. It is filled with fucking rednecks who hate hippies and want us all to burn in jail. Do you know the song *Bob Dylan's 115th Dream?*"

"For sure, about Captain Arab? I love how they burst out laughing right at the beginning and have to start over. You know they were stoned for sure."

"Well, everything is totally absurd in Bennett. I've been thrown in jail for being anti-war like I carried a harpoon into church."

Grandpa and Grandma reluctantly agreed that leaving for the summer was for the best. They had heard from my parents that the Steinmetz family was a good Christian family. They said they loved me and made me promise I'd come back for Christmas. Two days later, I was on a Greyhound rolling across the never-ending expanse of eastern Colorado, gazing in wonder at an emptiness that never seemed to end. But I had my music, and I'd busted out of jail.

Chapter 4: Asked for Collateral

The Greyhound stopped at every tiny town to let someone on or off. Most didn't even have bus stations, only an all-night gas station or a rundown motel. I sat across from the bathroom, and the noise and smell kept waking me up. It was a long, restless night.

"Oh fuck-goddam-shit!" A voice in the bathroom yelled.

A greasy, long blond head poked out the door and smiled when he saw me.

"Hey man, do you have a light?"

I hesitated. The guy had a scar on one cheek and was missing a couple teeth.

"You want to get high? Acapulco gold, and I dropped my fucking lighter in the shitter."

I hadn't smoked grass for a month; he was short and skinny. I could probably take him if he started anything. I grabbed my cigarettes and matches and glanced down the aisle of the sleeping bus. No one was stirring. I slipped into the tiny can and was pleasantly surprised to see a girl with long dark hair and darker eyes. She smiled at me as I squeezed in next to her. I handed him my matches, and he lit a fat joint, took a drag, and blew out into the exhaust fan. As I passed the joint, I told them I was changing buses in Des Moines. The greasy man told me the girl was his cousin, and they were going to Chicago to look for work. The girl didn't speak much but kept rubbing against my thigh, making me doubly high.

"For a twenty, she'll blow you," the man said as he threw the roach into the toilet and flushed.

I shook my head and stumbled out of the smoky bathroom. There was a long line. A man with a beat-up cowboy hat reached for the door, which slammed shut. Grunts came through the shaking door.

"Fucking hippies," the cowboy banged on the door. "Get the hell out of that bathroom before I tear off the goddamned door."

I quickly slipped into my seat.

The driver spoke on the intercom. "Passengers, please take your seats until the bathroom is accessible. Bathroom occupants, smoking in the toilet is prohibited.

I stared out the window, pissed off and depressed at capitalism, poverty and sexism. I was stoned for the first time on American grass but mostly felt dizzy, horny as hell, and missing both Rachel and Lillian. My head was exploding.

Headlights raced along Interstate 80, shooting crystal rays into my eyes. Each headlight shot glass shards through my chaotic brain. Then, mercifully, I fell asleep.

I woke as someone gently shook my arm.

"Wake up," the dark-haired girl whispered as she slid into the empty seat beside me. "You are good *hombre*. I am scared of that man. Take me *contigo*?"

I jabbed her with my elbow. The guy was walking up the aisle with his hand in his pocket and hellfire in his eyes. He grabbed both of our shoulders with steel-claw fingers and leaned over to hiss in my face.

"You trying to get it for free?"

"No, *Señor*," the girl gently touched his face and pulled a ten-dollar bill out of her bra.

"OK, good girl," he loosened his claw-like fingers. "But you're giving it too cheap."

He turned to me and shook a fist in my face. "I told you it was twenty, asshole, not ten. "Pay up," he ordered as he opened his fist, clicked a switchblade open and shut, then slipped it into his pocket, all within a few seconds.

"But I didn't..."

The girl's clutch on my arm and the fear in her eyes stopped me. I reached for a ten and handed it over. He dragged her back down the aisle and shoved her into the window seat.

I fell into a fitful sleep, too tired to open my eyes even when the bus stopped in Omaha.

I woke to the sun glinting off the Missouri River. Cottonwoods shook in the breeze. Bluffs towered over us as we crossed the river and passed into Iowa. The gold sun and pink clouds overhead cheered me up. I popped a Dylan tape into my cassette. A harsh grating America was scraping away my baby-blue innocence. I listened to Dylan for a hint of how to fight against all that.

We pulled into Des Moines, where I was changing buses. What was I going to do? I paused behind the row the girl was in. She turned to look at me, and the guy woke with a start. He reached into a jacket pocket, pulled out a knife, and cleaned his fingernails.

I walked by. I didn't even have the nerve to look the girl in the eyes. I was a total loser. I had a chance to make a difference in that girl's life and backed away. But what the hell could I have done? I mean, the guy had a knife, and how could I help that girl, even if we could get away from him? Could Bobby's parents have helped her? They would at least have known what to do. What kind of a revolutionary was I?

I waited a couple of hours for my bus. When I got to Dubuque, it was late evening, and I was sick and exhausted. And never so happy to see Bobby and his missionary mom standing in the bus station.

Dubuque had so much more going for it than Bennett. It was green instead of dusty brown, a pretty town with many parks, and they had a rock concert the first Saturday night I was there. The band played Top 40 hits that I didn't know. And there were dozens of hippies hanging around and emanating the sweet, tangy scent of marijuana. We were both too scared to score, but Bobby had a six-pack. We both got tipsy. It was the best time I'd had in a month—except for a few evenings with Lillian, but this was different. I was back with my best friend.

It was great being at the Steinmetz house. Bobby had a fantastic stereo with a bunch of excellent records. When he was at the bowling alley, I stayed in his room for hours listening with his headphones. Sometimes, I watched TV with his parents and their younger kids. I'd known them since they were little, and they treated me like part of the family. We all talked about India and how much we missed it. We ate hot South Indian curries a few times a week. It was a 500 percent improvement over Bennett.

It did get a bit awkward when I talked about Rachel. I didn't tell Bobby everything; I just said we'd become good friends and often hung out.

"And you guys probably made out a lot, too," He laughed, and I turned beet-red.

"But that wasn't until she'd broken up with you!"

"Hey, I don't blame you, man. She was a pretty good kisser!"

I talked more about our other friends and the changes at Kodai School. He left at the beginning of our hippie rebellion. So, I filled him in on the moon landing, our protests, the Black militant ministers, and all the radical stuff Rachel and I discovered together. Then, he got mad when Rachel called and asked for me without even saying hello to him.

Rachel talked with me for about a half hour. After five minutes, Bobby slammed the door on his way out of the house. She spoke about demonstrations and lectures she'd been to. I told her I saw many spray-painted STOP signs that were changed to "STOP THE WAR" signs. She told me about a revolutionary youth group she had joined but couldn't go into details over the phone. Dubuque was way ahead of Bennett, but compared to rebellious San Francisco, it was as dead as Kodai.

Then, I started working on the farm. The first day was ninety-five degrees and as humid as Bombay, but I never had to work there. That was the day our farmer had us literally shoveling shit out of a cow barn for ten hours. It was worse than mending fences and fixing buildings on the ranch. The dry heat of Colorado was nothing compared to the swampy stickiness of an Iowa summer. A drenching hot blanket of air sucked the sweat out of me in pints. I never could cool off. I had zero energy by the end of the day. And the shit-shoveling went on day after day for a whole week. I wondered who the hell I was anymore. I was a missionary baba-sahib a month ago. Boring but pretty high up on the social totem pole. Now, I was an American shit-sweeper, like the *bhangi* (sweepers who clean out toilets). I'd dropped from the top of the heap to an outcast in one month.

We finally finished the cow barn on my first Friday. Bobby worked all weekend at the bowling alley. And the next week, it was hay baling time. The farmer's son, Bobby, and I stood on a trailer in the fucking hot sun, lifting and stacking fifty-pound bales that shot out of the baler. The first bale bounced off the rack at the back of the wagon, hit me right in the chest, and knocked me down. As I staggered to lift it onto the stack, I lost my balance and fell again, almost getting hit by another bale. Bobby and the farmer's son burst out laughing. That really pissed me off. And the fucking bales kept firing at us. It was damn dangerous. Bobby teased me about it all day long. Then, told the story to the whole family that night like it was a big joke.

By Wednesday, I was already looking forward to the weekend so I could rest. And eat. Saturday night dinner was curry or biryani. And Sunday dinner was a big deal with the Steinmetz family. Mrs. S always cooked roasts or ham. They didn't try to get Bobby and me up for church, but we had to attend Sunday dinner. That Sunday, the family sat down to a leg of lamb, mashed potatoes, and roasted vegetables. My stomach was already growling. Bobby poured red wine from New York. Mr. Steinmetz said grace and then proposed a toast to the farmworkers. I was thrilled that they were big supporters of the grape boycott.

"I hear you are all in favor of the revolution," Mrs. S turned to me after sipping her wine.

"Yes, I am," I said proudly.

"So, you are against racism and war and poverty."

"Yes, of course."

"How are you going to get rid of them?"

"Well, I…I mean, we…"

"Mom, that's not fair. You're just trying to embarrass Jamie," Bobby tried to help me out.

"No, I'm not. I agree these are all evils, but I want to know Jamie's ideas on changing them."

"Well, through the movement, Mrs. Steinmetz. People change as they stand up against oppression, like the Blacks in Mississippi. Standing up for their voting rights broke the landowners' hold over them. It broke down the fear that trapped them. People stay poor because they can't organize and take power over their own lives. Women stay oppressed because they are afraid of men."

"A very wise statement," Mr. Steinmetz said.

"That all makes some sense. So, if you are against all of that, what are you in favor of?" Mrs. S asked.

"Well, a world that has moved beyond those things."

"What would that look like? Is that communism?"

"No, our system will be democratic, and everyone will have their freedom, and everyone will be equal, Black and white, women and men."

"Women, too? I do like that," Mrs. S smiled. "But how will it work? Who will run the businesses? How will you choose leaders?"

"The businesses? Well, I guess the people will."

"The people? Will you take my brother's garage away from him and give it to the people? Which people?"

"Well, I don't know. I mean, that would depend. Mrs. Steinmetz, I don't know all the answers. I'm new, just coming back from Kodai."

I could feel my face growing hot and glanced at Bobby. He was examining the bottom of his wine glass and surreptitiously reached for a refill.

"Jamie, I am glad you admit you don't have the answers. When I was in college in the early '40s, there were only two answers: capitalism or communism. And whichever side they were on, everyone thought their way was the only way. Some of the brightest people were the ones who thought Uncle Joe Stalin was their savior. They took the hardest fall when they learned he wasn't quite the hero they believed him to be. They were also hounded out of their jobs, and two families I knew lost their homes."

"Oh, I'm not a communist at all, Mrs. S," I said quickly but wished I could explain what I was.

"Enough talk. Let the boys eat, or they might turn into communists," Mr. Steinmetz said as he finished carving the roast.

Right after lunch, Rachel called again. She was very excited. Her picture of a Vietnam veteran burning his ribbons was on the front page of a Bay Area underground paper. And she'd gotten a call from someone with the Liberation News Service asking if they could put it on their wire. It was going all around the world. She went to a revolutionary meeting or took pictures at a women's clinic or demonstration every day. She spent evenings helping with flyers. She was even working on photos for a book on women's health. I listened to her with longing. Rachel said her women's group was studying the question of monogamy and its relationship with patriarchy. Her sister said she was done with men and declared herself a political lesbian. Rachel laughed.

"I can't see blaming all men for male chauvinism. Besides, I like men too much to give them up."

I laughed nervously. Again, I felt things were changing. Rachel was slipping farther and farther from my world. I was jealous of her being in the middle of the revolution while I was in the middle of the Midwest, where no one seemed to care about the war.

That night, while the family was watching TV, Bobby got a call from Mickey Carpenter. Mickey was hitch-hiking around, visiting Kodai friends, doing odd jobs or temps. The money was much better up north than down in Alabama, where his uncle was. He was in Kansas City and heading to Yellow Springs, Ohio, to visit Billy Peters. Billy graduated a year ahead of us and was at Antioch College. Mickey asked if he could stop by Dubuque on his way to Ohio. Was there any work he could do?

"Yeah," Bobby replied. "The farmer we're working for said he has to repair the roof of his barn. I don't suppose you could do that?"

"Why not? I worked with my brother for three weeks, roofing our grandma's house. How big a job? Is it the whole barn roof?"

"No, a tree branch broke through part of the roof, maybe a five-foot hole."

"I'd have to look at it, but I've fixed holes in the roofs of churches in Kerala. Depending on the damage, it might take me a week or two."

"Really? You know how to do that shit?" How much do you charge?"

"I'll do it for $3 an hour, cash at the end of each week."

"Carpenters get a lot more than that around here. He might be interested. I'll talk to him tomorrow." Bobby said.

"That's unfair that Mickey would get twice what we are," I said after we'd hung up.

Bobby laughed at me. "Unlike you, he knows how to work. Do you want to climb up on that rickety old roof and swing a hammer? I bet you couldn't last half an hour roofing."

"I bet I could. Have you ever done it?"

"No, but I carried shingles up the ladder when my uncle roofed his garage last summer. The first hour nearly killed me."

Mickey had helped his father build tiny churches in sweltering riverside villages in Kerala. He was big and strong and knew how to swing a hammer. He always got A's in shop class. His family were faith missionaries. They lived on whatever their supporting churches sent them, while Presbyterians and Lutherans paid their staff a salary. It was not a big salary, but they got paid monthly and provided scholarships to get their missionary kids through college. Mickey was expected to pay his own way.

He showed up a couple of days later. Along with a small backpack with clothes, he carried a tool bag. He had an Estwing hammer that he'd gotten from his uncle and a carpenter square, pliers, and a tool belt.

"Anything else I can borrow," he grinned.

Mickey spent a week fixing the barn roof while we finished baling the first crop of hay and then shoveled the shit out of another cow barn. It was in the 90s every day, and it was harder and nastier work than the ranch in Bennett. At least I didn't have to hang out with racists and warmongers. One evening, we drank beer at Bobby's bowling alley. Mickey told us about Antioch College, where he was heading. Billy, who'd graduated a year before us, lived there.

Antioch was a center of radicalism in Ohio, and Billy worked on a movement newspaper. Billy's roommate worked for a women's carpentry collective. They had more work than they could handle and were looking for help, even from a guy. I rubbed my bruises and picked splinters of hay out of my arms as I listened. Maybe I should check out Ohio.

Neal Young's voice filled my head. That was where Nixon's tin soldiers had cut us down at Kent State. But there were still radicals standing and fighting. Here I was, busting my gut, working on a hot farm. By the end of the week, Mickey had convinced me to join him for the trip to Ohio. I told the farmer and Bobby that I needed to take the week of July 4th off and would be back. As I packed, I took all my clothes with me just in case.

Bobby dropped us off on Monday morning on US 20 in East Dubuque, Illinois. Mickey and I were stuck on an entrance ramp south of Chicago at sundown. Semi-trucks roared past us, pickups zipped by, and car drivers occasionally looked but drove on by. It was getting dark, and we were surrounded by an industrial wasteland. Finally, a new Buick pulled over; the driver was dressed in a suit and was heading to Indianapolis. He waved for us to climb into the front seat, and we jumped in gladly. I put my head against the glass and drifted off to sleep. Mickey did the work of chatting with the driver to keep him awake, the hitchhiker's payment for a free ride. I woke up suddenly.

"Why are you getting off here?" Mickey asked, his voice tense. The man had pulled off I-65 onto a deserted country road.

"Just stopping by a place I know. It won't take long. We can get us a drink."

The man put his hand on Mickey's leg and moved it up his thigh. Mickey grabbed the man's hand and flung it away.

"Just help me come. I'll give you twenty bucks and drive you to the Ohio border."

"Let us out. Here, now!"

"If you don't play nice, you'll have a long, lonely walk. It is dangerous for hippies to be out at night in redneck Indiana."

The blue light of the dash reflected off the man's glasses and sharp yellow teeth as we raced down the gravel road. He started reaching into his coat pocket.

"What the hell are you reaching for?" Mickey shouted as he hit the man with his Estwing hammer. I hadn't even noticed him easing it out of his backpack.

The salesman slammed the brakes, and my head banged against the windshield. Mickey had the skinny man by the arm with his hammer cocked back, ready to pound right into his forehead. The man's hand was in his breast pocket.

"Fuck you, goddammit. You've broken my hand! I was gonna offer you money to blow me."

"Moore, go to his door and check out what this creep has in his pocket. I don't want to get shot in the back."

With shaking hands, I reached into the man's suit coat and pulled out a small pistol.

"Keep it pointed at him while I grab our backpacks."

We bailed out of the car onto the gravel road. Mickey grabbed the pistol from me and pointed it at the salesman. The tires slung gravel as the Buick spun around and raced back toward the interstate.

Mickey pitched the pistol as far into the cornfield as he could.

"We don't want to get picked up by a county deputy with a gun on us," Mickey said.

We spent the night in a ditch and walked three miles back to the highway at dawn. Cars and trucks whined along the interstate, but there was no traffic on the on-ramp. We ignored the "No Pedestrians" sign and walked toward the interstate. We weren't even halfway down the on-ramp when a cop screeched to a halt, flipped on his lights, and reversed up the ramp at high speed.

"You boys have trouble reading?" He pointed back toward the sign.

"No, sir."

"Hitchhiking on the interstate is a crime, boys. I'm going to have to take you in."

"But sir, we've been stuck since last night…" Mickey said.

"Well, a nice breakfast in jail should taste mighty good. It's either that or pay me the fine."

"How much is it?" Mickey asked.

"How much you got?" The deputy asked.

"A …" I was about to answer when Mickey jabbed me.

"How about twenty each?" he said.

"I'm gonna have to search your bags."

"Go ahead, sir, we're clean."

The cop got out and emptied our knapsacks onto the side of the road.

"The fine is $40 each," he said.

We pulled the bills out of our money belts.

"Thank you kindly, boys." He grinned as he handed each of us a ticket. Then, he ripped the duplicates out of his ticket book and tore them into shreds. He smiled at us and gunned his car toward the highway. Pink and yellow shreds floated in the morning breeze.

"That is why we call you pigs!" I yelled as loud as I could.

Mickey punched me hard on the shoulder. "We are fucking lucky he couldn't hear you. You got to treat these assholes with respect."

I wished I'd followed my parents' plan and stayed in India for an extra year.

Chapter 5: Telephones Ringing to Blow Your Mind

After two days of hitch-hiking hell, Mickey and I finally arrived in Yellow Springs. He called Billy from a pay phone. The setting sun and the towering elms bathed the town in a golden-green light.

"Far out, man!" I could hear Billy's loud voice clear. "I have a nice surprise for you fuckers."

A few minutes later, Billy drove up in an old Ford pickup. Sitting with him was Roger. He was our Kodai lights-out monitor and saved Charlie and Raghu from expulsion. He now had long blond hair and the build of an American football linebacker.

"Jump in the back, you fucking hippies," Billy yelled as he slammed on the brakes.

He drove to a run-down house a block off campus. Parked in front were a couple of pickups, a VW van painted with flowers, peace signs, and Dylan quotes. In front of the garage, an old car was up on blocks. A skinny guy wearing Army fatigues sat on the steps. His long hair curled over a guitar. He played the same chord over and over.

"That's Vinnie the Vet. Always say hello before you get too close to him. If you startle him, he might try to kill you. Still whacked out from 'Nam." Billy had dropped his voice to a whisper and then called out. "Hey Vinnie, how's the new song comin', man?"

Vinnie looked up at us with hollow eyes. He slipped a combat knife out of a sheath tied to his thigh and laid it on the steps beside him. Then, he went back to his guitar chord.

We climbed the steps in single file, staying as far from Vinnie as possible. We walked through the broken screen door into a riot of color. Red and yellow revolutionary posters, blue and red pottery, tie-dyed curtains, and a giant statue of two blue nudes on horseback charging the barricades waving AK-47s adorned the large living room. The blue, red, and yellow Viet Cong flag hung over the kitchen door. In the kitchen, a girl with a long brown braid stirred sizzling onions in a large cast-iron skillet. Mao Zedong pointed the way to the future from a poster on the wall, and the smell of frying onions and garlic filled the steamy room. I had finally found the America I was looking for.

"Hey guys, this is Shelley. Shelley, meet Mickey and Jamie, a couple more Kodai guys."

Shelley looked us over and nodded.

"She used to be my old lady but is kind of kicking me out 'because I don't help out enough," Billy said as we returned to the living room. Then, he lowered his voice and grinned. "But we're still making it. Sit down and relax, guys. I'll get you a beer."

Roger put a Jefferson Airplane album on the stereo and pulled out a big fat joint.

"You guys gotta try this stuff. Almost as good as Kodai flower tops."

I picked up a newspaper sitting from a stack on the coffee table. "Frelimo Rebels Ambush Portuguese Commander," the headline read. Who were Frelimo, and why were they fighting the Portuguese? My stoned mind soon learned that the Portuguese were fighting to hold onto their African colonies. As I read, my mind replayed those images of Indian army tanks and troops streaming past our compound on the way to Goa. Now, leftist guerillas were intent on pushing the Portuguese out of Mozambique, Angola, and Guinea Bissau. Wow! There were whole new revolutions I knew nothing about.

"Where can I get this newspaper?" I asked Billy.

"Oh, *The Guardian*, you can have that one," he replied. "That's last week's news. A new one came today, but Shelley is hogging it till she's read every last article."

I tore off the subscription form and put it in my wallet. I carefully folded the paper and placed it in my backpack.

"Hey, I smell something good," a voice boomed from the open screen door.

As the smoke drifted out, Vinnie drifted in. Apparently, he figured we weren't the enemy anymore. He joined us. As we drank beer and smoked, my thoughts floated on euphoric updrafts. Finally, finally, I'd found the movement. What had happened to it in the rest of the country? *Time* magazine, the Voice of America, and even the Indian papers in May were filled with protests ripping across America. Six students protesting the Cambodian invasion were killed at Kent State and Jackson State in Mississippi. A national student strike shut down most colleges and universities. It was all over when we landed at JFK in June. Nothing was going on. Gracie Slick's voice echoed through my head. Had I fallen through the wrong mirror, a post-Kent State crazy land where the movement had ceased to exist? Or maybe I had slipped into the rabbit holes of Bennett and Dubuque. The revolution was clearly alive and well in Yellow Springs, Ohio. Possibly, Grinnell would be another revolutionary oasis. Besides, I could now subscribe to *The Guardian* and stay plugged into the revolutionary movement.

A dozen people gathered around a large table for dinner, all women except Vinnie and our Kodai crew. Everyone was quiet as we passed the fresh salad, crumbly brown bread, red sauce, and spaghetti.

Part 3: Jamie Moore's 115th Nightmare

"Crap! No meat again?" Billy complained as he ladled sauce onto a mountain of spaghetti.

Shelley glared at him and then turned to us. "I know you are all Billy's friends, but we decide who to trust. I want you three to tell us specific facts about yourselves. First, what is your parents' class background? Second, what were they doing in India? Three, what are your current plans? And four, how do you think we can rekindle the movement in the fall?"

Wow! This was like a background check to figure out if we belonged in the movement.

Shelley was an artist. I later learned she was from a union family in Cleveland. Shelley was in SDS as a high school student in Cleveland. She got an honors scholarship to Antioch and became a regional organizer for SDS. She had supported Bernardine Dohrn and the SDS Revolutionary Youth Movement faction. Shelley broke with them when the Weathermen decided to launch an armed struggle and go underground. Shelley was on the national coordinating committee for the recent nationwide student strike. Now, her big question was what was to be done about the third American revolution.

Shelley presided at the dinner table like my mother did at tea. She had a United Steel Workers mug and used it as her gavel. She kept her mug full of cheap red wine this evening and waved at me. "You go first."

"My grandpa on my mom's side was a shipbuilder in Scotland," I started in on my history. "My mom was a nurse in World War II and became a missionary nurse afterward. On my dad's side, my grandpa was a missionary in India, but my grandma's family were miners in Colorado." I'd learned enough about Marxism to know it was essential to establish my working-class credentials. I explained that my parents' work gave poor and working-class people medical care and job skills. And weren't out to convert people.

"As far as the anti-war movement," I continued. "I don't know what the next step should be. Maybe a huge demonstration in the fall to show Nixon we aren't afraid of his tin soldiers."

Shelley nodded and turned to Roger.

"My dad was a coal miner in West Virginia and joined the Navy before the war to get out of the fucking coal mines. He learned to fix engines and worked up to be an engineer. They stationed him in the Persian Gulf. When the war was over, he got into the oil business in India, where he met a British nurse. They married, settled down, and ran an oil services company out of Bombay. We knew all the big shots in India's Congress party because they came to our house to eat beef and drink Scotch whisky when they were in town. As far as your movement, you have to go beyond student demonstrations. It would help if you thought big. You have to win elections and take over the government. And for that you need money, lots of it. You could hold rock

140

concerts and sell shit to raise real money. Then, buy a radio station in each town. Play good music and get the news out about the war and Nixon and those assholes. Political power comes from money, and I know just how you can get money."

Shelley nodded again, "How about you, Mickey?"

He explained that his parents were evangelists who were out to convert the heathen. His grandparents on both sides were red dirt farmers in Georgia, and he had no idea how to kickstart the movement. Despite what he said, Shelley was especially interested in Mickey and asked him more about his family. When he talked about his brother deserting the Navy, she leaned forward, her brown eyes never leaving his face. She asked several questions about the kind of work he'd done this summer. Mickey told her about a series of construction jobs in Georgia and fixing the barn in Iowa.

"So, you can roof? How about framing?" Shelley asked, her brown eyes boring into his, a hint of a smile on her lips.

"I've done that too. I can knock out a frame for a twelve-foot wall in two hours," Mickey grinned back, holding her gaze.

Shelley shook her head, "That's a little slow but not too bad. My dad's a union carpenter who had all girls but taught every one of us to swing a hammer before we were six years old. You better not be shitting me."

"I thought you were an artist," I said.

"So, working-class people can't be artists?" She swung her now stony brown eyes onto me.

"No, ... er, I mean yes, of course, they can," I muttered.

"We have a carpentry co-op to raise money for our projects," she told Mickey. "We have orders for two garages, an addition to a house, and a chicken coop. We could use your help."

"Four dollars an hour, cash only," Mickey said.

"We work as a co-op; we each take what we need to live on, and the rest goes to our projects," Shelley explained.

"My project is earning money for college, four dollars an hour."

"How about three-fifty?"

"I can live with three seventy-five."

"OK, we'll hire you for a two-week trial. If you don't prove your worth, you're gone."

"I'll be here till the fall."

Micky reached across the table and shook Shelley's hand. She grabbed his fingers and squeezed hard enough to make him wince. He tried to squeeze back, but she had him in her grip.

"Hey, you guys are blocking my way to the spaghetti," Billy protested.

"So, what kind of projects are you raising money for?" Roger asked.

"There's *The People's Voice,* the local underground paper. We're expanding into publishing. We want to buy our own press to tell the truth without worrying about whether someone will print it. People got to know the truth about the war and how the System is ripping them off."

"Yeah, we have to expose the lies of the corporate press," said a dark-haired girl sitting next to Shelley. She waved a fork in the air. Her rough hands showed she was in the carpentry collective.

"The bastards do more than fucking lie," Vinnie shouted and jumped to his feet. "They fucked my friends over and wasted the whole of fucking 'Nam with napalm. We gotta off all these motherfuckers."

"Vinnie, honey," she said smiling, "these are our friends here. We aren't quite there yet. Remember the stages of the struggle. We have a lot of work to build up our organizations before we can take the motherfuckers down."

Vinnie sat down and became lucid. "You are right, sweetie-pie. Remember meeting the VC down in Havana? Strangest trip—sitting and drinking rum with people who had tried to kill me a couple years before. I told them I would bring the war home. They said a revolution in America was decades away. I am ready to fight now!"

"We know you are, Vinnie," Shelley looked him in the eye and patted his hand. "But we need to build up our strength. You are one of our best workers in the co-op. And we're not just building garages. The money we make builds the movement."

"There are easier ways to raise money for your projects than swinging a hammer," Roger said.

"Really? We need a shitload of money to buy a printing press," Billy said.

"You work on fucking newspapers, Billy? You hardly know how to spell, shithead," Roger teased.

"Fuck you. I'm the editor."

"We're all editors, Billy. It's a collective." Shelley cut him down. "How would you raise money? By robbing banks?"

"No way, too risky. I'm not just traveling. I'm on a business trip," Roger said.

"What kind of business?" Shelley's eyes narrowed.

"Well, you guys aren't the only ones with radical projects. There are guerilla theater collectives, movie-making co-ops, food co-ops, and underground papers all over the country. They all need cash. I've helped a few of them, so I know what you're up against. An 11x17 offset press costs a few grand. You'll need ten or fifteen grand total for a camera, a plate burner, and fixing up a print shop."

"You know something about printing," Shelley said, but her eyes were still suspicious. "Go on."

"You need real capital. It's gonna take you forever to raise that building chicken coops."

"Yeah, but none of us are heiresses like people in The Weatherman. And they aren't giving us their money. How do you raise capital? Tell a bank we want a loan to overthrow capitalism?"

Roger burst into a giggle. All the guys joined him in a stoned laughing fit.

"I can see it," Roger slapped the table. "A bunch of stoned hippies in front of a desk, a guy in a blue suit turning bright red. 'You want fifteen thousand dollars for what?'"

"Yeah, like Dylan says," Vinnie burst in. "They ask for collateral. We pull down our pants."

Gales of male laughter shook the table, but I noticed the girls were quiet. I stopped laughing. I finally found the movement and didn't want to blow it. We were talking about how to finance the revolution. Roger's dad had built a multi-million-dollar business from scratch, and I was sure he'd passed those skills on to his son. Unlike the missionary kids, he always had enough money. He knew how to use it to make more money. We could use his help to fund the revolution.

"Sorry," Roger said, wiping his eyes and sipping wine. "I just had this vision of you all going into a bank in overalls and Mao caps."

He shook his head to get the image out and continued. "So, if you don't have money and can't get your capital from a bank, you get it by buying something low and selling high. And speaking of high, that is where I can help the good hippies of Yellow Springs."

"We are radicals, not hippies," Shelley said tersely.

Roger pulled an aluminum briefcase out of his backpack. Inside were rows and rows of neatly rolled lids of grass.

Vinnie whistled and reached over. He opened a plastic bag and stuck his nose in it. "Fucking good shit!" He passed it around, and the funky, acrid aroma of pure flower tops filled our nostrils.

"Pure Acapulco Gold. What is that going for around here?" Roger asked.

"When you can get it around here, it's at least forty bucks a lid."

"I can let you have it for two thousand a key," Roger said. "That's thirty-two lids with a little for yourselves. You guys could sell it for thirty or thirty-five. You will turn two thousand into nine grand in a week. Invest half of that in more inventory, rinse, and repeat. You will have all the capital you need for your print shop before the leaves turn. I'm delivering to half a dozen radical groups on the East Coast."

"Where did you get the weed?" Vinnie's girlfriend asked.

"Now that's an amazing story," Roger turned his sky-blue eyes on her. "My cousin is a captain in the Arizona National Guard."

"Fucking draft dodgers," Vinnie broke in.

Rodger ignored him and went on. "Last Christmas, I got high with him at his dad's house near Pittsburgh. He had a suitcase full of terrific shit and asked me if I could sell it at my college. By the end of the semester, I made more than enough for tuition for all four years."

He looked at Mickey and made his fingers into a gun. "Bang, you could have your college paid for just like that. Last week, my cousin called me and asked me to rent a big U-Haul to bring our quote for *grandma's furniture* back from Tucson. I drove there from Pittsburgh in two days. I stayed in motels on the way. In business, you don't have to scrape by and sleep in ditches like you assholes." Roger grinned at me and Mickey. "The next night, my cousin and I drove to a warehouse where we loaded long heavy crates. Then, we drove south and off a back road onto an Indian reservation. In a deserted arroyo, we met a Mexican guy wearing a red beret standing next to a military truck. I don't speak much Spanish, but he kept calling my cousin *compañero* and talking about *la revolución.* So, I figured he was with the Mexican guerilllas. We swapped what was in their truck for what was in ours. And now we have a truck full of Acapulco gold. My cousin wouldn't say what was in our crates, but I can guess."

"AR-15s for Acapulco gold," Vinnie smiled. "I'd say you got a damn good deal. My fucking rifle jammed every time I put it on automatic."

Roger looked around the room. The guys were all smiling, but the women were silent.

"I have commitments for most of our truckload, but I could let you have twenty kilos."

"Where's your truck?" Shelley asked.

"At a safe location. I'm not about to park next to Antioch with a couple tons of weed."

"Wow, we could raise thousands of dollars for all our projects," Billy was ecstatic. He turned to the dark-haired girl. "Peggy, you could get a loan from your parents to start us off."

"We need to have a closed collective meeting," Peggy said.

Billy rolled his eyes and got up to unplug the phone. Shelley put Coltrane on the stereo. She walked over to Mickey, put her hands on his shoulder, and leaned over him, her face inches from his. "The three of you should go for a walk, but you and your friends are welcome to crash here tonight. My room is upstairs at the end of the hall. The room next to mine is empty, and the couches are free, too."

Vinnie pulled the shades in the windows and shut the kitchen door. Mickey, Roger, and I walked out the back door and sat in the backyard. Roger lit a big fat joint. It was excellent weed, almost as good as Palani Hill's ganja. As we wandered, the setting sun lit the clouds on fire. Golden-pink light filled the sky, and revolutionary warmth filled my head. We walked until dark, and the moon began to rise.

Sometime later, Billy came storming out. "Goddam, they are stupid. They think this is a setup by the fucking Feds. They don't trust you, Roger, and they don't trust me. Shelley told me to leave the house tomorrow. She is fucking kicking me out! I knew she was kind of pissed, and I cooked so many curries that she loved! Goddamn their eyes. They think your cousin was put up to it by the CIA or at least is getting a nod and a wink from some higher-ups. Fuck them. I'll get the cash for a key or two. Let's go to a party across campus. Those dikes can all screw themselves."

We walked across campus through the hot Ohio summer night. Towering buckeyes and oaks blocked out the night sky, then opened to pools of brilliant moonlight.

"Free Bubby Seal!" I read some graffiti on a building wall.

"Illiterate revolutionaries," Roger said. "They can't even spell Bobby."

"Not so much illiterate as stoned out of their heads," Billy said. "In May, Antioch was a hotbed of activity. Then, right after the strike, a huge shipment of psychedelics came in, and people mellowed out. There are still a few meetings. And you can see radical movies every week, but most serious radicals left town or are lost in space."

"What does orange sunshine go for here?" Roger asked.

"Four bucks a tab, last I heard," Billy replied.

Roger let out a low whistle. "That's half the price down in Virginia. Do you know the dealers here? I could make a double profit on this trip."

"Yeah, but no one knows the distributor. The delivery is always super secretive. The dealers have to pool their orders. A friend of mine is the collector. He told me about it. He calls a payphone in Dayton the night before the deal is to go down. Someone tells him when and where to go, like a gas station or a McDonald's. When he gets there, he stands around till a black Ford Bronco comes by. The plates are always covered with mud, but the inside is spotless. There is a privacy wall between the front and back seats. They drive around while he passes the money up and gets a fat package of pure LSD. He gets a one percent commission from the distributor but doesn't take anything from the other dealers."

"So, unds like either the Mafia or the government," Roger said.

"No fucking way would the Feds do that," I said.

"Of course they would," Roger said. "The British did it all the time. Give people enough booze or opium, and they can't fight you. LSD was invented in a CIA experiment."

"I don't believe it," I said.

"Don't be naive," Billy replied. "I saw a story in *The Guardian* about the CIA shipping heroin from Thailand to L.A. If they do it, we can too. By any means necessary!"

Billy raised his fist.

That was the second time this summer I'd been called naive. But unlike Lillian, Billy knew what kind of shit was coming down. I wondered what Rachel would think of selling weed to finance the movement. She was a bit of a pothead, so she'd understand. Thinking of Rachel made me miss her even more. Still, she mentioned her guitar-playing friend seven times the last time we'd talked. She was probably sleeping with him but still called me her love. What I missed most was how Rachel and I could help each other figure out our big problems, whether politics or family issues.

"What kind of people will be at this party?" I asked.

"It's a fundraiser for *The Freedom's Star,* a new underground paper some other friends are starting. They have different politics, not as hard-core as Shelley and her friends, and they write more about music and culture. Not just politics and shit. They will be more interested in Roger's idea. They aren't as paranoid as those weather dykes."

Billy had long, curly brown hair, thick glasses, and a winning smile. He had a far-out head. There was no one better to have a rambling, stoned rap with. Mickey's long hair fell around his broad shoulders, and his chest had filled out from a couple of months of rich American food and hard work. Roger looked like a long-haired football player. As we walked into the party, I realized they looked pretty good compared to most strung-out hippies hanging around Yellow Springs. But I was gawky, skinny, and girl-shy. A chick with curly black hair and green eyes hugged Billy.

She turned to look at me but kept speaking to Billy. "Who are your friends?"

Billy introduced us to Rhonda. She was the art director of the new paper. Rhonda shook my hand firmly. I squeezed back, and she smiled. She wore a long cotton *jibbah* that reached halfway down her long thighs. Her legs were covered with silky black hair, which intrigued me and, at the same time, freaked me out. I'd never seen a girl with hairy legs.

"And are you from India too?" she asked me as she led us to the table with the drinks.

"Yeah, I am. I like your *jibbah.*"

"Thanks, I bought it in Poona. I did a semester abroad there last year."

"Poona? No shit. That is less than a hundred miles from where I grew up."

She handed me a glass of Southern Comfort.

"Do you speak Marathi?" she asked in American-accented Marathi.

"*Maza maher basha* (my mother tongue)," I replied with a huge grin.

We stood against a wall, talking about India. Her green eyes locked on mine. Someone shouted her name.

"Oh shit, I have to get the brownies into the oven. Don't you go away? I like talking with you." She tousled my hair and turned away.

I took a gulp of the whisky. It burned all the way down, but I liked its sweet orange taste. Kodaikanal was in the dry state of Tamilnadu, so I'd never tried whisky before. Billy came over, pulled out a ball of hash, and started passing a pipe around. After a few tokes, I felt wobbly. I refilled my empty glass and went to sit on the couch for a bit. That was the last thing I remembered until waking up on the front porch of People's House with the taste of vomit in my mouth. Rodger and Mickey had half-carried me back. I felt like total crap. My head ached; my stomach was ready to heave again but was completely empty.

"You stupid shit," Roger said as he came out onto the porch and handed me a cup of coffee. "If you hadn't gotten so drunk, you could've had that pretty dark-haired chick. She tried to wake you up once, but then Billy took over."

"He took over helping me out?"

"No, you fuckhead. He took over helping *her* out."

Rhonda got Shelley out of Billy's heart that first night. He came by about lunchtime with his pickup to clear his stuff out of People's House. The four Kodai guys moved Billy's stuff to Freedom Star House, where Rhonda met us on the porch. I felt like a stupid shit when I saw her, but she gave me a hug and a quick kiss on the cheek.

"Sorry you got sick last night," she said.

Rhonda led us into the dining room. The collective for the new underground paper listened to Roger's proposal. They didn't have the ambition to set up a print shop and lacked the revolutionary fervor of *The People's Voice*. But they scraped together cash for a couple of keys of Acapulco gold.

Roger fronted Billy ten lids, and then, with all his customers satisfied, he hit the road. Mickey stayed in Yellow Springs. Billy and I drove to his parents' house in Columbus. He said I could crash there for as long as I wanted.

Mickey spent the rest of the summer at People's House, working with the building collective and sleeping with Shelley. Billy and I got night jobs stocking shelves at the local A&P. I had the pet food aisle. But it was a fun place to work. Marshall, the supervisor, was a guy in his 40s who always smelled of whiskey. The only other person on the shift was Saul, the night janitor. He told us that if we lasted beyond the summer, we'd have to join the union. He told me that the union kept the working class from being crushed. I was very impressed.

One night, I was helping him unload janitorial supplies from a delivery truck.

"You in college too, kid?"

"Not yet. I start in the fall."

"In this world, there are only two classes of people."

"Yeah?"

Saul was the first Jewish person I'd met. I knew Marx was Jewish, too, and I figured Saul was an organizer. I was excited that he was about to open up about his socialist ideas.

"Two classes," he repeated. "The educated and the working stiff. Get an education, kid, or you'll end up like me."

After that, Saul ignored me because he figured I'd be gone in a month or two.

Billy and I would get stoned a couple times a night with another college kid and then race to see who could stock their aisle first. Shelves had to pass inspection by Marshall, who had a bug up his ass about how all the cans and boxes had to line up. I never won. I was fast but usually had to redo my shelves. Sometimes, though, I'd get sick from looking at the stacks of fancy dog and cat food. The money Americans spent on pet toys and treats would feed our *mahli* and his family for a year. What kind of fucking world was this anyway?

On our days off, we'd go down to Yellow Springs on Billy's motorbike. Sometimes, on a dark summer night flying down I-70, Billy would turn off the headlight, and we'd soar into the darkness at eighty miles per hour, screaming our heads off. We'd visit Mickey and party at the Freedom Star House. Their newspaper was starting to take off. By then, Rhonda had picked Billy. I'd sleep on the couch. Then, we'd make a couple hundred loose joints from Roger's latest shipment. We'd load up with copies of the *Freedom Star.* We made pretty good money selling the paper and our own brand of loose joints wrapped in cinnamon-flavored papers in Columbus. Indian ganja, we told our customers.

To avoid narcs, we'd take turns selling the paper on a corner. The other one watched from a nearby burger joint, scoping out safe customers and telling them where they could find a bright green pleasure machine. Narcs were easy to spot in Columbus in those days. They were always young white guys with short hair but wearing hippie clothes. We probably lost the business of a few engineering students who wanted to get high, but we didn't get busted.

I spent my spare time reading all the radical books and papers I could handle. One morning in mid-August, Rachel called and woke me up.

"Jamie? Are you still there?"

"Yeah, I'm just tired. I work nights."

"Oh yeah, I forgot. I really wanted to call and talk to you about us. You meant so much to me, but we're really in different places right now," Rachel said. Her voice sounded deeper.

"Yeah. So, I probably shouldn't come to San Francisco, right?"

"Oh Jamie, I'd love to see you, but ... have you bought your ticket?"

"No, not yet."

"It might just make things harder."

"...Umm, yeah. OK."

"You sound really out of it. I really want to talk this through with you, though, Jamie. Do you want to call me back later?"

"Sure, I'll do that."

But I never did. I just drank half a bottle of Scotch and called in sick that night. When Billy and I went down to Yellow Springs that weekend, I talked with Mickey. He was sympathetic but said the same thing as Rachel. It's time to move on. After dinner, he tried to introduce me to a woman in his carpentry collective. But I did the same thing as that night at the Freedom Star House. I got falling down drunk. What was wrong with me? I could not feel at ease around a woman who turned me on. Still, it wasn't a bad summer, even if things did not turn out as I had planned. I did find the movement. I used the money I saved for a flight to San Francisco to go out to Denver and patch things up with my grandparents before I went to college. And it was a blast hanging out with Billy.

He wrote a column for *The Freedom Star* on Dylan and the politics of rock music. Like many people in those days, Billy was obsessed with the hidden meanings of each Dylan song, especially songs from *Bringing It All Back Home.* That was Bob's Book of Revelations about the Revolution. The Weather faction of SDS had chosen their name from *Subterranean Homesick Blues.* But Billy figured the absolute truth was in one of the other songs, maybe the *115th Dream.* That was my favorite, but all the songs were filled with perfect metaphors about surviving the shit that was coming down across Amerika. Billy figured that if we could decipher what Dylan was saying, it would guide us to a successful revolution. Who was the Pope of Eruke? Maybe the CIA director? And who was Ahab? Was he a metaphor for Marxist revolutionaries so obsessed with killing the capitalist white whale that they were ready to see the ship of the movement go down?

I wasn't sure about all that, but you had to agree with him on one thing. The way Dylan sang proved that he understood what was happening here, unlike Mr. Jones. And it was too dangerous for him to lay it out as he used to in his folksongs. If Dylan said what he knew in plain English, he'd have ended up like Malcolm, Martin, and all the Black Panther leaders, shot dead or locked away for life. So, he spoke in parables like Jesus. Christian Tom from Kodai was right. Dylan truly was our prophet.

Part 4: Winter in America: 1970-1971

Chapter 1: Couldn't See for Snow Was Blowing

There were big parties on both North and South Campus on the first night of Grinnell's freshman orientation. I was drinking beer with Wendell, a short, tubby, long-hair from suburban Chicago. Two sophomore women offered us a bottle of Southern Comfort. Sometime later, I was outside wrenching my guts out. When my stomach stopped its spasms, I stumbled against the trunk of a towering cottonwood. Steadying my spinning world, I slowly slid down the trunk to the thick, cool grass. Silver stars speckled the dark Iowa sky.

What the hell was I thinking? I would never touch Southern Comfort again.

The following day, I woke up in my own room. My new roommates were standing by the door talking.

"Hey, you finally woke up," the short one with curly brown hair said.

"Yeah, hell of a party last night," I mumbled as I pulled on my jeans.

"My flight was delayed, so I fuckin' missed it. But hey, I'm Fred Stein from Jersey." He stuck out his hand.

"And I'm Jack from a small town in Minnesota," the tall guy said.

"Hi, I'm Jamie. I grew up in India."

"From India? You don't look Indian," Fred remarked.

"Yeah, parents were missionaries. You're from Jersey? Like the island between England and France?"

"No, you ignorant fuck. Jersey like in New Jersey," Fred said, shaking his head and walking into the hall.

"Wow, he gets pissed off easily," Jack whispered. "Is everyone from New Jersey like that, or is it 'cause he's Jewish?"

"How do you know he's Jewish?" I said as Fred walked back into the room for his toothbrush.

"My name, you dumbass. How many Steins do you know who aren't Jewish?" he asked.

"I dunno, I've never met anyone named Stein," I said.

"I never met a Jew before," Jack said.

"My God! I'm stuck in fucking Iowa living with a bunch of ignorant Aryans," Fred exclaimed. "Let's go to the Student Forum for breakfast. But it will be a miracle if they have edible bagels in these cornfields."

I wondered what an edible bagel was and followed along. I found out they were chewy bread in the shape of a doughnut. Fred deemed the bagels acceptable but grumbled as the three new roommates hung out together. Jack didn't say much.

The next day, I got on Jack's wrong side, too. I couldn't find my hairbrush, so I used his. When he returned from his shower, he discovered my curly blonde hair on his brush.

"Did you use my brush?" Jack asked in shock.

"Well, yeah. I've lost mine."

"Who the hell said you could use my brush? You used my shampoo, too, didn't you?"

"I didn't have any, but I'm going to town and buying all that stuff today. Then, you can use mine anytime."

"Why would I want to do that?" Jack acted grossed out as if I'd suggested we share toothbrushes or something. He slammed the door to his tiny bedroom.

In Kodai, we always used each other's stuff, and they used yours. If you had something you didn't want to share, you kept it in your locked drawer. It wasn't as if I rummaged through his drawers or anything. But it seemed to bug the hell out of Americans if you took their personal stuff. Jack hardly spoke to me after that.

I'd had roommates who didn't like me before. But what really bothered me about Grinnell in late August 1970 was the invisibility of the anti-war movement. People talked about the May Revolution. The college had exploded in rebellion against the invasion of Cambodia and then shut down over the Kent State massacre. The students and some faculty made the campus an anti-war organizing base. They used the college station to broadcast news about the national strike. They printed flyers and news sheets and marched through the town. They turned every flag upside down to show that America was in crisis. A few students busted some windows.

Then, a platoon of vets from the American Legion marched onto campus, rifles over their shoulders, and turned the college flag right side up. They mounted a 24-hour armed guard to protect the flag. The administration canceled classes for the year and sent the students home.

By the time classes started back up in the fall, everyone seemed to have forgotten about the war. I asked many people what was happening, but they were mostly freshmen and didn't know. When I opened my first checking account with money from my family, I pulled the yellowing subscription form for *The Guardian* out of my wallet and wrote my first check. At least I'd stay in touch with the movement through America's leading radical paper. I kept looking around for signs of anti-war activity.

Finally, flyers from the Student Anti-war Committee went up in the second week of classes. They called an organizing meeting to plan a massive protest at the state capital. I got there right at seven o'clock. Fifty people were milling around the South Lounge of the Forum. After ten or fifteen minutes, a tall guy with a scraggly beard and a blue Mao cap called the meeting to order.

"The Student Anti-war Committee is calling for a boycott of classes until the administration agrees to pay for buses to get us to the protest."

A short guy with curly black hair jumped to his feet. "That is bullshit, man. Who decided that? We gotta focus on the war, not the college administration. They are against the war, too. And what's another march going to do? We need direct action against the military machine."

"Fuck yes, we'll shut it down, but we gotta get the people to Des Moines first!"

"No, what we need is to elect Congressmen to cut off funds for the war," a third guy shouted.

A dozen others jumped into the fray. Arguments swirled around the room like hornets. Everyone had a plan, and no one wanted to listen. I sat in the back of the room, trying to follow the debate. Students drifted away as the meeting went on and on. At about nine-thirty, the last Student Democrat walked out of the room, leaving the field to the direct-action faction.

"Fuck you all," the chairman yelled at the retreating Democrats. "The system is fucking evil, man. You will never reform it."

"So, who's organizing the demo?" a woman with a blond Afro asked.

"Go ahead, Joe. Looks like you are volunteering," the tall guy replied.

I'd never heard of a woman being called Joe. I remembered a Johnny Cash song about a boy named Sue. There was so much about America that I did not understand.

"You do the shouting and make the women do the work. Fuck you, Larry," Joe glared at him.

"I accept your offer, any time of the day or night," Larry grinned.

"Sex and shouting, is that all you care about? Someone has to organize. I'll do it if you and Peter promise to drive your vans. We don't have student support to force the college to hire busses, and we don't have time to raise hundreds of bucks."

"I'm in," Larry said and glanced at Peter, who nodded in agreement. ". It's a deal. You calculate the odds so well, JoJo; you should have been a gambler. Now let's go get high." He pumped his fist in the air. The remaining dozen or so activists got up to leave.

"Hey," Joe turned to me. "You're new. Will you distribute leaflets for us?"

"Sure, but I don't know many people. I can pass them out in my dorm."

"Cool, and your classes too. I'll get some printed tomorrow. Want to meet in the Forum at 12:30?"

"Sure."

"Come on, Jo-Jo," Larry shouted from the door. "Everyone is on their way over to Adam's place."

"He's out of town, remember?"

"Oh shit, that's right." He turned and bellowed into the night, "Hold up, people, we'll have to party in Luce Lounge. Adam's not around."

The tall radical led the party in the correct direction.

"Do you want to come along?" Joe asked.

I most definitely did. These were the real radicals on campus, the remnants of Iowa's most militant SDS chapter. And I kind of dug this girl named Joe.

As we left, Joe asked a girl named Nancy what she thought about the bombing at the Army Research Center in Madison. Nancy was petite and had dark, curly hair. She replied that the "war against the war" was a big mistake. To stop the war, we needed to organize outside the campuses, and violence on behalf of the peace movement undermined our cause.

It was another warm Iowa night. The stars sparkled in the dark sky as brilliantly as they did in Kodai or Sangli. I followed behind Joe and Nancy as we made our way out of the Forum talking radical politics—the Weathermen versus the Maoist Progressive Labor Party, the police shoot-out with the Panthers in Philly, and an article about the new communist movement in *The Guardian*. Nancy had read that Vietnamese Communists met with SDS leaders in Cuba. And the Vietnamese said that America was not ready for armed struggle. That was what the crazy vet in Yellow Springs had said as well. Maybe he wasn't so crazy. I kept quiet except for asking a question now and then. The group was well ahead of the three of us. We made our way across campus, stopping every time Joe or Nancy got passionate about a point they were making, which was pretty often. Then, we walked on till the next flash of intensity. Those two were like a meteor shower.

By the time we got to Luce Lounge, I was in love with both women, and my head was exploding with new ideas. Maybe Grinnell would work out after all. Peter started passing around a bottle of Southern Comfort and a few joints. I had learned my lesson with Southern Comfort but toked up happily. A stereo filled the air with Jefferson Airplane. Luce Hall was a coed dorm right next to mine. I figured that was where Joe and the other woman lived. I sat on a couch next to them. People were dancing and making out.

Peter leaned over the turntable and changed the record. He grabbed Larry's Mao hat and put it on his head like a crown, waving for us to gather around him. Twelve radicals knelt in front of the stereo cabinet. Peter started the music.

Boom-Bppm. nna-nnA-nNA-NNA. Jimi's guitar invited us into "Purple Haze." Peter held a plate covered with a monogrammed purple handkerchief. He lifted the silk, revealing small squares of blotter paper, and raised the plate to the sky. Jimi's guitar pumped pressure waves through the air.

"To rock and revolution," Peter said, passing the plate around.

Larry took two pieces of paper and put one under Joe's tongue and one under his, and then they kissed. Damn, he must be her boyfriend. Joe's petite friend shook her head when Peter offered the plate, and then he turned to me.

"What's this?" I asked.

"Purple haze," he said as I slipped the paper under my tongue.

I knew the name of the song, so I turned to Nancy. "What's in the blotter paper?"

"A kind of LSD called purple haze."

"Oh, shit!"

"Is this your first time?"

"Oh, no."

"If you haven't tripped before, you need a guide," she said.

"Don't worry, I have," I reassured her. It couldn't be much stronger than the opiated hash I'd had in Kodai.

Nancy looked at me closely. "You really have?"

"Oh, yeah. See, I grew up in India, and we had it in pills there. Not blotter paper." I lied.

"Oh, OK."

Hendrix was deep into "Manic Depression" as I tried to follow a complex discussion about sexual politics between Joe and Nancy. I took a toke on a joint and listened to the music. It didn't feel much different than a good Kodai ganja high, but the sound was marvelous. I could see the dark blue air waves vibrating to the rhythm of the bass guitar. The blue waves pulled purple darkness through the shimmering glass windows and pumped it into our bodies. As Jimi's deep voice prayed for forgiveness, an eerie high-pitched howling flew in from the prairie night. The pulsing and howling synchronized, growing louder and louder. Energy waves exploded, bouncing off walls and breaking over the furniture, smashing everything. I jumped up, ready to run, but no one else had noticed. They were still talking, laughing, making out. I looked around wild-eyed and then sat back down alone.

A crystal ringing turned my head toward the stereo. Jimi was announcing a new movement. Peter and the tall guy were talking revolution. Joe and Nancy were talking women's liberation. One couple didn't speak.

Instead, they were engaging in direct action for copulation. Faces changed from intense angelic beauty to horrific ugliness and back as I stared at them. The music played louder, and Hendrix asked where Joe was going with a gun. Joe's boyfriend pulled her up and started to act out the song.

"Hey, Joe," he sang, grasping his heart. "Are you gonna shoot your baby down? Shoot him down now?"

Her flashing smile revealed sparkling icepick teeth. She grew ten feet tall, and sonic bullets flew out of her mouth, shattering my bones and turning me into a jellyfish. I melted into the rug and dripped through the floorboards into a dark green basement.

Somehow, I ended up back in my bed but not asleep. I watched the shadows on my wall as the acid alternatively froze and then burned the marrow of my bones. Finally, I saw a painful grey dawn and fell asleep.

I didn't get out of bed until late in the afternoon. I went to the Forum and ordered a plate of scrambled eggs. Strange flashes of light crossed my eyes. I sat down, and Dylan was playing in my head, asking me what the price was for doing acid twice. The medicine had scrambled up my head. I saw scrambled brains and toast served on a plate with a side of toast. I rushed to the bathroom and threw up violently. Acid was worse than drinking Southern Comfort. I swore I was never going to trip again. I was up till dawn and then slept through all my morning classes.

Joe caught me as I was leaving the Forum. "Hey, you were supposed to meet me at noon, remember?"

"Oh, shit, I'm sorry. After last night ..."

"First time with purple haze?"

I nodded.

"That is strong shit. I only take a quarter hit. Anyway, don't worry about it. Hand these out in ARH. Classes get out in ten minutes. I'm going to stand in front of the library."

She handed me a stack of flyers for the demo at the Iowa Capitol.

The leaflet demanded "No More War" in bold black letters that stretched across a sketch of the Iowa statehouse. Impressive art for scratching on a wax stencil. The flyer called on us to gather outside the Forum at nine AM on Saturday and caravan to Des Moines. We chatted for a bit longer. She suggested that I take a class next semester by Adam Mansour, a Marxist professor. I thanked her and went to hand out the flyers right away. I handed half of them out to students streaming out of classes. Most people took them and stuffed them into their pockets or backpacks. Then, I posted flyers on each floor of my dorm. If doors were open, I knocked and handed a flyer to people and asked if they would go. Most people were non-committal, but at least six said they would go. And one senior said he could drive. I wrote down his name and room number. It would be my first anti-war demo, and I was helping organize it.

The evening before the demo, I walked up the tracks that ran through the middle of campus. I walked until the sunset. As I was coming back, people were shouting and crying out their windows. A cacophony of Hendrix music swallowed the campus; I looked up at a dark purple sky. Slowly, the songs all came together. People stopped playing their records and tuned into KDIC, the campus radio station. A voice solemnly read a news story announcing a rock god's death. The voice then announced they would repeatedly play each of Hendrix's records until dawn.

Hundreds of students gathered in the field outside Darby Gymnasium. People were handing out acid for a free-will donation. I took part in the acid wake despite my harrowing experience the week before. Lying on my back, I watched a blood-red moon rise above the trees. I floated through a long, green, purple night like a kite tethered to the blood moon. Something was dying—was it me? I awoke as part of a cottonwood tree in front of Reed Hall. My skin had turned to bark, and my legs were tree roots partially buried in the ground. I watched for hours as night turned into day. A Chicago & Northwestern train rolled down the tracks fifty feet from my tree. Workers opened the Forum, and lights came on. Bio and pre-med students walked by me without a glance, heading to their eight o'clock classes. They couldn't see me because I was part of the tree. I watched as Peter and Joe and her boyfriend waited outside the Forum for the mass of demonstrators. I tried to get up, but my back was fused to the trunk, rooted to the earth, immobilized. Nancy and another woman showed up, and then a few more people. By nine-thirty, they only had enough people to fill two vans. No one else had even brought a car.

"Sweet dreams, you fucking upper-class hippies," Joe's boyfriend shouted across the tracks to the silent dormitories. I stared at him with my tree-root eyes. He gave my tree the finger.

Two weeks later Janis Joplin died. I went and bought a bottle of Southern Comfort and got drunk while the campus radio played her songs all night long. From then on, I usually had a four o'clock joint, and then I watched the war on TV. A constant stream of body bags flew in from Saigon. Nixon announced the withdrawal of 40,000 troops but kept up the massive bombing campaigns.

The government was indicting movement leaders. Black Panthers kept getting shot, and their houses were blown up. A hundred thousand people marched against the war in DC, but the fighting went on. Every day, some new shockwave blew through America. What were Grinnell students doing? Pretty much studying and getting high. And so was I, but not much studying.

What could I do? I wasn't part of this country. I looked American but was really from India or another planet.

I just stayed stoned and studied sometimes. All my classes were incredibly dull. You first had to take the intro class for that department to get into exciting courses. I listened to professors introduce me to anthropology, economics, and sociology, explaining why each was the best of all academic disciplines. The assigned readings were abstract, theoretical bullshit. Still, the worst was Intro to Humanities, where we had to read the Greek classics. Who cared? I wrote many letters to Kodai friends, even Rachel, who never answered. I wrote to Lillian from Colorado. She did write back for a month and then told me she had a new, steady boyfriend. I smoked even more dope and listened to music all day long. I wrote terrible poetry and recorded my strange dreams, filling two notebooks with ramblings about God and revolution. In my mind, I recreated every hour of each day from my senior year in Kodai. We had it so great; why were we so desperate to get out of there?

On weekends, Bobby and I would get together and drop acid or mescaline or whatever we could afford. I had bad trips often, but I kept on doing it. We hitchhiked back and forth, from Ames to Grinnell, or Grinnell to Ames, almost every weekend, even when the weather turned cold and gray. The sub-zero wind chills and exhaust fumes on I-80 made me hate Iowa and Amerika even more. So, many people passed you by. It was a fucking fascist country, and no one cared about the rest of the world. I stopped talking to Amerikans, and even in class, I never spoke.

One Friday in November, I noted in my journal that I'd spoken eighty-nine words in the previous four days. If I could return to India, everything would be much better. By the end of the semester, I failed Humanities. For the first time in my life, I'd gotten an F and didn't care. I also had incompletes in Anthro and So, ciology. Econ was the only one that held some interest because one professor had been a Marxist in the thirties. He was wounded in WWII and told exceptional stories about his war experiences. He challenged the students to think about the way economics affected their lives.

But I had it with Iowa and Amerika and college. I was ready to drop out and go back to India, where I belonged. I wrote a letter home asking my parents to let me return as I planned to drop out after Christmas anyway. Just before Thanksgiving, I saw an invitation for Thanksgiving Dinner tacked to a bulletin board in the mail room. Churches in town were reaching out to the student body to repair bridges the May protests had broken. I was getting pretty sick of SAGA food. And the word Presbyterian caught my eye. I was up early the Sunday before Thanksgiving and thought I'd check out the Presbyterian church. Something kept me there for the whole service, and I saw Nancy as I walked out. She introduced me to the farmer who'd invited her to Thanksgiving dinner. And both of us went to that farm for Turkey Day. While waiting for dinner, the farmer's six-year-old daughter asked if I was Big Bird. When I said I wasn't a bird, she grabbed me by hand and led me to the TV.

"See!" The girl said, pointing to the Sesame Stree character. "You are tall like Big Bird, and his hair is like yours too."

I watched Sesame Street for a while and then started imitating Big Bird, to the little girl's delight.

In early December, I got a letter from England. It was from Billy, my Dylan-obsessed Kodai friend. He had gotten a draft notice and left for England the following week. Whoa! That hit kind of close. I figured I'd better stay in school and sign up for the second semester. I actually got exciting classes. Because I'd passed Intro to Econ, I got into a class on Development Economics taught by Blackjack Dawson, the most demanding Econ professor. But he had spent years working in Uganda, so I figured he knew about poverty. I still hadn't decided about God, so I signed up for a class on Comparative Religion. I also did an independent study in sociology with a professor who was an expert on the Russian Revolution. I got into the seminar with Adam Mansour, the radical prof Joe had told me about.

Just before Christmas break, I got a response from my dad to my request to return to India. In a tersely worded letter, he reminded me they had offered me that choice before I left. They could not afford to fly me back to India, and he warned me that if I dropped out, I'd better get a job because I'd be supporting myself. He told me that the church scholarship only lasted until I was twenty-one. And turning my back on that money was a big mistake. That bummed me out but reinforced my decision to come back the next semester. Billy's letter had made it clear that I had a choice of staying in college or getting drafted. Then, I could either die in Vietnam or leave Amerika, and since my parents wouldn't fly me back to India, where would I go? With my new classes, I could figure out what I really believed in. After that, if I survived my first year at Grinnell and got drafted, my parents might let me return to India.

Bobby invited me to Dubuque for Christmas. He got a ride for us partway, and then we'd hitch the rest. They picked me up in an old green Pontiac on a dark afternoon that smelled like snow. Bobby's friend dropped us off on Interstate 80 outside Iowa City. It was snowing hard, but we caught a ride almost immediately. It was a young professor at Cornell College in Mt. Vernon. He suggested we stay the night in one of the college dorms because a blizzard was coming, and we still had seventy miles to Dubuque. We refused his offer, and he dropped us off at the Maid-Rite Café, which doubled as the town's Greyhound station. He gave us ten bucks for a meal. The bus wasn't coming for a few hours, and we didn't want to waste the money, so we walked to the edge of town and started hitching. Fortunately, someone from Grinnell's Presbyterian Church had given me their son's old parka. When the elderly couple dropped it off at my dorm, they asked me about winter boots. I told them my canvas jungle boots were plenty warm. Ignoring my protest, they dropped a pair of old Sorrels at the dorm. The snow came down thick and heavy. Only two cars passed us by. Then, we had to jump into a snowbank to avoid a snowplow. After that, Bobby insisted we head back to the Maid-Rite and wait for the bus. The snow lay six inches deep and was a slog to walk through. I would have had frostbite if it wasn't for those Presbyterian boots. We almost missed the bus. We saw it pulling in when we were still two blocks away. We tried to run along the sidewalk but instead stumbled and slid. We ran into the middle of the snowy street, so the bus would have to stop. Or run us over. Anything was better than that winter hell. I decided I officially hated Amerika worse than ever.

Chapter 2: Faith Lost and Found

Bobby's mom was standing inside the Dubuque Greyhound terminal when we arrived. She hugged me and asked, "Did you run away from me or the hard work on the farm last summer?"

"The work, I guess," I stammered and turned red.

"Good answer. You missionary kids had such a rough life in India," she said with a smile and tousled my long hair. "Your hair is as big a mess as Bobby's. I will teach you two how to take care of that long hair. And if you don't, I'll sneak in one morning and cut it all off."

Bobby drove us home while his mom grilled me about classes, teased me about girls, and asked what life after the Revolution would be like. I now knew to laugh off her teasing. Besides, next semester, I would figure out what I believed in. I was happy I'd survived my first semester. I was glad to be back with Bobby's family, people who knew Kodai wasn't a town in Wyoming and loved Indian food as much as I did. When we got to the house, Mrs. Steinmetz heated up a fragrant shrimp curry that warmed my stomach and heart.

We slept till late afternoon the next day. It was Christmas Eve, and it snowed again. Large flakes floated into the yellow light above the door and settled onto the deck. Bobby and I sipped cheap wine and watched it fall. We listened to Dylan's *Self Portrait* album, a collection of old-time music that wasn't his best. We put on *Blonde on Blonde* instead. I had found a safe home in America.

"It's been over three weeks since my last trip," Bobby said.

"Yeah, that was my last time, too. The Night of the Talking Vending Machines."

"That was fucking weird," Bobby laughed. "The Coke machine actually does have recorded audio messages."

"But all the machines were talking to us that night."

"And following us around, or so we thought. It was a hellish trip."

"Most of mine turn out that way. Not too sure I'm in a rush to do it again," I explained.

"Really? You're usually the one who suggests it."

"Because I thought you liked tripping,"

"No, I usually have a bummer, and it's kind of expensive."

"Yeah, a waste of money. Let's just stop."

"Fuck, yes."

The wind picked up, and the snow came down heavier. The family den looked over an unfenced yard that opened onto a grassy field. The rest of

Bobby's family were at a watch night service.

We spent the rest of our vacation eating, watching TV, sleeping, and going out to buy a six-pack or some cheap wine. We didn't get high even once, and I actually felt all right. Good even.

After the break, when I returned to my dorm room, two Christmas presents were on my bed. The first was a hairbrush with a note that read, "This is yours. Please don't use mine. Maybe I'm a little uptight, but having someone use my hairbrush bugs me." The second was a twelve-pack of Hamm's. The note on it said, "Let's drink this tonight and watch the Vikings playoff game." I wasn't a big football fan, but by the end of the twelve-pack, I was yelling at the referees and shouting for the Vikes along with Jack.

The following day, I had a treasure trove in my mailbox. There were Christmas cards with checks from my family, letters from Kodai friends, and even a radical New Year's card from Rachel.

With the money from my grandparents, I bought Jack a copy of *Blonde on Blonde* as a selfish Christmas present. I wanted to make a tape of it. I now had my own music and my first American friend. The new semester was starting out a whole lot better than the old.

My classes were also a complete U-turn. Howard Buerkle, the Comparative Religions prof, made everyone feel comfortable. This led to deep discussions about our beliefs. We read James Cone, a founder of Black liberation theology, who produced a powerful argument for revolutionary Christianity. And I loved Rabindranath Tagore, the first Indian Nobel Laureate. Tagore's sensual yet spiritual poetry gave me a whole new take on God. And his love poems made me even more desperate for a soulmate to make love with.

When I mentioned that to Jack, he laughed. "You're as desperate to get laid as I am."

He and I were in Development Econ together, and that class was challenging. We read a book each week and then had to write a short paper summarizing and analyzing the book. Blackjack Dawson made you work, but he laid out the issues facing post-colonial countries. How could they develop capitalism with little or no capital? He was no Marxist but said the government had to lead. That and the Marshall Plan was how the Japanese and the Germans had recovered from World War II. Now, they were fast becoming manufacturing giants. His class explained the poverty and underdevelopment I'd seen in India.

My Russian Revolution independent was even better. The professor was a second-generation Russian with ancestors on both the Red and White sides of the Russian Civil War. He pushed me to examine the pros and cons of the revolution. I learned about the long and brutal struggle against the

Tsar, the horror of WWI, the fights between various revolutionary factions, and Lenin's triumphant coup when the Bolsheviks were at the crest of their popularity. Literature, theater, and art blossomed in the early days after the October Revolution. The rights of women became a reality in the larger cities. Neighborhood and workplace democracy spread through people's assemblies known as soviets. However, the Russian Civil War saw brutal massacres by both the Reds and the Whites. Lenin's death and the seizure of power by Stalin led to the successive elimination of every other leader. Thousands of revolutionary veterans were rounded up and killed or sent to gulags in Siberia. Every revolution went through this Thermidorian reaction, according to a book on the French Revolution. Both the French and the Russian Revolutions followed that pattern. First, pent-up anger swept away crumbling old regimes. The people's demand for liberty, equality, and fraternity washed away walls of repression like spring floods as the revolution swept away the ancient horrors, leading to a burst of creative community. Then, a reaction set in. Each of these beautiful new societies was frozen into a horrific caricature of the utopian dream. To hold onto power, revolutionaries often aborted the birthing of the new society. It was chilling. How could our new American revolution avoid a Thermidorian reaction?

The best class of all was Adam Mansour's seminar on socialism and capitalism. The young professor had long black hair and a hooked nose. He wore jeans and red shirts and was an unabashed Marxist-Leninist.

On the first day of class, he asked us, "How many of you subscribe to *The Guardian*?"

I proudly raised my hand, along with Joe and one or two others.

"Consider it required reading each week," Mansour said.

I loved that class. We studied events that had a direct bearing on the Vietnam War. We read Edgar Snow's *Red Star Over China*. William Hinton's *Fanshen* showed the changes the revolution brought to a small village. It reminded me of our *mahli*'s tiny hometown by the Krishna River. We even read Mao himself. Mao made a lot of sense and had a simple, almost poetic writing style. We also read *Monopoly Capital*, a critique of the American economy of the sixties. Each class was a lively debate on the crumbling capitalist system, how to change it, and a call to action against the war. After class, the debates often moved out into the hallways. The passionate debates continued in the Forum and then at late-night parties at Adam's house.

On the very first day of Mansour's class, I saw Nancy. She was the pretty friend of Joe's I'd met at my first and only anti-war meeting. I sat with her in the back, and we talked a bit. She was an Econ major whose primary subject was women in the economy. Nancy was the quiet type. She wasn't part of the set clustered around the dynamic, young professor. And I never saw her in the cafeteria. But we sat together after that.

My new classes sparked a drive to learn, and I got excited about studying. There were so many new ideas to explore. I began finding my way to answer the big questions of love, God, revolution, and my purpose in life. While I had outgrown my Sunday School faith way back in my sophomore year of high school, I still knew there was a purpose to my life. And now I was getting the chance to figure it out for myself. Every night after supper, I'd haul a colossal armload of books to Burling Library and study until 10:45. When they'd blink the lights, I'd gather up my heavy load of books while my mind raced around the world. I was in St. Petersburg with Lenin and Trotsky, sitting with Marx in the British Library, visiting Hanoi, Saigon, and Havana, or relaxing under bright Bengali stars in the gardens of Tagore's mansion in Calcutta. For the rest of that winter, James Cone and Tagore wrestled for my soul against Marx and Mao.

As I walked into the library on a Saturday in January, one of the librarians called me over. "Hey, I see you come in every day with a huge armload of books. A few carrels have opened up. Would you like to sign up for one?"

I was puzzled, "What kind of carols—like a Christmas song?"

"No," the librarian laughed sympathetically. "A library carrel. It's a desk assigned to you. You can keep your books there, so you don't have to carry them around with you."

"Oh, that kind of carrel," I said, feeling like an ignorant freshman. "Yeah, sure, that would be great."

She led me up the stairs to a row of carrels on the east wall. As she showed me to an empty one, Nancy looked up from the next one over.

"Hey," she smiled shyly.

It hit me how cute she was. Her green eyes smiled from a tousled head of curly brown hair. She had rosy cheeks and a little button nose.

"Hey," I said back.

The librarian smiled and left.

"What are you doing your first paper for Mansour on?" Nancy asked.

"Uh, I don't know for sure, maybe the May Fourth student movement in China."

"Yeah? That's pretty cool."

"It is kind of freaky that it was the same date as Kent State."

"For sure."

"What are you doing yours on?" I asked.

"Women leaders in the Chinese Revolution,"

"Cool." I wasn't sure what to say next. So, I sat down and started reading. I read about the early days of Sun Yat-sen. I soon got lost in the intrigues of turn-of-the-century Chinese politics. These battles raged from Peking to Tokyo and back to Shanghai.

"Are you hungry?" a voice asked. I was startled and dropped my book.

"Huh?" I looked up into Nancy's smiling eyes. They reminded me of jade green rice fields in Tamilnadu. "Oh, um, sure. What time is it?"

"One-thirty."

"Oh shit, I guess we missed lunch."

"My girlfriend made me a couple of sandwiches. You could have one of them, and we can get some soup at the Forum."

Nancy and I walked out of Burling and into a snowstorm. She had zipped up her parka; her lunch pail was in a fur-gloved hand. I held my old coat shut as it was missing a few buttons. My blond hair turned white with snow in the time we'd walked a hundred yards to the Forum. Nancy held the door open for me, and I rushed in, rubbing my bare hands together.

"You're not used to freezing weather," she observed. "Where are you from?"

"India."

"You look and sound American, more or less. How'd your family end up in India?" she asked and paused, ready to listen to my answer.

For once, I was happy to explain. Usually, explaining our unusual background was a painful process. People asked stupid questions like, "Did you ride elephants to school?" When you did try to tell them what it was like, most people got bored and wanted to drop the subject. Lots of people didn't even believe I was from India, implying I made it up just to be cool. Nancy was different. As we stood in line to order our soup, she asked about the history and culture of India.

When we sat down, Nancy pulled sandwiches out of her lunch pail. Her sandwiches were made with heavy brown bread that crumbled as I took a bite. Bits of bean sprouts and cheddar cheese fell onto the table.

"I'm sorry," I mumbled.

"Don't be," Nancy smiled. "I'm still learning to bake bread. This batch is really crumbly. Sally makes great bread."

"Who's Sally?"

"My roommate who bakes good bread."

"I never knew a cheese sandwich could taste so good."

Nancy laughed. "You remind me of my younger brother, Fred."

I flushed a bit. "How old is he?"

"He's a freshman, too, at Columbia. He wanted to get as far away from Iowa as possible."

"Why?"

"Because we're from a farm about fifty miles from here, and he wants to see the world."

"Don't you?"

"Of course, but I got a great scholarship here. And there are good study-abroad opportunities. Last semester, I went to Costa Rica, and I'm going to London next fall. My senior paper will discuss the intersection between the English feminist and labor movements."

"Labor feminists?" I asked, a bit puzzled.

"Sure, socialist labor and women's suffrage were interwoven back then. Have you read Engels on the woman question?"

"Um, no," I said, munching on my sandwich. "What's the question that Engels had about women?"

"That is the same thing my brother Joey asked! The Woman Question, you know, like the National Question. It's just a term the early socialists used for an issue or topic," Nancy explained without a hint of condescension.

"Hmm, that's kind of a weird way to say it." I finished the second half of my cheese sandwich. "These are great sandwiches. I'd never met a girl who could bake before."

"Woman," Nancy corrected.

"Huh?"

"Do people call you a boy?"

"Sometimes."

"Do you like that?"

"No."

"Well, they call us girls until we're thirty or forty, and I don't like it one bit. If I'm old enough to have a baby, I should be called a woman." Nancy's voice deepened while her volume rose.

"Yeah, that makes a lot of sense. None of us likes to be put down."

"Exactly." Nancy examined me.

"I really do like this bread," I said, cleaning up the last of my tomato soup with a piece of the crust. "Do you have a kitchen in your dorm?"

"No," Nancy shook her head at me. "I live in an apartment with my girlfriend over on State Street, south of Fourth Ave."

So, that's why she was never in the cafeteria.

"I love those crunchy nuts in the bread."

"Sunflower seeds. Haven't you had them before?" Nancy asked.

I shook my head.

"You are different, a bit clueless, but very smart," she smiled. "You're different from most Grinnell guys in a good way. Most guys are condescending."

We finished our lunch and returned to the library. Nancy picked up her backpack from her carrel.

"I'm heading home before the snow gets too deep. But I've been thinking," she paused and looked at me intently, "have you ever been to a CR session?"

"CR? What's that?"

"Consciousness-raising. It is like the criticism and self-criticism sessions the Chinese do. Except we focus on our internalized sexism," Nancy explained.

"How can women be sexist against themselves?"

"Let me count the ways, Jamie. Male chauvinism couldn't survive if women didn't go along with it. We are all raised to fit into the boxes the System has built for us."

"Hmm, like the poor peasants in China who wouldn't stand up to the landlords until the revolution came?"

"Exactly, I'm leading an intro session at Women's House next Tuesday night. It's for both women and men. Why don't you come and check it out?" Nancy asked.

"OK, sure."

She paused and looked out a big glass wall. The leafless oaks caught the light from the library, creating a web against the darkness.

"Next weekend is going to be really strange. Sally and I are going for dinner at my parents' farm. It will be the first time she has met them."

"Oh, OK. That sounds good."

"Please wish me luck."

"Sure. Good luck," I said, not understanding why Nancy needed it to have dinner with her parents and a friend.

That night, I couldn't sleep. Nancy's pretty face and smile filled my mind. Her green eyes stared at me out of the darkness every time I shut my eyes. I played *Blonde on Blonde* on my tape player. I flipped the cassette over. Dylan sang "I Want You," and I certainly did. Fantasizing about Nancy, I finally fell asleep as the grey fingers of dawn crept through the blinds.

I went to Women's House the following week to check out the Consciousness Raising session. Nancy gave a short talk at the beginning. She then led us in a frank but sympathetic discussion about personal sexual issues. Most people were open and trusting and talked about traumas they'd experienced, even rapes and sexual abuse by teachers. I was too embarrassed to say much. I thought my only sexual issue was that I was almost nineteen and still didn't know how to come on to a girl, or rather, a woman. Nancy explained how each person's traumas were connected to the patriarchal, commodity-based System. She had a kind yet analytical way of laying things out. She helped us see how we had internalized sexism and male supremacy, either by accepting demeaning roles or forcing them on others.

Nancy pointed out that both women and racial minorities maintained their own chains. She said white men were also damaged by our role of domination. It stunted our humanity and forced us to repress our feelings and those of others. I was super impressed at how Nancy guided the discussion. My problem was that she was prettier than ever. And I couldn't help looking at the nipples that poked against her tight t-shirt. I was getting turned on, but that was precisely the oppressive thinking she was talking about—treating women as sexual objects. Then, we started discussing the need for everyone, especially women, to liberate themselves. We each had to take the initiative to explore our own sexuality. By the end of the night, I was thoroughly confused about what I should do with my feelings for her. I finally figured I had to wait for her to take the initiative. It would be oppressive for me to make the first move.

At the end of the meeting, Nancy introduced Sally, her girlfriend.

"Hey," Sally shook my hand, squeezing until it hurt.

"Hi. Are you in Grinnell too? I haven't seen you around."

"No, I graduated last year. I work the evening shift at the hospital. I'm helping Nancy get through school. Then, we'll move to Chicago, where I've been accepted into Rush Medical School. She's going to work while I'm in med school."

"Wow, that is cool. You must be really good friends helping each other out like that."

Sally looked quizzically at me and smiled. "Yeah, we're the best of friends."

During the next month or two, Nancy and I spent most evenings studying together. We would take breaks and debate anti-war tactics, if and how the revolution could change America into a socialist country, and how it would impact stereotypes of women. We talked about the radical movements sweeping Latin America and what she had learned from her time in Costa Rica. We chatted a lot about the problems of counterculture and analyzed the sexist lyrics of our favorite songs.

I studied every evening except Saturday, when I partied with Jack and the other guys at Reed Hall. I only saw Bobby about once a month. We both kept our promise to stop chemicals, and he was doing better at school, too. Grinnell was going well except for one thing. When the winds of March blew across campus, I didn't want to be sexist, but Nancy still hadn't taken the initiative. She hadn't given me a hint of an opening, and I was falling harder and harder in love with her.

On the Tuesday before Spring Break, intense rains washed away all the snow. A warm wind blew from the south as Nancy and I left the library the next night. The smell of earth told us winter was over. A thrill of happiness rushed through my chest—something I hadn't felt since leaving India. A wave of love for Nancy welled up from deep inside. I had to tell her how I felt before I exploded.

"You want to go for a walk up the tracks?" I asked.

Nancy looked a bit surprised but agreed. We walked down to the railroad tracks separating the dorms from the Forum and academic buildings. Nancy balanced on one rail, but I kept slipping off.

"How can you balance so well?"

"I used to do ballet and ice skating," she explained. "My parents wanted me to do all the frilly girlie things, but I've been a big disappointment."

"I don't know why. You're smart," I said.

"Well, my orientation mainly," she said quietly.

I guess they didn't like her being a leftist, I thought. Just then, I slipped off the rail again. My foot caught on a railroad spike, and I would've tumbled face-first onto the rocks if Nancy hadn't hopped off and grabbed me.

"Here, try this," she said, mounting the rail again. "Walk on the rail and lean away, holding my hand to keep your balance."

With her help, I managed to stay on all the way across Eighth Avenue. As we walked by the football field, I slipped off again. Still holding Nancy's hand, I playfully pulled her off the rail and caught her other arm.

"Nancy," I said, standing close and looking into her eyes. "I've gotta tell you how much I like you."

Nancy's face turned white, and she let go of my hand. "Well, I like you a lot too, but…as a friend."

I blanched and let go of her arm.

"A close friend. You are one of the best guys I know, but you do know about Sally and me?"

"What does that have to do with it? I mean, she's your best friend and roommate."

"Yes, Jamie! And she is also my lover."

Oh my God. My mouth dropped open, and I couldn't close it. Cold claws twisted my stomach until I felt like I was going to heave.

"You mean you really didn't get that? I've talked about our plans a lot, and it's so obvious that we're both lesbians. Everyone knows that! I tried hard to make it clear that you and I are platonic friends. You're like a brother to me. You knew that, right?" Nancy was getting frustrated.

"No, I didn't." I shook my head and looked away up the tracks. "You were right about me. The first time we talked, I am fucking clueless and so stupid."

A long blast of a train whistle came through the night, and a headlight rounded the curve. I started running up the tracks.

"Jamie," Nancy shouted and started after me.

The train whistle blew repeatedly.

I could run fast, but she grabbed my arm as we crossed 10th Avenue and pulled me away from the tracks. The train roared onto campus.

"You're acting a bit crazy, man. I didn't trust the way you were running toward that train."

I looked at her and felt myself shaking with the ground as the train lumbered by.

"Just because I'm a woman doesn't mean you can outrun me. I was a track star in high school."

She looped her arm through mine and guided me across an open field. She turned to look at me. Hot tears were streaming down my face. I kept shaking my head.

"Am I the first gay person that you know?"

I nodded my head. Nancy held my arm close to her side and patted it with her other hand.

"Well, probably not, but the first out person you know."

"Out person? What does that mean?"

"Coming out of the closet means not hiding anymore and being proud to be gay."

I looked at her, my eyes widening.

"Don't be too hard on yourself, Jamie. We were all raised to see homosexuality as a complete taboo. Not being gay, you knew nothing about it. Still, somehow, you knew our friendship wasn't sexual. I believe your reticence was based on something more than shyness. You were picking up on what was going on with us. But you've never known gay people. So, how could you recognize my clues?"

I nodded.

Nancy squeezed my arm. "Hey, take a lesson from Mao's essay *On Contradiction*. You are learning the difference between external and internal conditions. Between what you wanted and what was real on the outside."

"What?"

"Inside, you want and need a lover. Our relationship is one of good friends. Your internal desires prevented you from seeing that."

For a minute, I stopped heaping abuse on myself to think that through.

Nancy and I walked through the soft spring night. Iowa stars the size of corn kernels burned in the dark sky.

"Look, Jamie, as your friend and comrade, I will tell you the truth. You are an attractive, thoughtful man. There are tons of women who would love to be with you, but not me. I'm gay. Break out of your shyness and meet them, dude."

I said nothing. Nancy kept talking about how hard it had been as a young girl. How she'd always felt different. How she was teased and bullied. She spoke about coming out at Grinnell and how that had changed her life. She walked me down Elm Street. In the autumn, it had been a golden leafy tunnel. Now, the many-fingered branches reached for the skies above yellow streetlights. We walked silently for a couple of blocks. Her hands on my arm and her body next to mine were reassuring. She wasn't afraid to touch me.

"You told me how hard it was for you to get used to the States," Nancy started speaking again. "Maybe you should think about the Costa Rica semester. It is a beautiful country. The way you describe Kodai, I'm sure it will seem familiar. It is about the same latitude, and San Jose is up on a plateau near volcanoes and mountains. On weekends, you can take a train or a bus to amazing beaches on the Atlantic or Pacific coasts. They have a strong student movement. I bet you'd feel more at home than in this cold country. You could study the economics of imperialism. And many beautiful, radical women down there would be happy to fall in love with you. Very few of them will admit to being lesbians. I found that out from a couple of conversations where I felt as stupid and out of place as you do."

I laughed through my tears, and she held me until they stopped flowing. Then, I walked up the stairs to my dorm, finished a bottle of brandy left over from the previous weekend's party, and fell hard asleep.

Over spring break, Bobby and I hitchhiked south to visit Mickey and other Kodai friends. We camped at a beach outside Gulfport and partied heartily until it was time to return to school. Billy and I hitched back north in a hard, cold rain. When I returned, I kept my nose in my books and only got drunk with the guys on weekends. I was safe there. No lesbians to fall in love with. Nancy tried to introduce me to straight feminists she knew. They were as pretty and intelligent as Nancy, but I rarely talked much with them. I was consumed with lust and guilt at the same time. How could I initiate a sexual encounter without being a male chauvinist aggressor?

In some ways, I hadn't moved beyond the echoes of Victorian mores that passed as twentieth-century, middle-class Christian values. Romantic attractions were something moral men cherished in private. They could achieve their sexual goals through proper courtship. But that was a male-dominated system, too. There seemed no way out but to wait for a woman to take the initiative with me. So, I read, studied, wrote papers, and debated God and politics in class, with my friends, and in my head. I agreed with Nancy and Sally on personal and social issues. But they were both confirmed atheists, and I was still trying to figure it out. My drinking and smoking buddies in Reed Hall liked to debate sports and philosophy more than politics. They were all against the war except for one guy with an ROTC scholarship, Gary Berger, whose room was across from ours. His roommate, Rod Eaton, was a theater major and a Baha'i. Others on the floor were agnostics, recovering Catholics, or exploring Eastern religions. Debates in Rod and Gary's room lasted well into the night.

Nancy and I kept studying together. We shared a fascination with how the Chinese revolution changed personal relationships. We tried to figure out how social systems ingrained subordination into some people and domination into others. And a bit of both into everyone. I told her about our *mahli* back home in Sangli. He was subservient to me, all Europeans, and even our cook. But he ruled his wife and children with an iron fist. Nancy described a pamphlet called "Control, Conflict and Change" by James Foreman, a leader of SNCC (Student Nonviolent Coordinating Committee). It talked about the psychological control mechanisms, which were patterns for social relationships. In class society, these were all relationships of domination and subordination. Our culture and education programmed the patterns into our heads. The revolution had to lead people into conflict with these control mechanisms and break them down.

"Wow, that makes so much fucking sense," I responded.

"You know, drugs are a control mechanism as well," Nancy said. We were walking over to the Forum for coffee. It was the first warm night in April, and you could see the stars.

"Now you're going to get all Presbyterian on me about drugs and drinking," I teased her.

"The church we were raised in is part of the capitalist system. But that doesn't mean everything we learned is a lie," she shot back.

"Well..."

"I'm serious. Drugs dissipated the anti-war movement last year right after the national strike."

"Umm, I missed the Kent State stuff," I mumbled. It was one of my biggest regrets. I had followed the protests in the news. But it was the end of our senior year, and I was too busy partying with my friends to think about doing anything. That was her point, I guess.

"And remember last fall?" Nancy asked. "Remember that acid party after the anti-war committee meeting in September? That trip did you in, didn't it?"

"Well, kind of."

"You didn't come to any anti-war meetings after that night."

"Well, there weren't any, were there?"

"Of course, there were," Nancy said. "We kept having meetings and movies and speakers. You never showed up. I was sad because you were the only few first-year guys at that meeting."

She was right. I turned on to psychedelics and dropped out of the movement. I told her what I learned from Mrs. Grant back in Kodai. "Einstein said that energy cannot be created or destroyed. But human energy is creative or destructive. If you prevent people from creating, they turn destructive. And they either take it out on themselves or on others."

"That is profound," Nancy said as we sipped our coffee.

Studying was now my creative outlet, bringing me out of my fog. The crucial issues on my mind, other than sex, were stopping the war and whether there was a God. Tagore and Mao wrestled for my soul, but the battle was over by the end of the semester. Socialist theories showed we had to change the system to end the war. After the Vietnam War, there would be another one. Wars were essential for capitalism. Mansour had a Marxist analysis that explained the insanity of our world. It gave me concrete conclusions and a path forward. Spiritualism only produced mushy answers. There was a solution to the fucked-up world we lived in, and it was political. And if there was anything I'd learned from Nancy, it was that the political was personal and vice versa.

The source of the anger that had torn me apart in Kodai was no longer a faceless monster. It was not a mysterious, ticking time bomb. I could now name it. The theory I learned from Adam Mansour and Nancy, from Mao, Lenin, Marx, and Engels, puts all the pieces together. There was a method behind the madness of domination, greed, and exploitation. And the way to overcome it was a revolution.

And revolution was sweeping the world. The starving people on the streets of Bombay and the mud huts in the villages that fell apart every monsoon weren't unhappy accidents. They were the result of opulent hotels and the towers of corporate capitalism. Even the archaic sexual rules that ripped through me like a cross-cut saw were part of that same System. And I wasn't alone. The Cubans, the Vietnamese, and the Black Panthers all taught us how to hone and direct our anger. We were part of a world revolutionary movement from Grinnell to Guinea-Bissau to Saigon to Soweto. We were tearing down the old world and building a new one. That was the meaning of my life. I'd been searching for that sense of purpose ever since I started thinking. I knew what I believed in for the first time since my old beliefs blew apart in that My Lai Thanksgiving storm.

In early May, I signed up for the Costa Rica semester. In late August, I would be off to study imperialism in action. Maybe I would meet some of those pretty activists Nancy had talked about. But first, I had to face the threat hanging over me for years—the Draft.

Chapter 3: Waiting for the Sky to Fall

I went back to Colorado for the summer. My grandpa got me a job stocking shelves at Walgreens in downtown Denver. I mostly stayed at their small house on Yates Street in northwest Denver. I watched TV, read The Guardian, or walked around Sloan's Lake when I wasn't working. Most weekends, my grandparents took me out to Bennett to attend church. Lillian spent the summer in Boulder with her new fiancé, which spared me the embarrassment of seeing her.

Grandpa was building a deck on the back of the pastor's manse, a house provided by the church. He taught me some carpentry skills under Colorado's dry, hot sun. Until then, I never thought you had to learn to hammer a nail. Really, how hard could it be? Or so I thought when Grandpa asked me if I could swing a hammer. Sure! Of course!

On my first swing, I hit my thumb with the hammer. Grandpa removed his cap and watched me. I got the nail in with no more damage to me but a few dings in the deck. I sent the second nail pinging through the air. It thwacked the aluminum siding and barely missed a window.

"Obviously, you spent precious little time in the Sangli carpentry shop," he said.

Grandpa spent the next *hour* teaching me how to hammer a nail. It pissed me off at the time. Still, I began to respect what it takes to learn a skill. A real carpenter spends years hammering, sawing, measuring, and learning a few new things each day. Grandpa had spent the last twenty-five years building congregations, but he'd also built his share of houses. After that afternoon, I spent weekends in Bennett helping with the deck.

At the end of a long, sweltering afternoon, we sat in the backyard with Grandma, sipping Cokes as the sun slipped toward the mountains. Grandpa told stories about their days in India. I talked about my memories of Sangli. The house sat on a rise at the edge of town, and you could see for miles and miles. Sometimes, we would watch a storm approach. Moisture rolling up from the Gulf of Mexico would meet the cool air from the Rockies. Tornadoes and baseball-sized hail would come out of nowhere.

When a storm was far away, Grandma would be the first to notice because she had lost family to a tornado when she was a girl. Grandpa and I would look at it with mild interest and return to our hammering or talking. If Grandma mentioned it again, the thunderclouds would be towering and dark. You could see the rain and lightning streaking down. A twinge of concern would cross Grandpa's leathery face, but he would pray for it to pass north over open range. Now, we would all watch the storm. Sometimes, I could see fierce winds shaking trees and flattening wheat fields. One time, the light turned a sickening shade of green. I remembered the Thanksgiving storm in Sangli, the day my old world had blown apart.

As I saw the clouds reach greedily toward the earth, trying to suck us into the sky, Grandma cried, "Run for the shelter."

A funnel touched down and pulled apart a barn a few miles away. We ran to the northwest corner of the basement.

The tornado missed the town of Bennett that afternoon. But in the middle of the night, I woke up shaking. After all those years, the storm I feared most was about to arrive. My draft lottery.

When we were kids, we played Cowboys 'n' Indians or Americans 'n' Viet Cong. At thirteen or fourteen, we sort of noticed the war. At sixteen or seventeen, we paid more attention. It still wasn't as important as friends, dating, grades, or sports. Still, you probably knew someone who'd been in Vietnam. But we tried to ignore it until you turned eighteen. Then, you knew your next birthday would bring dark clouds ready to rip your world to shreds and maybe put you deep into the earth.

You had to decide. Were you going to run for shelter? Or face the storm racing across the fields? How were you going to serve your country— by resisting an immoral war or going to Vietnam? I turned nineteen in the summer of 1971. It was my time to decide.

The draft had changed. A wave of resistance had filled the jails and disrupted draft boards across the country. There had been many complaints about local draft boards favoring upper-class kids. Most of the infantry was Black or brown. The Selective Service started a lottery based on birthdates to make the draft more equal. The luck of the draw would determine your place in line.

The draft lottery was prime time on all the networks. Even *Perry Mason* was pre-empted for the televised event of the summer. I sat between my grandparents on the edge of the couch as we watched their old black and white TV. Aging *white* men in suits, Senators, Representatives, and Selective Service officials stood in a room making small talk. Walter Cronkite provided pre-event commentary. The goal, he said, was to make the draft lottery fair. No more local draft boards that let the rich kids slide and put the poor into the infantry in Vietnam. Now, it would be a completely random process. The goal was to randomly sort each day of the year into an arbitrary sequence, one to three-hundred-and-sixty-six since 1952 was a leap year. That sequence of days would determine what order people were called up in. If your birthday matched number one, you would be called up first. If your birthday was three-hundred-and-sixty-sixth on the list, you wouldn't go to war unless Russia attacked us, and then we'd all be dead anyway.

The method of ordering the year's dates, and thus our birthdays, had to be completely random. Any day should have an equal chance of being chosen as one or three hundred sixty-six. There was one list for the whole country, and the method had to be perfectly transparent. TV was the medium of choice in the sixties, and game shows were the rage. What could be better than a nationally televised game to determine the fate of all nineteen-year-old males?

I watched, horrified, as a Presidential Marine Guard rolled out two clear plastic barrels. Each was filled with ping pong balls. One set of ping pong balls had a sequential number, from one to three-hundred-and-sixty-six. The other set was marked with the dates of the year. My birthday was one of them, and Charlie's and Mickey's and everyone born that year. They would spin the barrels, one after the other. A man in a suit would reach in and pull out a ball, matching each birthday to its lucky or unlucky number.

If your number was low, you were sure to go. A Country Joe and the Fish song played in my head, *"Don't ask me. I don't give a damn; next stop is Vietnam."*

Walter Cronkite assured us that this method was a step forward for America. It restored our core value of equality. It would improve the transparency of the draft and help restore some trust in our government. Two Marines walked up to the barrels, grabbed a crank, and gave each barrel a spin. A congressman in a black suit and heavy-rimmed glasses approached one barrel. It stopped spinning. He pulled out a ping pong ball with a date. He pulled his glasses down to the tip of his nose. He read the date and then looked up at the camera.

"Ju-u-u-ly the first," he announced.

A fat, bald senator pulled out a number from the other barrel and read it.

"Number two hundred and eighty-four," he smiled into the camera.

I had a notepad with the birthdays of my college roommates, Jack and Fred, and all my male Kodai friends. So far, all of them were safe.

The second spin and the senators and congressmen heeded their call. The date was March 22. They drew out the suspense like we were waiting for a big door prize. The senator was squinting at a ping pong ball with a number on it and shouted self-importantly, "Three-hundred-and-forty-five."

Across the country, from Alaska to Key West, boys born on 3/22/1952 jumped off the couch and celebrated. Last year, they had called up through 195. This year, the word was they wouldn't even go that high because Nixon was "Vietnamizing" the war and slowly drawing down American troops.

They spun the barrels again. Again, the grim suspense. October 25th.

A drum-roll on the hearts of thousands of young men across the country…
"Number Ten."

"Oh shit. Frantzie," I blurted out and then mumbled apologies to my grandparents as I stared at my sheet. "They got my friend Frantz."

Grandpa looked at me and nodded grimly. Grandma was glued to the TV set.

Dates and the numbers whipped across the prairie like hail.

"J-u-u-ne…" I leaned so far forward that I fell off the couch to my knees.

"Tee-wennnntee," This was it. This was my fate.

"June Twentieth," The man repeated. OK, not quite.

The bald guy was getting bored. He calmly read his ping pong ball.

"Number thirty," he said calmly.

I exhaled, missed by a hair. But, oh my God, that's Mickey's birthday.

"That's one of my best friends," I said, turning to my grandparents.

Grandma took my hand and pulled me back to the couch.

"We're praying real hard for him and for you."

The grim lottery continued. My birthday was pulled about halfway through.

"June 21,"

"296."

I jumped through the roof. The dark axe that hung over my life was gone. I was free. I settled back on the couch, but a cold fear crept up my back. Mickey, with a birthday one day before mine, was going to a certain death, and I was celebrating.

Chapter 4: The Land of Eternal Spring

I was still flying high a few weeks later, and I hadn't smoked weed for months. In the Miami airport, I met other students who were part of the Central America program and took notice of a blue-eyed girl with curly hair. She reminded me of sweet Anna in Korea. I hadn't thought of her in years.

We boarded the plane, and I was disappointed to see her take a seat four rows ahead of mine. But as I lay back in my seat and sipped a rum and coke, my mind moved on. I had been reading about the revolutionary movements across Latin America. Che Guevara had been killed five years earlier. Still, his words and actions inspired a new generation of revolutionaries from Chile to Mexico. An article in *The Guardian* said revolutionary students in Chile were organizing armed units to defend Allende's revolution. The Sandinistas were waging a guerilla war against the Somoza dictatorship in Nicaragua. Would there be Sandinistas in Costa Rica?

The jet engines roared, and the 707 was set to fly. The force pushed me back against the seat, and my heart soared as the plane rose from the tarmac. I was leaving the USA to study imperialism in action. I hadn't been this happy since dancing under the starlit sky on the circus sands. I was on my way to discover my fate, driven deep beneath the waves of the Bay of Bengal. I would find my place in the worldwide revolution.

Epilogue

During college, Jamie, Nancy, and thousands of other students were introduced to Marxism. But it wasn't ideas that radicalized them. It was their personal experience of oppression. Theory connected to their reality and helped make sense of it.

Young people worldwide began to see that the Vietnam War was not a mistake. It was an outcome of the American system of settler colonialism. That system, along with the coal and oil found in Native lands, enabled the United States to surpass no-longer quite so-Great Britain and France. And become the leader of the capitalist world.

A friend explained that he became a Marxist in high school civics class. A teacher assigned *The Communist Manifesto*. The teacher wanted the kids to be able to argue against student radicals, so he told them everything that was wrong with the *Manifesto*. My friend decided that the *Manifesto* explained his life as a working-class kid much better than the rest of the civics class.

Racism was inherent to the colonization of darker-skinned nations. Rape and harassment of women was the result of another pillar of the system, patriarchy. Military domination is inherent to nation-states. They all came together with a vengeance in the Vietnam War that killed over 3 million people. But, the war was one part of global decolonization that gave the nations of Asia, Africa, and Latin America political independence. And so was the social revolution that started with the Montgomery bus boycott. It partially de-colonized African Americans. Anti-Black racism was delegitimized, and legal segregation was outlawed. A peace movement stopped a war for the first time in history. Male supremacy was gravely weakened as the Women's Liberation Movement opened economic and cultural doors for women and LGBTQIA2S+ people to fight their way to human rights. There were permanent successes before the first televised revolution was aborted.

A new generation faces new challenges and must find their way forward. They are not alone.

And Now What?

A Contest

NOTE TO READERS #2

Rock music was our North Star, pointing our way forward. Or sideways, up or down. However, we chose to interpret the songs of Dylan, the Beatles, the Doors, and many other rock stars. I will run a contest for the first year of this book's publication. If you identify 50% or more of the nods to rock 'n' roll prophets, you will win a prize that might be cooking a curry dinner when I come through your town on a book tour. Or a free copy of the next book in the series, *On the Road Through Maggie's Farm,* or a package of my favorite Indian spices.

To enter the contest, send an email to RobbieOrrWrites@gmail.com. Put *"Rock Prophets Contest"* in the subject line of the email. And list the page #, the text of the allusion, and who was the singer or songwriter.

Thank You

I greatly appreciate you reading my book. Writing it was a gift that helped me learn who I was and who I am. I genuinely hope it has encouraged you to examine yourself and the world we are living in.

A Call to Action

• Whatever issue you care about, please do something about it today. Only by working together can we solve the myriad problems facing us. You can't solve them all, but you can pick one issue and take some steps to improve it. And please investigate political and social movements such as 350.org, Democratic Socialists of America, or local LGBTQIA2S+ activists. Start by googling, but don't stop there.

• Please write to me at RobbieOrrWrites@gmail.com to discuss ways to repair our broken world.

• Visit RobbieOrrWrites.com and sign up for my newsletter. Connect with me online on Facebook or at RedVoltBooks.com/Robbie Orr.

COMING SOON

On the Road Through Maggie's Farm: The Birthing of a Revolutionary

On the Road to Maggie's Farm opens with Jamie landing in Costa Rica. Jamie continues his cross-cultural personal and political revolution as he naively tries to connect with revolutionary students. At first, he is treated as a gringo spy. Eventually, the Costa Rican radicals find a mission for him, and Jamie finds a Sandinista lover. After a transformative romance, she is ordered to return to Nicaragua, and Jamie forlornly returns to the US. Soon, the 1972 antiwar upsurge sweeps Jamie into a new circle of young activists.

The novel shows how historical events, relationships, and rebel music can transform kids into revolutionaries. It follows their bad breaks and setbacks, where they fumbled, fell, and moved on. It explores how gender conflicts demand politics be personal and not abstract. It also shows how the Sixties movements led to the New Communist Movement.

On the Road Through Maggie's Farm will be published in 2025.

Breaking Blonde on Blonde: An Inside Out Revolution

The third novel opens in the Twin Cities of Minneapolis and St. Paul in the fall of 1974. The Twin Cities were a center of radical activism and culture. There were a dozen community-run food coops. A Black organizer who had been a SNCC and Black communist determined the coops could be a base for a multi-racial working-class movement. He organized clandestinely and initiated the tumultuous Coop Wars (see https://coopwars.com). These events, documented in the Coop Wars movie, tore the Twin Cities Left and counterculture apart. Breaking Blonde shows how Jamie's circle of friends was divided into opposing camps. One group accepted the gospel of Marxism-Leninism, and the other their sworn enemy. Jamie and his lover think they are becoming professional revolutionaries, but their organization becomes a cult. And their life goes down a long, strange rabbit hole. The story shows how and why intelligent people can transform into blind believers, like frogs in a slowly heating pot. The novel also covers their strenuous efforts to recover. This story is a cautionary tale for dedicated activists.

Breaking Blonde on Blonde is still a work in progress. How long? As BB King used to sing, "Someday, baby!"

Author Bio

Credit: Photo by Ibrahim El-Amin

Author Bio:

Raised in India as a missionary kid, Robbie Orr's life was transformed by the decolonization wave sweeping the world in the mid-twentieth Century. His mission became de-colonizing US American culture and his own mind. He was an anti-war activist and Maoist cadre until that wave passed with the collapse of South African apartheid and Russian-style communism. Robbie has devoted the last four decades of his life to raising a family, studying justice healing, organizing with the National Writers Union and Democratic Socialists of America, and writing articles, book reviews, poetry, and novels.

www.ingramcontent.com/pod-product-compliance
Lightning Source LLC
Chambersburg PA
CBHW022154240626
47153CB00007B/2657